~BACKBEAT~

MASON MALONE

ISBN - 978-0-9912058-7-5

Other books by Mason Malone

The Chamala Quest - 2018

The Polyandrist - 2018

Dedication

This book is dedicated to struggling songwriters, musicians, authors and artists all over the world. I salute each and every one of you for your tireless efforts to bring your creations to life.

Foreword

The term backbeat refers to the second and fourth beat in a four-beat measure. In popular music it's usually a crisp rap on the snare drum that comprises the backbeat. When the guitarist, pianist or sax player venture off on a solo during an extended jam it's the steady backbeat cutting through the drone of other instruments that keeps the tempo and holds the sound together.

I was introduced to music at a young age. My parents gave me a guitar for Christmas one year. I took to it immediately. Learning to play it instilled in me a sense of pride and self-confidence. And in those days, I didn't have much of either. I practiced hard and became accomplished enough on bass guitar to play in a garage band. I went on to play in several bands, performing at parties and in nightclubs. One notable highlight in my short-lived career was playing alongside Bo Diddley during one of his concert performances.

I never made it big. In fact, I never even made a decent living playing music. In truth, wealth and fame weren't the things that drew me into the profession. It was the subculture. The on and offstage camaraderie and mentoring from bandmates. Acknowledgment and acceptance by my peers. That was the lure. That and the groupies, of course.

My career as a musician began when I was fifteen and was over before I turned twenty-four. In the course of it I learned many valuable life lessons while paying dues in seedy bars and nightclubs in rough parts of the city. And I'm thankful for every one of them. Those lessons still provide me with guidance, fifty years later. They are my backbeat. When my life's path wanders off-tempo and I start to lose my way, I listen for the backbeat to guide me home, once more.

Prologue
Detroit 2004

The place was a dive, to put it kindly. Located two blocks off the main thoroughfare, it was squeezed in between an auto repair shop and a beauty salon. The smell of engine oil and brake fluid mixing with the scent of hair spray and shampoo greeted the bar patrons as they walked from the parking lot into Eddie's Cocktail Lounge and Dance Club. A dimly lit sign hanging on the blacked-out storefront advertised Happy Hour from 3 to 7 and live music Saturdays.

It was 1:40 AM Saturday night—or rather Sunday morning. The band had just finished their last set and were packing up to go. Trevor watched his wife, Grace, chatting with people, passing out business cards and letting everyone know the band was available for private parties. Trevor played bass for the band. Grace was the vocalist, business manager and public relations person all rolled into one.

"We sounded good tonight, didn't we?" Ray, the sax player said to Trevor as he was leaving.

"We always do," Trevor replied. "See you at practice, Tuesday."

The guitarist, keyboard and horn players followed Ray, leaving only the drummer, Isiah.

"Are you almost ready to go?" Isiah asked Trevor.

Trevor scanned across the room to where Grace was sitting at the bar talking with Eddie Marshall, the nightclub owner. The bartender was placing a drink in front of her.

"It looks like we'll be here a while longer."

"This is a rough area. I can stick around, if you like."

"They're all rough, these days, Isiah. You go ahead. We'll be alright. Chandra will be waiting up for you. No sense making her worry."

"Alright, then. See you Tuesday."

Isiah left without arguing further, but not without trepidation. He and Trevor had been as close as brother ever since the first band they put together, five years before.

Aside from Trevor and Grace, only the nightclub staff and a handful of patrons remained. Trevor was exhausted and anxious to leave. Their son, Dylan had been sick with bronchitis for two days, keeping them up most of the night caring for him. He knew Grace was every bit as tired as him, but there she was, taking care of business the way she always did. The bartender set a fresh drink in front of her. Trevor sighed and went to sit at a table in a dark corner where he could shut his eyes while he waited.

He immediately dozed off, but was roused awake a minute later when the front door banged open. A large man entered, stumbling as he did. He wore a long coat and a cap pulled low over his ears and forehead. Trevor watched him slowly work his way to the bar, probably hoping for one last drink before closing. Aaron, the bartender, saw him approaching. He noticed the unsteady walk and glassy eyes.

"The bar is closed, sir," Aaron called to him.

The man stopped just outside of arm's reach. His eyes met Aaron's as he steadied himself and stood erect.

"That's alright. I didn't come here to drink."

The sudden change in his demeanor unnerved Aaron, but he did his best to hide it. Watching the man in his peripheral vision, he picked up a towel, wiped across the bar top, bent over and placed it nonchalantly onto a shelf below, grabbing a handgun next to it as he did. The gun made a barely audible, but distinctive scraping sound as he slid it toward him. For Aaron, it was a fatal mistake.

Before he could raise the gun above the level of the bar top the man produced a shotgun from beneath his coat and shot Aaron in the chest. The impact of the blast propelled Aaron backward for six feet and put a hole through his chest the size of a man's fist. He was dead before he hit the floor. The gunman racked another shell into the chamber.

Trevor sat at the table, frozen in place, knowing he should run or take cover, but unable to do either. Grace was still sitting at the bar next to Bobby Marshall and a few others. The big man in the long coat swung the shotgun on them.

"Empty your wallets, purses, pockets and give me everything in the cash drawer," he ordered.

Everyone was in a state of shock after seeing Aaron brutally killed. Nobody reacted immediately.

"Now!" the gunman bellowed.

Bobby hesitated. Either he was frozen in fear or he was stalling while he figured a way around giving the thief his money. Trevor couldn't just stand by and watch with Grace in the line of fire. He was on his feet before he realized it and running toward the gunman. If he could get to him while his attention was focused on the people gathered around the bar maybe Trevor could wrestle the shotgun away from him.

Only ten steps away from the gunman Trevor's foot struck a discarded beer can at the edge of the small dance floor. The sound reverberated through the nightclub. Trevor pushed hard as the gunman's head turned his way. Three long strides and Trevor would collide with him. The gunman whirled and swung the shotgun to point at Trevor's midsection. Trevor made a desperate leap. The shotgun roared. Trevor's body seemed to hang in midair momentarily, then plummeted to the ground at the gunman's feet.

Grace shrieked hysterically at the sight of Trevor being shot. A river of blood poured from his body. She couldn't force herself to look away. With the gunman distracted Bobby Marshall seized the opportunity, drawing a handgun from a shoulder holster inside his jacket. The gunman had just racked another shell into the chamber and was turning back toward the bar when Bobby shot him in the chest. It wasn't enough to stop him from pulling the trigger and hitting Grace before he fell.

~~~

Isiah's phone rang at 4:05 AM. He was sound asleep. His wife, Chandra, shook him roughly.

"What?" he grumbled.

"Answer your phone, and tell whoever it is not to call here at this time of night."

Isiah felt in the dark for the phone on the bedside table, knocking it to the floor, instead. Chandra switched on a lamp. By Isiah's count the phone sounded eight times before he finally answered.

"Hello?"

"This is Lieutenant Reed with the Detroit Police Department," the voice on the line said. "Who am I speaking with?"

"What's this about?" Isiah asked warily.

"I'm trying to contact the family of Trevor Pruitt. This number was the first of his phone contacts. Are you Isiah?"

"Yes sir, I am." Guilt surged within Isiah. Something has happened to Trevor. Why else would a policeman be calling at four in the morning? He never should have left Trevor and Grace at the club. A bad neighborhood, drunken drivers on the highway. Too many possibilities and none of them good.

"What's your relation to Mr. Pruitt?" Reed asked next.

"He's a close friend. What's happened to him?"

"He sustained injuries from an incident at a nightclub, early this morning. Do you know if he has family here in Detroit? His parents or any siblings, perhaps?"

"He's an only child and he's not close to his parents. Hasn't talked to them in years as far as I know. I'm the closest thing to family he has, other than his wife, Grace, and his son, Dylan. How badly is he injured?"

Reed was quiet for a long moment. Debating how much he should say.

"Officer?" Isiah prompted.

"Mr. Pruitt is at Sisters of Mercy Hospital, in the ICU. It's not good, I'm sorry to say. You should probably hurry over there."

~~~

An hour later Isiah sat in the waiting area of the ICU. Getting information about Trevor's condition was next to impossible. He wasn't out of surgery, yet. That was all they would say.

"Uncle Ise," a small voice called out.

Isiah turned to see three-year-old Dylan in footed pajamas hurrying toward him with outstretched hands. Isiah bent low to scoop Dylan into his arms.

"Hello little man."

"Where's my mommy and daddy?"

"I don't know, Dylan. I just got here. How'd you get here?"

"She brought me," Dylan said, pointing at a woman who then stepped forward.

"I'm Carol Hart with the Victim's Support Unit of the Detroit PD. I brought this young man down to see his father."

"I haven't been able to find out anything about Trevor or Grace. Do you have any information on either of them?"

Hart glances at Dylan, then back at Isiah, letting him know it's something she can't discuss in front of the boy.

"Will you keep an eye on Dylan while I check in at the desk?"

Isiah watched Hart as she spoke with the same ICU personnel who had basically stonewalled him a few minutes earlier. They seemed to be more forthcoming with her. After a brief conversation she returned to Isiah.

"I'm going to take him in to see his father, now."

"How is Trevor? And, what about Grace?"

She raised her hand to ward off his questions.

"I'll come back in a minute."

She took Dylan by the hand and disappeared through a door. True to her word, she was back in a minute, though it seemed much longer to Isiah.

"I told Mr. Pruitt you were here. He'd like to see you, but first he needs to explain what has happened to his son. An attempted armed robbery took place at Eddie's Cocktail Lounge early this morning near 2:00 AM. I'm sorry to have to tell you this. Both Trevor and Grace Pruitt were shot by the robber. Grace Pruitt died at the scene. Trevor's injuries are severe. He isn't expected to live through the day."

Isiah felt as if he himself had been struck by a shotgun blast. His knees wobbled. Hart grabbed his arm to steady him. An ICU nurse motioned for him to come with her. Trevor wanted to see him.

"I'll wait here," Hart said.

Through a door and down a hallway Isiah followed where the nurse led him. She pointed to a room, then left him. He slowly pushed open the door. Trevor was lying on a bed surrounded by an array of monitoring devices, wires, tubes and medical gadgetry. His torso was wrapped from his shoulders to his waist with blood-soaked gauze. His face was as pale as the sheet beneath him. Little Dylan was lying next to him with his face pressed against Trevor's neck, sobbing uncontrollably. Isiah struggled to maintain his composure.

"I'm sorry, Trevor. I never should have left you."

Trevor tried to speak, but couldn't.

"It's alright, man. Don't try to talk."

"Got to," Trevor croaked. "Got to tell you."

The light in his eyes was just a flicker, threatening to go out any second. Isiah didn't try to stop him, again.

"Grace is gone and I don't have much time."

"I know."

"You're the only one we trust. We put it in writing when Dylan was nine months old."

Trevor's eyes went to Dylan, then back to Isiah.

"Please, brother. Take care of him for us."

"Anything you want. You know that, Trevor."

"You hear that, Dylan. You're going to live with Isiah, Chandra and Nikki. Won't that be fun? Your momma and I will be watching over you every minute from heaven."

"Nooo!" Dylan wailed.

Trevor blinked away the tears in order to have one final look at his son. Then, his eyes closed forever. The monitors sounded an alert. A doctor and two nurses came in. Isiah took Dylan in his arms and left the room.

~1~

Like a complete unknown, like a rolling stone

My name is Dylan, as in Bob Dylan. My parents liked his music, I think. I can't be sure because they died when I was three, before I got to know them very well. After they died, my father's best friend, Isiah Jones, took me in. For the last fifteen years I've lived with him, his wife Chandra and their daughter, Nikki. They've been really good to me and I know it hasn't been easy for them.

I'm like an unwanted pregnancy. The child they didn't plan for and could ill afford. To make matters worse, I don't look like I belong in their family. You see, I'm Caucasian. As white as snow. Isiah, Chandra and Nikki are African American, with skin the color of dark chocolate. I won't kid you. At times, it can be awkward. People often stare at the four of us when we're out together in public, as if wanting an explanation.

"Never mind them," Isiah says when he sees me staring back. "They're just curious. They don't mean nothing by it."

When we're home together, we're like any other family. Any other that I know of at any rate. We eat dinner together most evenings and often watch TV or a movie afterward. Nikki yells at me like I'm her younger brother, though she's quick to remind me I'm not. We slept in the same bedroom until she turned twelve and started to grow boobs. After that I got my own room, next to the furnace in the basement.

I didn't like it at first. It was dark and musty smelling. Isiah helped me get past that.

"There comes a time when a man needs his privacy. I had a room like this when I was your age. I personalized it, put some posters on the wall, set my drums up in one corner. I'll help you fix it up. It'll do fine."

Isiah has played the role of father to me, but I don't call him dad. We call each other by our first names, Isiah and Dylan. I use his last name as my own, because it makes things easier. He gives me advice if I ask for it. We joke around a lot and talk about music. Sometimes he tells me about the things he did with my real dad, Trevor Pruitt. They were close friends then, the way Isiah and me are now. I don't know where I'd be if he hadn't taken me in. Once I asked him why he did.

"Trevor would have done the same for me. That's just how it was between us."

Chandra and I on the other hand have never become close. Don't get me wrong. She's never mean to me. For whatever reason, there's an invisible wall between us and I can only speculate as to why that is. Maybe it has to do with Nikki, and wanting her to feel she's their number one priority. There's another possibility, though. One time I heard her talking to Isiah, when they thought I was out of earshot.

"I understand why you feel obligated to take care of Dylan. I do, and I respect you for that. He's a good boy, but he's not your son. Don't you want a son of your own? Someone to pass on your name to? We always planned to have more children. Has that changed?"

"Plans always change, whether we want them to or not. I love Dylan as much as if he were my own. Even if I didn't, I'm not sure we can afford more children. Food, clothes and school for Nikki and Dylan is about to break us, as it is."

Nikki is a year older than me. From the moment Isiah brought me home and said I'd be staying with them, Nikki has hated me. I understand why. Before that, she was the center of attention. Everything Isiah and Chandra did, every decision they made revolved around her. Learning to share her house and family with me hasn't been easy for her. Growing up, we were constantly arguing over anything and everything. They were usually loud and occasionally physical. Last year she went away to college. The day before leaving she took me aside for a heart-to-heart.

"My room is off limits to you, Dylan. Understand? And, that goes for anything else of mine. Keep your sticky fingers off my stuff."

"What are you going to do, dust your things for fingerprints each time you come home?"

"I don't have to. You'll leave greasy smudges on everything you touch. And even if you don't, I have little cameras hidden everywhere."

"You do not."

"Touch my stuff and you'll find out. And what I do to you won't be pretty, I promise you that."

I'm bigger than Nikki, by four inches and thirty pounds, but she still intimidates me. She's the main reason I don't have a girlfriend and probably never will. If she's not picking on me about my long shaggy hair and stick thin figure—a mop with legs is how she puts it—it's my flaccid muscles or lack of athletic prowess.

The constant barrage of insults and criticisms keeps my self-esteem in a perpetual nose dive. The other day I overheard two girls talking about me.

One said to the other, "He's not bad looking."

What does that even mean? He's not so ugly I'd barf if he kissed me?

A few months ago I turned eighteen. In another month I'll graduate from high school. I can't wait. I'm sure most schools have cliques and rivalries between students, but I bet there aren't many that have gang bangers recruiting new members in the hallways as the teachers walk by and pretend not to see. The last couple of years there have been scary, to say the least. But to be honest, what lies ahead after graduation scares me more.

College really isn't an option. That's okay. Academics aren't my strong suit. Throughout school I struggled to make a passing grade in every class except for one—Music Theory. The teachers think I have Attention Deficit Disorder. That's not the problem. It's difficult to concentrate on studying when you're constantly looking over your shoulder.

Although she's never said as much, I'm sure Chandra expects me to move out soon after graduation. I've been racking my brain trying to think of how I can. It occupies my thoughts twenty-four hours a day. I lie awake at night unable to put it out of my mind. There aren't a lot of jobs available for someone with my limited skills. Even the cheapest places to rent cost more than I can make working at a burger joint. Short of winning the lottery, I'm pretty much screwed.

~2~

While my guitar gently weeps

After school most days my friends and I stop by the music store. It's an eclectic mix of people who frequent Sticks, Strings and Brass—spanning the entire spectrum of mankind. All ages, genders, races, religions, sexual preferences and music genres. The one and only thing the mass of people crowding into the store have in common is their interest in music. That makes it a safe haven for misfits like me. Check your political differences and gang affiliations at the door and come on in.

The friends I mentioned are Truman, Maddie and Josh. During the last couple of years, we've been drawn together out of necessity. We're outcasts. A bunch of mutts. It's the glue that binds us. That and the need to have someone watching your back. Flying solo can be dangerous in this city. You're easy prey to the thugs and gang members who lurk in alleys and abandoned buildings. Those same bad guys come into SS&B, but inside the store they transform into singers and musicians.

Four guys and two women are coming out of the store as we reach the entrance. Hip-hoppers. I recognize them from other times I've been here. We step aside to let them by. No one makes eye contact. Just as well. Inside the door we quickly make our way to the west wall. That's where the electric guitars and basses hang on display. Truman heads straight for a Fender Stratocaster with a natural finish and a maple fretboard.

I find a Fender Jazz Bass, take it off its hook and sit on an amplifier to play. It's an updated version of the Jazz Bass my father played way back when. I still have it. After his death, Isiah recovered it from the nightclub and stored it until I was older. I take it out of the case occasionally, wipe it off, attempt to tune it and pluck at the strings, though I'm not very good at it.

"You suck on bass, Dylan," Truman chides.

He laughs. Maddie and Josh join in. It doesn't bother me. I'm used to them ribbing me. I'd worry if they didn't.

"Is that so?" I retort. "Well, you suck worse than me."

"That may be, but at least I do it on tempo. You can't even get that much right. Oh, I forgot. You white people ain't got no sense of rhythm."

More laughter follows.

"Here, I'll show you the way, Dylan," says Josh.

He begins snapping his fingers at around sixty beats per minute.

"Hell, no," Truman says. "Way too slow. Like this."

He snaps his fingers at closer to ninety BPM. Maddie tries to match his pace, but lags behind. The three of them snapping their fingers sounds like a cricket infestation.

"Alright, you guys. I give up," I tell them. I hang the bass back on the wall. "I'll be back by the drums if anyone's interested."

"I'll come with," Maddie says.

Electronic drums are set up in a corner of the store. I don headphones and position myself behind the drums. Maddie puts on headphones and stands in front. I start things off by tapping my fingers on the snare pad while working the bass drum pedal with my foot. Maddie handles the tom toms and cymbals. We're having fun. She's getting into it. Her head is bobbing and her hips are swaying back and forth.

I'm enjoying watching her move. I've never told her so, but I'm into her in a big way. It didn't start out that way with us. To be honest, in the beginning all I felt for her was pity. She moved to the city in the middle of the last school year. It was that same old story. New town, new school, no friends. I'd see her hanging around before and after school, looking lost and lonely. When I walked by her I'd nod or maybe say hey, just to be nice. She would drop her head and look at her feet without replying. One day Truman and I were walking past her after school.

"Hey," I say.

She looks away as always. I take a few more steps and stop.

"We're going to SS&B," I tell her. "You can come too if you want."

She shrugs her shoulders and nods. We lead the way and she follows a few steps behind. Several weeks later she tells us she didn't know then what SS&B was. The idea of following strangers to some unknown place scared her half to death, but whatever happened wasn't going to be any worse than the hellacious loneliness she was going through.

A hand appears from behind me. Then another appears beside it as Josh crowds in next to me. A competition begins. Which one of us can strike the most drum pads the quickest. The noise in my headphones is deafening. It has to be the same for Maddie, but she's loving it just the same. Josh is having fun, too, but he doesn't have headphones on, so he can't hear what a racket we're making.

A store employee comes close enough to be sure we see her. She raises her eyebrows. That's all it takes. We all stop at once because we don't want to get kicked out, or worse, be told we can't return. She mouths, *thank you.* We skulk away with our hands in our pockets.

We find Truman. He still has the Stratocaster and as we approach he's stretching the B string on the fifteenth fret as far as he can. His mouth forms an O and his eyes are rolled back so only white shows through the slits of his lids. I'm sure he's paying tribute to one famous guitarist or another, but for the life of me I couldn't tell you which one.

The store employee is still watching us.

"We may want to leave," I suggest. "I think we've maxed out our welcome for today."

"Oh, man," Truman complains. "I was just getting warmed up. I was about to take things to the next level. I'm not lying."

"Yeah. It sounded like it. Stay if you want, but I better leave."

"Same here," Josh says.

Truman looks at Maddie, who shrugs her shoulders to let him know she's leaving too.

"Alright, then. There's always tomorrow."

He carefully hangs the Stratocaster on its hook and follows us toward the exit. We're out the door and already starting down the street when he calls us back.

"Hey! Check this out. It's a Songwriter of the Year contest."

Taped to the storefront glass next to the entrance is a sheet of paper announcing the event. It lists the sponsors, some of the biggest names in the music industry. It gives the rules and deadline for song submissions. We all crowd in to read the fine print.

"Look at all the prizes," Josh says. "A hundred grand if you win. Ten thousand for the runner-up. All kinds of guitars, drums and amplifiers. We should do this."

"What do you know about writing a song?" I ask.

"I didn't say *I*. I said *we*. We should do this."

"Alright, then. What do *we* know about writing a song?"

"We can learn. How hard can it be? Look here."

He points to a line on another sheet of paper taped to the glass. Billboard's 100 best songs of the year.

"*I like it*, by Cardi B and somebody else. It's the number one song on this list. Have you heard it?"

"No," I say. "I don't listen to hip-hop, but that doesn't mean anything. A whole lot of people like hip-hop and most of them like Cardi B, too."

"That's not the point. What I'm saying is, the song isn't much. Without Cardi B shaking her ass on the video, the song would have never made this list. I think we could write one ten times better than that."

"I think we should try," Maddie puts in. "I mean, it's not like we have a lot else going on. Look at it like this, Dylan. Can you think of any other way to put your hands on one hundred grand?"

~3~

Ebony and ivory live together in perfect harmony

Truman Dixon is an African American with five half-sisters he barely knows. His parents divorced shortly after he was born. His mother remarried and had three daughters with her second husband. His father remarried and had two daughters with his second wife. Everyone is happy these days, except for Truman. He's caught in the middle. At his mother's house, he's the son of the other man. At his father's house, he's the son of that other woman.

Before we became friends, I saw Truman around school some, and every now and again I saw him outside of school, but we never spoke. He's small. About five-foot-six and no more than one hundred twenty-five pounds. He has a tall flattop haircut and wears glasses that give him a nerdish appearance. A few of the school bullies call him names. Like shrimp and runt. He always keeps to himself and never does anything that might draw the attention of the alpha males. I noticed this about him because it's something we have in common. During our first conversation, I learned we had other things in common, as well.

"You like music?" he asks.

We're both hanging around after school. Both by ourselves. Both with nowhere better to be.

"Who doesn't?" I reply.

He pulls his earbud out and offers it to me.

"Check this out. I want to know what you think."

17

I insert the earbud. He pushes play. It starts with drums and bass. After a minute, 70s style, distorted electric guitar begins playing. It sounds familiar, but I'm not an aficionado of rock guitarists from that era.

"He's pretty good. Who is it?"

"That's Jeff Beck. He's one of the best there ever was. The song is called Freeway Jam."

"Cool," I say. "Do you play guitar?"

"A little, but nothing like him. I hope to be that good someday. It takes a lot of practice. Hey, you want to go over to Sticks, Strings and Brass. I'll show you some of the guitar licks I've been working on."

That's how my friendship with Truman began almost two years ago. We don't talk much about our families. He knows my real parents died when I was young, and a friend of my father took me in, but he doesn't know the family I live with is black. I know his parents separated when he was young and he has a bunch of half-sisters who don't like him. That's about it.

We joke around a lot, and there aren't many subjects that are off limits. However, a while back Truman started using the N word around me. We'd be kidding around and he'd say something like, "You ain't telling this niggah nothing he don't know, already."

It made me uncomfortable to hear him talk that way. I saw it as a bad habit I didn't want to pick up. I can't imagine what would happen if I let that slip while having dinner with Isiah, Chandra and Nikki. Isiah has never raised a hand to me. Not once. That might be the proverbial straw to break the camel's back.

"I really wish you wouldn't use that word, Truman."

"What word? Niggah?"

"Yeah, that one. A lot of people find it offensive. What if someone overhears you?"

"So what if they do. You mean you've never said it?"

"No, I never have."

"You're trying to tell me you've never once in your life used that word to refer to a black person."

"That's what I'm telling you. I'll swear it on a stack of bibles."

"Damn, Dylan. You might be the strangest white boy I've ever met."

"Truman, you don't know the half of it."

I don't know whether it's because of his size or if it has to do with his five half-sisters who treat him like a stranger. He's painfully shy around women. Breaks out in a sweat and stutters if a woman speaks to him. When Truman and I saw Maddie that first day, I couldn't help but notice how timid she seemed to be. Just like him. I thought the two of them might hit it off. It didn't work that way. It took a long time for them to warm to one another.

Maddie, short for Madeleine, was the epitome of an Indiana farm girl when she arrived in Detroit. Slightly overweight, pasty skin, unkempt hair and a sad face. I could picture her getting up at sunrise to milk a cow and feed the pigs. She had a homey, down-to-earth quality about her that felt out of place in the urban environment. I liked that about her. She was easy to be around. I could simply be myself. Nothing forced or contrived.

After a few months around us she started to come out of her shell. It happened slowly, a little at a time. Something different about her hair one day. A dress instead of jeans another day. And then, a flush to her cheeks and a gleam in her eyes. The transformation was subtle, but it wasn't lost on me. She picks me up when I'm feeling down. I catch myself smiling for no reason just being with her.

I can tell the change in Maddie has affected Truman as well. I worry it might come between us one day. I sure hope not. There was a period when I found myself feeling jealous of other guys who smiled or even looked at Maddie. I'm hoping she never picked up on it. It was wrong to feel that way. She doesn't belong to me, after all. If she meets someone and falls in love with them, I can handle it. In fact, it almost happened, or at least I thought it had.

~4~

Now if six turned out to be nine, I don't mind

Truman, Maddie and I are at the mall on a Saturday in early November. It's unusual for us to go to the mall, but it's a cold and rainy day and the mall is warm and dry. There are a lot of people thinking the same as us that day because the place is packed. We sit on a two-foot-high wall surrounding a pool of water with coins at the bottom and a gurgling fountain in the middle. I'm enjoying watching the different types of people come and go, and the variety of clothing they wear. Maddie sees something displayed in a store window and goes in for a closer look. Truman and I stay put. She's gone for what seems like a long time. I become concerned.

"Do you think we should go check on her?" I ask Truman.

"Give her five more minutes."

She comes into view before the five minutes are up, walking toward us with a good-looking guy beside her. He's a tall, lean Latino kid about our age, fashionably dressed with a pompadour haircut.

"Who's that with her?" Truman asks.

"I don't recognize him."

A moment later Maddie and this new guy are standing in front of us.

"This is Josh," she says. "We have a couple of classes together. He's here by himself, so I told him to come hang with us. Josh, this is Dylan and that's Truman."

I don't think we were rude to Josh that day, but we didn't welcome him into the fold with open arms, either. Nonetheless, he became a regular member of our group after that. It took Truman and me a while to get used to the four of us as opposed to the three of us. Four didn't seem right. It's like adding a fourth musketeer, a fourth stooge or a fourth blind mouse. Maddie sensed my discomfort and took me aside one day.

"Why don't you like Josh? He's a real nice guy. Is it because of me? He thinks you and Truman are jealous of my relationship with him. Are you?"

I wasn't about to confirm his suspicions on that matter.

"No, of course not. You, me and Truman are just friends. That's all. If you and Josh are…, uh, you know, more than friends, we're okay with that."

"Who said we were more than friends?"

"No one said it. I'm just saying if you are, it's okay."

"I'm not sure what you mean by *okay*, but it's not that way with Josh and me. And if it was, that wouldn't change how it is with us. That day when you invited me to come with you and Truman. That meant a lot to me. I was in a bad place, then. I didn't have a single friend in this city. I don't know why you did it, but it made a big difference. The day I saw Josh alone at the mall, I could tell he was in that same bad place. I thought about what you did for me and I wanted to pass it on."

"You make it sound like I saved your life. It was no big deal. We were going to SS&B whether you came with us or not."

"Trust me. It was a big deal to me, Dylan."

We stand there in silence for a moment. Maddie has something on her mind. Something more she wants to say. I wait her out.

"If I tell you something, will you promise not to tell anyone else, not even Truman?"

"Sure. I guess."

"No, Dylan. Promise not to tell. This is important."

"Alright. I promise I won't tell anyone."

"It's about Josh. He's different from you and Truman. I don't want you to hold it against him."

"We won't. I mean, heck, almost everyone is different from Truman and me. We're used to it."

Maddie has to smile at that.

"That's so true. You guys are one of a kind. But that's not exactly what I meant by different. You see, Josh is gay."

You could have knocked me over with a feather. I didn't have a clue, but I feel the need to appear more cosmopolitan in Maddie's eyes.

"I know."

"You do? Since when?"

"I saw some of the signs early on," I lie.

She's doubtful, but lets it slide.

"Those times when Josh and I are talking in low voices, so you and Truman can't hear what we're saying. That's what we're talking about. Him being gay and whether or not he should come out."

"He hasn't told anyone other than you?"

"He's told a few people. Guys like him. He told me he's had sex with one or two guys. His family doesn't know he's gay."

"He's had sex? He's one up on me, then."

"Oh, really? You're a virgin?"

"Uh…, I'm not saying."

"I'm a virgin. It's nothing to be ashamed of."

"It's not that I'm ashamed. It's just not something I want everyone to know about, that's all."

Which is the main reason I don't want to discuss it with her. I can picture her pulling Josh or Truman aside and telling them all about it, the same way she told me about Josh. I'm beginning to wonder if anyone's secret is safe with her.

She can sense my concern. She tries to reassure me.

"Dylan, I want you to know if there is ever anything you need to talk about you can come to me. No matter what it is, it won't go any further. My lips are sealed."

"Good of you to offer, Maddie, but there's nothing I want to share."

~ 5 ~

Hot town, summer in the city

I witness classmates of mine actually sobbing on the last day of school. Seriously. Hands covering their faces, tears streaming down their cheeks, unabashedly bawling like the world is coming to an end. It must be a disorder akin to Stockholm syndrome. That's the only explanation I can come up with.

I'm halfway through the day before I remember it's the last time I'll ever see the inside of a classroom. That's how preoccupied I am. After seeing the notice for the songwriter's contest, Josh, Truman, Maddie and I have a long discussion on the feasibility of entering. Afterward we take a vote. It's unanimous. We decide to enter the contest and make a solid attempt to win.

With that decided, we first have to work out the logistics. We can write the lyrics individually or together as a group. That can be done almost anywhere. The music has to be created and recorded some place where we won't be disturbing anyone and won't be disturbed by anyone. I have a place in mind, but need to run it by the owners. Isiah and Chandra.

"There's this big contest taking place," I say, to break the ice.

It's during dinner on a Wednesday evening. We're having macaroni and cheese. One of my favorites.

"Uh-huh," Chandra replies, with indifference.

"A songwriter's contest."

They both pause mid-bite, glance at one another, then at me.

"The winner gets one hundred thousand dollars and a recording deal."

It's obvious I'm working up to something.

"That's a lot of money," Chandra says. "But what does it have to do with us?"

"I'm going to enter."

It comes out weak, like I'm not quite convinced myself.

Chandra starts to say something, but Isiah speaks over her.

"I think that's a fine idea, Dylan."

Chandra seems ready to argue the statement. Isiah isn't having it.

"I know Trevor would be proud. Have you finished the song you're going to enter in the contest?"

"Actually, we haven't started it, yet."

"We? Someone else is helping you with it?"

"There are four of us. Truman, Maddie, Josh and me. The deadline to enter is August 1st."

"Four heads is better than one. I'm happy to see you get involved in this. I can't think of a better way to spend your time over the summer."

"Finding a job would be better," Chandra says.

I half expected that to come up.

"We've discussed that. Truman, Maddie, Josh and me. We're going to look for jobs and work on our song as we have time."

She doesn't comment, but I can tell she isn't appeased. I have to ask them and it's now or never.

"I need a favor."

Chandra does that thing where she lowers her chin and looks over the top of her glasses at me. It always makes me nervous.

"What do you need?"

"We need a place to rehearse and put together the music. Would it be alright if we used my room in the basement? We'll try to keep the sound level down, so we don't bother you."

"I don't know if I...," Chandra starts to say. Isiah cuts in.

"I think that would be okay for a couple of hours at a time, a few days a week. Is that what you had in mind?"

"We haven't gotten that far with planning. Six hours a week over three days would probably be plenty."

"Wait a minute," Chandra says. "I haven't said yes, yet. We're not through discussing this."

"Come on, Chandra. What's it going to hurt?" Isiah says.

"I don't know anything about these friends of yours, Dylan. Where did you meet them? What kind of families do they come from? Have they been in trouble with the law? Do you know the answer to those questions?"

"Did you know any of that about me before we started dating?" Isiah asks. "Dylan, why don't you bring your friends by for us to meet them."

"Sure, I can do that. When?"

"This weekend sometime. Is that alright with you, Chandra?"

"I suppose so, but I still haven't said yes, yet."

"Thank you both. You'll like my friends."

I get up from the table and take my dish to the sink, pleased with the course of the conversation.

"Dylan," Chandra calls to me.

"Yes?"

"Don't forget. Nikki will be home from college for the summer in a few days. You'll have to consult with her before you schedule any rehearsals."

I'd forgotten all about Nikki.

"Crap," I mutter under my breath.

"What's that, Dylan?"

"I said I'd forgotten about Nikki. I'll be sure to discuss it with her when she gets here."

I'm afraid I know how that discussion will go before it ever starts. I know how it will end, as well. There never seems to be any winning with Nikki. The more diplomatic I try to be, the more obstinate she becomes.

~6~

She's a brick …. house

There's something I haven't told you about Nikki. On one plane it's difficult for me to admit. On another level it's more than a little creepy. Nikki is absolutely gorgeous. To be totally honest, she might be the hottest girl on the planet. There, I said it. She gets her looks from Chandra, who is without a doubt a very attractive older woman. I bet she was really something twenty years ago. I'm not sure how Isiah ended up with her. As much as I love him, Isiah is butt ugly.

Nikki wasn't anything special when we were kids. Even in her early teens her legs, arms and ears seemed out of proportion with the rest of her body. Her last year in high school it all started to come together. She was easily the most popular girl in her senior class. The guys chased her around like hounds after a fox. She went through them at the rate of two a week, toying with them the way a cat does with a mouse. Teasing, manipulating and tantalizing them until they begged for mercy.

I informed my friends of the possibility my basement room could be used for rehearsals. Then, I told them it was contingent on making a good impression on Isiah and Chandra.

"What are your parents like?" Josh asks.

"They're not my parents. I've lived with them for fifteen years. They're great people. Isiah is supportive of what we're doing. Chandra isn't sure she wants strangers in her house. Just be yourselves when you meet her. That's all we can do."

Isiah, Chandra and I agree on Sunday afternoon at 1:30 as the time. I pass that on to Truman, Maddie and Josh. Nikki comes home Saturday, parties late with friends and sleeps until noon the next day. She isn't told about this rehearsal thing until thirty minutes before my friends are due to arrive. It doesn't go over well.

"What! Here, in my house? Why wasn't I told before now?"

"Calm down, Nikki," Chandra soothes. "I haven't had a chance to tell you. You were out last night and slept until a short while ago. Dylan's friends are going to be here at one thirty. I'd like you to meet them, if you feel up to it. That way you can make mention of any certain time when their rehearsals would be inconvenient for you."

"Oh, you can be sure I'll do that."

The gang arrives on time. I usher them in. They look petrified.

"Don't worry. You're going to do fine," I tell them.

They follow me into the kitchen where Isiah and Chandra are sitting at the dining table. Maddie doesn't wait for an introduction.

"Hi," she says, crossing the room. "I'm Madeleine Lee. Call me Maddie. You must be Isiah and Chandra. Dylan has told me all about you."

Josh follows her lead, extending his hand to Isiah and then to Chandra.

"I'm Josh Martinez. It's good to meet you."

So far things are going well.

"This is Truman Dixon," I say.

He parts his lips preparing to speak. At that precise moment, Nikki enters. She quickly scans the faces in the room, going from Josh to Maddie and pausing on Truman.

He's frozen in place, staring at Nikki with his mouth gaping open.

Did I mention how agonizingly shy Truman can be around girls?

Nikki's mouth spreads to display two rows of sparkling white teeth. There's nothing friendly about it. It's more like a wolf curling its lips back and baring its teeth before pouncing on its prey.

"What are you looking at?" she says.

A rhetorical question, of course.

"Uh…, uh…, uh…," Truman stutters.

Isiah intercedes.

"Would anyone like a soda?"

A chorus of *I dos* reverberates in the small room. I grab the cans from the refrigerator and pass them out.

"I'm just curious," Isiah says. "What made you all decide to enter this songwriting contest?"

We look at one another for a moment. I recall Truman seeing the notice taped to the glass at SS&B.

"It was Truman's idea. He found out about it, first."

Give credit where it's due, I figure. Truman is able to divert his attention away from Nikki long enough to speak to Isiah.

"I just happened to see this sheet of paper in the window at the music store, Sticks, Strings and Brass. When it comes to writing a song, I don't even know where to start. I wouldn't attempt it if these three weren't willing to give it a shot."

"Same here," Josh agrees.

"And here," Maddie chimes in.

This seems to please Isiah. Although he seldom talks about it, I know his days as a musician hold many special memories. The gigs and rehearsals, and the camaraderie with the other band members. It all adds up to a thousand memorable moments. He's in our corner. Chandra and Nikki are another matter.

"If we let you rehearse here, I have a few rules I expect you to follow," Chandra says.

"I have a few rules, myself," Nikki says.

"In a minute, Nikki. There's no smoking in this house. Not cigarettes or anything else. And no alcohol. None of you are old enough to drink legally. You clean up after yourselves. And you keep the volume at a reasonable level."

"That's no problem," I say. "We can do those things. Right guys?"

They all nod vigorously.

"No one goes anywhere near my room. Put that at the top of the list of rules. Stay away from my room."

"Is that all, Nikki?" Chandra asks.

"For now."

"What time of day are you thinking about?" Chandra asks next. "I'm thinking afternoon would be best. Nikki sometimes sleeps late. And you should wrap up before 4:30. That's what time some of the neighbors get home from work."

Things were going better than I expected.

"How about this? We'll start no earlier than one and quit no later than four on Tuesdays and Thursdays."

She thought about it a moment, then nodded once.

"Okay."

~7~

Running on empty, running blind, running behind

The toughest thing about writing a song is deciding where to begin. We agree to mull it over individually beforehand, thinking we'll compare notes at our first rehearsal. I toss ideas around in my head, jot down words and pluck tunes on my dad's bass. Nothing. If each of the others comes up with as much it's going to be a rough start.

Tuesday, Isiah and Chandra are at their respective jobs until five or so. Nikki is who knows where doing who knows what. Not home, in other words. Monday, Chandra reminded her of our rehearsal saying she might want to leave the house while it was going on.

"I don't have to go anywhere if I don't want to," Nikki says, just to be contrary, something she excels at.

It isn't as if she's staying home to read a book. Her day planner is filled with shopping, seeing friends and hanging out where she'll be seen.

The gang arrives together right on time. I invite them in. On the way to my room Truman keeps looking around.

"She's not here," I tell him.

"Who?" he asks, unconvincingly.

"Who wants to go first," I ask, once we are situated inside my basement room with the door closed.

We're seated on stools and chairs I borrowed from elsewhere in the house, looking at one another expectantly. It's as I feared it would be. Between the four of us we have zip.

"You guys are into different styles of music than I am," Maddie says. "I was afraid you wouldn't like my ideas."

"Right now, any idea is better than what we have," Truman points out.

"That's true, but I sort of feel the same way as Maddie," Josh says. "I like a different kind of music than you do. I think we need to establish some ground rules before we go further."

"Every successful group has a leader," Truman says. "We should vote on which one of us would be best for the job."

"I vote for Dylan," Maddie says.

"I second it," Josh says.

"Hold on a minute," I say. "We're looking at this wrong. There must be a thousand different ways to write a song. If we start making rules for how we're going to do it, we only limit ourselves. Rules are restrictions. They stem the flow of creativity. We're blocking our flow by worrying about things that don't matter."

No one speaks for a long moment. They stare at me like I'm speaking in a foreign language.

Then, Truman says, "Damn, Dylan. That was heavy. You were telling us we don't need a leader and at the same time you were leading us exactly where we need to go. You've got my vote. Tell us what to do next."

"I appreciate you three voting for me, but I don't know if I want to be the leader. We just need to start somewhere and hopefully things will come together in time. Did anyone write down any lyrics?"

More silence and looking at one another.

"I'll take that as a big no. What about a word? One word that you like how it sounds or its meaning? We can start with one word. Maybe we use it in the title. We can try building the lyrics around that one word."

"How about Stratocaster," Truman suggests.

Because he falls asleep every night dreaming of owning a guitar by that name the word is never far from his thoughts. I don't want to discourage him, but at the same time it doesn't feel right for a hit song.

"There aren't many things that rhyme with Stratocaster," I say.

"Sure there are."

To prove his point, he begins rapping lyrics.

"I'll be the master, when I get my Stratocaster. You can put me out to pasture, cause I've got my Stratocaster. Won't nobody play faster, than me on my Stratocaster. It would be a disaster, if someone stole my Stratocaster. See, and that's off the top of my head. I could come up with others if I had more time to think about it."

I clap for his performance, albeit not very enthusiastically.

"Not bad, Truman," Maddie says. "But Stratocaster doesn't feel right to me. I'm not sure that many people know what it is. Sorry."

"That's okay. It doesn't hurt my feelings. I got things started. Someone else think of a word."

"Jazz Bass," I say, just to get a laugh.

"What if we focus on the meaning of the word?" Josh says. "A word that makes you think of being free and happy, or free like floating through the air."

"I like the concept," I say. "That thing where the astronauts float around weightless in the space capsule, they call that zero g-force. Is that what you mean?"

"Yeah, sort of."

"Zero g-force," Truman repeats. "It's catchy, but most people won't understand what it is."

"Yeah, probably not. It's the first thing that came to mind when Josh said floating through the air."

"You've been quiet, Maddie. Have you got a word?"

"I thought of one, but I don't think you'll like it."

"You can't think that way," Truman says. "Screw us if we don't like it. That's what you have to tell yourself. Go ahead and say it."

"Alright. What about suspend. That's sort of like floating."

She grimaces as she says it, like she expects it to be shot down. I don't comment initially. Instead, I let the word echo through my head and try to imagine it in a song with a little reverb to soften its edges and smooth it out.

Something about the word is familiar. It's triggering a memory. One which is locked away and difficult to access. Truman raps a few lines with the word.

"I hope you don't mind my friend, but I think I'm gonna suspend. There's no need to pretend, you didn't see me suspend. Now don't you be offended, when I get myself suspended."

We all clap this time.

"Truman," I say. "Have I ever told you how much I hate hip-hop?"

"About a hundred times. That's okay. I hate it too. I can't help it if I have a natural ability for rap singing. It must be in my genes."

"Hip-hop aside, I like the way it sounds. Suspend."

It pleases Maddie to make a contribution. Seeing the smile on her face pleases me.

"I think we should work with it and see what happens," I say. "Everyone start putting phrases together using a form of the word. Suspend, suspended suspending. Okay? The next thing we need to work on is the music. You may have noticed we don't have much in the way of instruments."

"I have a miniature keyboard," Maddie says. "I've had it since I was ten. It's really just a toy."

"Bring it next time. It can't hurt."

"I have a harmonica," Josh says.

"It's one more instrument. For now, we have a harmonica, a keyboard and a bass guitar. Once we have the song together we may need to rent some instruments in order to record it."

"That will take money," Josh says. "And...,"

No need to finish that sentence. Between the four of us we couldn't scrape together enough dough to rent a Jew's harp.

"Maybe we can find part-time jobs," Maddie says.

"Maybe," I reply, though I don't like my chances.

~8~

Takin' what they're givin' cause I'm workin' for a livin'

I'm amazed at our good fortune. Truman hears about a job opportunity at Bubba's Catfish Restaurant. We go there to inquire about it and are both hired on the spot. I can't believe it. Ten bucks an hour, five hours a day, six days a week. No skill, no experience, no problem. After the first day of work, I understand why there isn't a long line of applicants competing for the job.

We begin our workday at 6:00 AM, Monday through Saturday and are off at 11:00. The lunch crowd packs the place from 11:00 to 2:00. The big draw is the all-you-can-eat fried catfish buffet. At 10:00 PM each night, after the dinner crowd leaves, they turn off the six frying vats in the kitchen. By the time we get there at six, the grease has cooled enough for us to begin cleaning up. I've never seen so much grease. It's everywhere. Literally. If I live to be two hundred I'll never eat fried food again.

"What do you think that is?" I ask Truman.

I've come across something blackened and crispy at the bottom of a vat after draining the grease through a filter into a holding tank. It's an odd shape for catfish and though I'm no marine biologist, I don't think catfish have feet.

"I don't know and I don't care. Throw it in the trash and don't think about it no more. That kind of thing will give you nightmares."

He's right. I'll be better off if I don't closely scrutinize certain things. I won't lie to you. There isn't much I like about the job, other than the money. With money we have hope, confidence and more options.

Josh finds work, too, making evening deliveries for Anthony's Pizzeria.

Maddie surprises us all. She doesn't tell us beforehand. Maybe it was a spur-of-the-moment decision. She walks into Sticks, Strings and Brass, asks for a job application and starts work two days later. I'm so jealous I can't see straight. Truman is furious with her, but he'll get over it.

The money we earn will take care of renting the equipment necessary to record our contest-winning song. The different work schedules make rehearsing difficult, though. Since Truman and I work the same hours, we're able to get together three times a week. The only thing is we seem to be going in different directions, musically speaking.

"Let's take it from the top," Truman says.

At three in the afternoon Truman, Josh and I are tweaking the latest version of our song, 'Suspend'. Maddie can't be there because of her job at SS&B. Josh has to be at the pizzeria in thirty minutes.

"The world's coming to an end," Truman raps.

Boomp-duh-duh-boomp-duh-boomp, I pluck on the bass.

Josh slaps his thighs in 4/4 time while using his tongue against the roof of his mouth to simulate a hi-hat sound.

"Chic-ca" slap "chic-ca" slap "chic-ca" slap slap.

"I'm unable to comprehend," comes the next line.

Boomp-duh-duh-boomp-duh-boomp. "Chic-ca" slap "chic-ca" slap.

"If I'm unable to defend." Boomp-duh-duh, "chic-ca" slap slap.

"My soul will certainly suspend." Boomp-duh, "chic-ca" slap.

We end the song there, knowing Josh has to go.

"Sorry to cut out on you guys, but my boss is a real pain about me being there on time."

"That's okay. We understand. Do what you have to do and we'll see you next time."

"What do you think?" Truman asks, after Josh is gone.

"About the song?"

"Of course about the song, dumb-ass. What else would I be asking you about?"

"Can I be honest?"

"It won't make any difference if I begged you to lie to me. You're going to go ahead and tell me what you think, no matter how badly you hurt my feelings. You know that."

"As I've already stated on several previous occasions, I hate hip-hop. Maybe if I explained what it is I dislike about it, you'll have a better understanding of why I'm dead set against submitting a hip-hop song as our entry in the contest."

"I doubt it, but go ahead, anyway."

"The first thing I dislike about it is this. All hip-hop artists sound angry. I don't like listening to angry people. Another thing is it's repetitious. Every song sounds like the one before. It seems to me hip-hop artists sell more records because of their bad-boy persona than because of the music."

"Is that it?"

"Isn't that enough?"

Truman isn't taking my criticism well. I can't really blame him. It isn't given constructively. I don't suggest how we can improve on the song. I shoot it down unfairly.

"Maybe I'm being too critical. You do great with lyrics. You're real creative. All I'm saying is I think it would be better to soften the song overall. So it appeals to a wider audience."

"You are being too critical. You always are, but that's just you. I can take it. I'm not thin-skinned. What you said about softening the song. I've been thinking the same thing. What it needs is a woman's touch. That's where Maddie comes in, but she's working in the afternoons. Is there any chance we could get together here in the evening after she gets off?"

"I'd have to run it by Isiah and Chandra. I don't know how they'll feel about it. Then there's Nikki. Most likely she won't be home before midnight, but if she is home she'll pitch a fit over it."

"Speaking of your sister...,"

"She's not my sister and we weren't speaking of her."

"Speaking of Nikki, then. That fine looking black girl that lives here."

"Don't go there, Truman. I'm telling you as a friend, she'll rip your heart out and stomp all over it."

"Maybe you could put in a good word for me. Tell her what a fine upstanding young man I am."

"A good word from me won't help. She hates my guts."

"Maybe you can warn her to stay away from me, then. You know. Try some reverse psychology on her."

"Stay away from you? What? Like I want you all to myself. I don't think so dude. I'm going to tell you one more time. She's dangerous. You're playing with fire. Stay away from her if you value your sanity."

"I see what you're doing, now. You're trying some of that reverse psychology on me. Aren't you?"

"I'm only trying to save you from yourself, but I sense my advice is falling on deaf ears."

"My ears are just fine. I think I see what's going on here. You've got a thing for her. That's why you keep saying she's not your sister and I need to stay away from her. You want her for yourself."

If it was anyone other than Truman saying that to me I'd have him in a headlock until he took it back.

"You're wrong about that. I don't see her as my sister because she doesn't see me as her brother. It's mutual. We hate each other. We only tolerate one another because Isiah and Chandra make us."

"I see. This sounds like a case of unrequited love if you ask me."

I'm used to Truman needling me, but even he can go too far.

"For the last time, I don't have a thing for Nikki and you shouldn't either. If you're not going to listen, then all I've got to say is don't come crying to me after Nikki chews you up and spits you out."

~9~

All you got to do is pick up your telephone

Having money in my pocket feels strangely unfamiliar. Not that I can't get used to it. For my entire life, right up until my first payday at Bubba's, I walked around with only what I'd been given to cover the necessities for that day. Lunch money, bus fare, change for a soda, that sort of thing. Things were easier then. I'm convinced money complicates much more than it simplifies. I guess I'll get used to that, too.

The first thing I purchase is a prepaid cellular phone, so I can stay in contact with the others. They do the same. This is going to be hard for most people to believe, but none of the four of us ever had a cell phone before now. The first call I make is to Truman, who calls Josh, who calls Maddie, who calls me.

"Hi Dylan. This feels so strange talking to you on the phone."

"I know what you mean. I've gotten used to seeing your lips move when you talk."

I've gotten used to so many other things about her, as well. Things I probably shouldn't tell her. Like the strand of her curly red hair that's always falling down over one eye, and the way she flicks it back with her finger. The way her nose turns up when she smiles or the way her eyes dance when she laughs.

"How are things at SS&B?" I say.

"I love working here. Everyone is real nice. I've missed being at the rehearsals with you guys. How are things going?"

"Not great. I feel like we're in a rut. Truman and I were talking yesterday. We think our song needs female input. I still have to get permission from Isiah and Chandra, but we were wondering if you could come by after work for rehearsal. It wouldn't be every night."

"I'd like to do that. I'm feeling left out as it is. What about tonight? I'm off work in an hour. There's a bus stop at the corner. I could come straight there instead of going home."

"Umm…, Chandra and Isiah won't be home before you get off."

"We can do it tomorrow night if you'd rather."

I'm eager to make some progress on the song. I'm excited about seeing Maddie, too. Josh is working. Truman probably won't be able to make it over on such short notice. I don't think Chandra and Isiah will object if it's only Maddie and me.

"We can do it tonight. Josh and Truman won't be here. It won't be as noisy if it's just you and me. I'm sure Isiah and Chandra won't mind."

"Just you and me?" Maddie asks, sounding apprehensive.

"Is that okay with you?"

"Umm…, I guess."

"So I'll see you around six?"

"I'm not sure what time the bus comes. It should be about then. I'll call if it's going to be much later. Bye."

"Bye."

"You'll see who around six?" Nikki says.

I didn't hear her come in and don't know how long she's been listening.

"That was Maddie. She wants to show me something."

"Oh, I bet she does. I bet you want to show her something, too."

"That's not what I mean. It has to do with the song we're working on for the contest."

Nikki flashes a knowing grin.

"Are you sure that's all it is? Because I've seen how you look at her. You've got it bad for her. Does she feel the same about you? Probably not is what I'm guessing. But then how could she? I mean look at you."

"Give it a rest, Nikki. Don't you have anything better to do than criticize me and my friends?"

"I didn't say anything about your friends. Let me ask you something. Have you ever been intimate with a girl?"

No one is better at getting under my skin than Nikki.

"None of your business," I shout. "Have you?"

"That's what I thought. That is so pathetic. Eighteen years old and never kissed a girl. Would you like me to teach you how? If you don't hold your lips right or if you close your eyes too soon it might gross her out. It could ruin everything. I'll let you borrow my Barbie doll so you can practice for the big moment."

I'm red-faced and trembling with anger, but I manage to keep my voice level.

"Nikki, please go away."

"I'm just trying to help you keep from making a fool of yourself. But if you don't want my help, then I guess I'll leave."

She walks away snickering at me. One day she's going to push me too far and I'll go off on her. She better hope Isiah is around to pull me off of her when it happens. That's all I have to say about it.

Chandra is so tired when she gets home all she wants to do is kick off her shoes and put on something comfortable. I tell her only that Maddie is coming over. Nothing more.

"That's good, Dylan. She seems like a nice girl. I've had a long, hard day. I'm going to lie down for a bit."

Maddie arrives ten minutes later.

"Hi, Dylan," she says, as I open the door and invite her in.

I lead her toward the basement. We've taken only two steps before Nikki appears from somewhere.

"Well, hi Maddie," she says in a sickly-sweet manner. "It's nice of you to drop in on little Dylan like this. The poor boy has so few friends. Dylan, you behave yourself with this girl. You hear? I don't want you treating her like those others."

"Nikki, would you please go back in your room and stop bothering us?"

"Oh my. There's that temper of yours. I better do as you say, because I wouldn't want you hitting me again."

She walks away snickering. Again. I pretend it doesn't bother me and continue toward my room. Maddie hurries to keep up.

"It was nice seeing you again," she calls over her shoulder to Nikki. To me she says, "She's awfully nice."

"Trust me. She's really not."

"You don't really hit her do you?"

"No. Or at least not since I was four."

"I didn't think so. She doesn't look like she's been knocked around much. She seems like the sort who can hold her own in a fight."

"I wouldn't bet against her. That's for sure."

~10~

She takes just like a woman

My basement room seems even smaller than usual as Maddie and I descend the stairs. And considerably warmer, as well. I feel sweat beading on my forehead and dampening my armpits. I try to remember when I last brushed my teeth or used deodorant.

"You want a soda?" I ask.

"No thanks. You said rehearsals weren't going great and you feel like you're in a rut. What seems to be the problem?"

"I can't put my finger on it. We rewrite, add and delete lines. Each time we play the song with the new lines, Truman starts rapping them to the same beat as before. It feels like I'm being sucked into a hole that I can't climb out of."

"Oh, come on. It's not that bad. Have you told Truman how you feel?"

"Yes. More than once. The thing is, he feels the song needs something more, too. We just don't know what. Maybe if we soften it some. I know hip-hop music is popular, but it has a hard edge to it. I'm picturing something more flowing and melodic. You know what I mean?"

"I think so. Let's try some things. Play a few notes on your bass and I'll hum a melody. Maybe we'll hit on something we like."

I turn my amplifier on, dial the volume back to the lowest setting and begin plucking the strings.

boomp-boomp-duh-duh-boomp.

"Slow it down a little. Try putting more space between the notes and letting them reverberate longer. See how that sounds."

I do what she asks of me.

boooomp—duuhh—duuhh—

I switch it up, moving randomly to other notes.

Maddie hums softly, letting her voice modulate, grow louder, then softer. Her lips part. A sensual moan escapes. It sends a chill up my back. I realize I'm holding my breath. I exhale.

"Mmm—mmm—mmm-ah-mmm—mmm—mmm."

A melody is taking shape.

"Right there," she says to me. "That note and the one before it. Play those two back and forth."

I do.

boompf—buumpf—boompf—buumpf—

She hums a melody. It's more structured than before. It sounds familiar.

"I think I've heard this before."

"It's a song by Carrie Underwood."

"I don't think I know anything by her. She's a country singer, isn't she?"

"That's right. She's one of my favorites, but I listen to a lot of others."

"I didn't realize you like country music. That's interesting."

"My mother was into old-time country western. People like Loretta Lynn and Tammy Wynette. Growing up listening to that stuff had a big influence on me."

I didn't see this coming. Though maybe I should have. Maddie's down-home, farm girl persona goes hand in hand with country western music. This creates a whole new dilemma for me. If there is any genre of music I hate more than hip-hop, it's country western. Maddie picks up on this.

"Is it a problem if I like country music?"

"Of course not. I hadn't considered it a possibility for the contest. That's all."

"Dylan, you're being too narrow-minded. First, it can't be hip-hop, now it can't be country. What's next? How do you feel about salsa?"

I answer her question with a grimace.

"See. That's what I mean. Wasn't it you who said there must be a thousand ways to write a song and we shouldn't restrict our creativity, or something like that. Take a page from your own book or practice what you preach, in other words."

I know she's right. What bothers me is that it wasn't more obvious to me before now.

"You're right. I'm sorry. Truman tells me I'm too critical, sometimes. I'll work on it. You want to do some more?"

"Yes, I do. Will it help if I keep time?"

"It couldn't hurt."

Maddie starts things off, swaying and snapping her fingers at a moderate pace. I walk my fingers up and then down the fretboard in C major scale, thankful I learned something in the music theory class I took. Maddie improvises a few lines.

"Yeah, baby you know what I mean. You make me feel so good."

Be objective, I tell myself.

"Whoa, don't you feel it too. Talk to me, baby."

I like the way it sounds. Sweet and sultry. She picks up the tempo. I try to match it. I don't know if we're creating anything we can use later, but we're having fun. After ten minutes of intense jamming Maddie signals to stop. She's sweating and breathing hard. I have a passing thought involving Nikki walking in right about now and making false assumptions about what's going on here. My phone sounds a call coming in.

"Hello," I answer.

"Dylan, what's up? Did you talk to Maddie, yet?"

It's Truman. I put my fingers to my lips to shush Maddie.

"Not yet. Chandra needed my help with something, so I've been kind of busy. I'm still working on it. Can I call you back in a while?"

"Don't worry about it. I'll talk to you tomorrow at Bubba's."

"Okay, later."

I can feel Maddie's eyes burning into me as I disconnect.

"That was Truman?" she asks.

Not a question, really. She knows it was him.

"Yeah. He called to see how things were going."

Then, why did you hush me? And what was that about helping Chandra?"

I'm caught in a lie, there's no denying it. Covering up one lie with another has never worked well for me, so I decide to come clean and tell a version of the truth.

"I wasn't sure Chandra would be okay with us rehearsing this late, but I knew she wouldn't mind if it was just you and me. I didn't tell Truman that because I thought it might hurt his feelings."

"You could have told me that. I would have understood."

"I probably should have explained earlier. There was the thing with Nikki and then we came down here. We started playing and I didn't think about it after that."

Neither of us speaks for a long moment. I look at her looking back at me and can't get a sense of what she's thinking.

Then she asks, "Do you like me? People don't lie to those they like."

"Of course I like you. You're one of my best friends. I didn't lie to you about Truman, I just didn't tell you everything all at once."

"Did you want to be alone with me? Is that why you didn't let Truman know I was coming over here?"

I'm not sure I'm ready to confess that to her. I haven't even admitted it to myself, yet. I need to be careful how I phrase this.

"If I say yes, I wanted it to be just us here today, will it upset you?"

She steps closer, takes one of my hands and squeezes it between both of hers. At five foot three, the top of her head comes to my nose. Her face is downcast looking at my hand. Her hair is full of smells of the city. Cigarette smoke, bus fumes and shampoo long ago rinsed away. I inhale deeply. She raises her eyes to meet mine.

"I like Truman and Josh. They'll always be my friends. I feel differently about you. I have since the first. It's nice to be with you like this. I hope we can do it again."

"Me, too," I say. "Do you want to rehearse more?"

"Not really. If it's alright with you, I'd like to do exactly what we're doing a while longer."

"Okay."

I put my free arm around her waist and pull her closer. She presses her face to my chest and I rest my chin on her head. It has been a long time since my body was against another like this. Isiah and Chandra hugged me when I was younger, but not these days. Body contact with Nikki has always been in the form of a hit or kick. Being held and caressed is something I haven't experienced since my parents died.

~11~

You were always on my mind

I t's after dark when Maddie is ready to leave. I follow her up the stairs from my room. Isiah is in the front room watching TV by himself. He's into the show and doesn't notice us at first.

"Hi, Mr. Jones," Maddie says.

He's startled momentarily, but quickly recovers.

"Hello, Maddie. I didn't know you were here. It's good to see you. How are the rehearsals going?"

Since there hasn't been any sound coming from the basement, I'm pretty sure Isiah knows we haven't been rehearsing.

"I think they're going well," Maddie says.

She looks at me, so I nod in agreement.

"I'm glad to hear it. I'm happy to see young people like you get involved in something like this. I have a lot of good memories of the days when I played in a band."

"Dylan said you played drums. Do you still play occasionally?"

"No. Not for a long time."

His reply is given wistfully. For a moment he's somewhere else. A faraway place in another era, I presume.

"I'm going to ride the bus with Maddie, to be sure she gets home okay."

"That's a good idea. You be careful. And call me if you have any problems. Goodnight, Maddie."

The round trip to Maddie's place and back is uneventful. I see her home safely and return without incident. I undress and plop down on the mattress on the concrete floor of my room. An hour earlier, Maddie lay here beside me. It's not what you think. We didn't make out or anything. Our clothing never even got ruffled. For a couple of hours we felt the warmth of our bodies touching against one another. Nothing more. I really needed that. I breathe in her scent as I lie back and drift off.

Deep and restful sleep eludes me most nights. My eyes shut, but my brain continues to churn out images from my past. On this night the image is that of my mother. It's been so long I don't recognize her immediately.

"Dylan," she calls to me. "It's me, your mom."

I don't answer because I don't trust what I'm seeing.

"Don't be mad at me," she says.

"I'm not," I reply, but in truth I'm furious.

Who wouldn't be furious with a mother who abandoned them as a child? She comes closer. Her arms reach out and wrap around me pulling me to her.

"You don't know how much I've missed you. I'm so sorry we had to leave. It wasn't our choice."

I know this is true. I've heard what happened. She doesn't deserve to be the target of my anger, but I've held on to it waiting to release it on someone or something for all this time.

"Why?" I ask.

It comes out as an accusation. One hundred questions rolled into that one word. Why you? Why me? Why then and there? I wish the memory of my parents was crystal clear, but it's not. I'd like to be able to recall everything they ever said to me because I'm sure they dished out a lot of important advice from time to time.

She doesn't try to explain. How can she? I often wonder if they somehow anticipated their deaths and suspected I'd be left on my own. A premonition, perhaps. I feel her hand softly stroke my hair. Close to my ear she begins singing. The voice is so familiar. It's the same one she used to lull me asleep when I was a baby.

I shut my eyes for only a second. When I open them again, she's gone and the clock next to my bed says five fifteen. There's no time to think about the dream or vision or whatever the visit from my mother can be called. I'm due at Bubba's Catfish Restaurant in forty-five minutes. I dress and run to catch the bus. I arrive ten minutes late, which means I'll have to work that much harder to be done by eleven.

"Are you okay?" Truman asks.

We've been at work for an hour and I haven't said a word.

"Yeah. I'm a little distracted, that's all."

"Does it have to do with our song?"

It doesn't, but I'm not about to tell him my dead mother came to visit me, or that the words of a song she sang are bouncing around in my head.

"That's part of it," I say, instead.

"You worry too much, Dylan. It will come together. I know it will. You just have to relax and let it happen."

"I'll try."

We don't have rehearsal scheduled today. The door to Nikki's room is closed when I get home at noon. I tiptoe past to go shower. After I've cleaned the grease off, I sequester myself in my room. All morning at Bubba's I thought about the words my mother sang last night. I need to write them down before I forget.

Verse 1
The greatest force known to man cannot compare with love
Love can overcome all obstacles, to lift you high above
Love will wrap you in its grasp, and comfort you all night
Watch over you as you sleep, until the morning light
Verse 2
My love for you is the greatest gift that I have to give
Like a blanket it will keep you warm, as long as I may live
And if something should happen to me and I'm no longer here
I'll leave my love behind with you, to help you persevere
Chorus
Love will transcend heaven and hell to reach you anywhere
In times of need, think of me, and somehow I will appear
Love will transcend the worlds between us, I know this to be true
Open up your heart to love and feel it coming through
Verse 3
Life can take some twists and turns that catch you unprepared
And if I'm not around I don't want you to be scared
There may be times you find yourself facing loneliness and dread
I may not be there in the flesh, but remember what I said
Repeat Chorus

~12~

I've got sunshine on a cloudy day

It's been fourteen hours since the song was delivered to me and I'm still unsure of exactly what took place. I know most people will laugh at me if I tell them. Hell, I'd laugh too if someone told me their dead mother sang to them last night. I don't intend to share that part with the others.

Not yet, anyway. I am anxious to see what they think of the lyrics, though. I'll get together with Truman and Josh tomorrow and sing it the way I heard it. If they like it, maybe Maddie can come over after work so she can hear it.

Speaking of Maddie. I've been busy with the lyrics and haven't thought of her. I should probably call her tonight after she gets off. It's what she'd expect after last night, I think. Is it presumptuous of me to think of her as my girlfriend? Probably, but I don't know. I've never had a girlfriend.

How do we go from just being friends to being a couple? There must be a transition period of some kind. I wish there was someone I could ask about such things. Truman and Josh don't know any more than I do. Isiah and I never discuss those things. Nikki is a self-professed expert on boy/girl relationship etiquette, but no way am I going to her with this.

Five o'clock comes. Maddie is leaving work about now. I think about her waiting at the bus stop. It's a twenty-minute ride to where she gets off to walk home. I give it until six. That should be plenty of time. I punch in her number and listen to it ring three times before she picks up.

"Hi," she answers.

She's breathing hard.

"It's me, Dylan. Did I catch you at a bad time?"

"I know it's you. I recognized the number. No, you didn't catch me at a bad time. I'm walking home from the bus stop. I'm glad you called. I've been thinking about you."

I breathe a sigh of relief.

"I've been thinking about you, too. Hey, guess what."

"What?"

"I wrote a song. It sort of came to me in my sleep."

"A whole song? You mean from start to finish with words and music?"

"Yes. I wrote the lyrics down. The music is in my head."

"I want to hear it."

I'm really shy when it comes to singing. I don't even sing in the shower.

"I don't know if I can."

"Why not? Just sing the first couple of lines."

"I don't think I can do it justice, singing a cappella over the phone. I'll wait until the next time I see you."

"I've got an idea. Let's meet at Riverfront Park. There's always stuff going on there."

"Now?"

"Sure. Why not? It'll be fun. Meet me at the intersection of Orleans Street and Atwater in an hour."

She hangs up before I can say no. Which is just as well. Spending the evening hanging with Maddie. It does sound like fun.

I catch up with her at the agreed upon time and place. For three hours we stroll the river walk, talking and laughing like we're the only ones there. We eat sausages on a stick and later have ice cream.

"I've had a great time," I say. "I hate for it to end, but I have to be at Bubba's at six. By the time I see you home and make it back to my house it will be midnight."

"I'm not letting you go until you sing your song."

I hadn't forgotten. I was hoping she had.

"I didn't bring the lyrics with me. I'm not sure I can remember them."

"Quit stalling, Dylan. Sing what you can remember. What's the first line? Sing that."

I glance around to see if anyone is nearby. No one is, so I begin.

"The greatest force known to man cannot compare with love."

I stop there, hoping that's enough.

"Go on."

"Love can overcome all obstacles, to lift you high above."

"I like it a lot," Maddie says. "I really do. This came to you while you slept? Like in a dream?"

"More or less."

"That's amazing. We've been struggling to come up with the words and music for the song. I was beginning to wonder if we ever would. Then you put together the whole thing in one night. What are you not telling me?"

It's uncanny how girls always seem to know when you're holding out on them.

"I'll admit I haven't told you everything, but it's for the best. We've been getting along so well. I don't want you to think I'm weird."

"I'm not going to think that. We talked about this last night, after Truman called. I want us to feel like we can trust one another. There shouldn't be secrets between us."

Keeping it from her might do more damage than telling her, I decide.

"I don't know what the technical term is. Last night my mother visited me. She sang the song. I recalled the lyrics and wrote them down."

"Your mother? Chandra?"

"No. Chandra isn't my mother. I mean my real mother. The one who died fifteen years ago."

"She came to visit you?"

"I know how that sounds."

"You mean like a ghost?"

"More like a dream, only so real it couldn't have been a dream."

"You remember a minute ago when I said I wouldn't think you were weird? Well, I take it back."

~13~

Tell me something I don't know

Halfway through our shift at Bubba's we get a ten-minute break. It's the same routine every day. We get coffee in a Styrofoam cup and sit in the alley behind the restaurant to drink it. It stinks like hell back there because it's where all the trash containers are kept. But, it's the only place to sit where we don't have to worry about transferring the grease from our clothing to furniture or walls.

"There's something I need to tell you."

I owe it to Truman to tell him about Maddie and me. After all, I've known him longer.

"If you're going to tell me you're gay, I don't want to hear it."

"I'm not gay."

This would be the ideal moment to out Josh, but I won't. Maddie swore me to secrecy. And besides, Truman doesn't need to know.

"It's about Maddie and me," I continue.

"What about it?" he's says, as if the subject doesn't interest him.

"We're kind of seeing each other."

"You're kind of seeing each other or you are? There's a difference. And if I have to point that out to you, it just may be that you're kind of not seeing her at all."

"We had our first date last night. We went to Riverfront Park."

"Really?" His interest is piqued, finally. "Did you…?"

He does this thing with his hands which is supposed to indicate two people in the act of copulation.

"Come on, Truman. Don't be crude. This is Maddie we're talking about."

"Yes, and I've seen the way you two look at each other. I knew it was just a matter of time until you got together."

"You did? Really? I didn't know it was that obvious."

"About as obvious as a nun in a brothel."

"Are you okay with it? I mean, I know you like Maddie, too."

"Oh, I like Maddie, but not like that. You two have my blessing. Don't worry about that another second."

"Thanks, man. I'm glad I got this off my chest."

"So, if you haven't gone all the way with her, what have you done?"

"None of your business."

"Has there been any preliminary exploration?"

"No. We're not ready. I kissed her goodnight. That's it."

"That's it?! You're a young man in the prime of your life. Your hormones are raging. You kissed her and that's it? That's pathetic."

"That's what Nikki would say."

"Speaking of Nikki, how is that fine young woman doing?"

I knew the second it passed my lips I shouldn't have mentioned Nikki.

"You really need to forget you ever saw her."

"I'd like to, but I can't. Can you take a picture of her with your phone and send it to me?"

"No."

"Maybe while she's sleeping. You could open the door real quiet, sneak inside and snap a picture of her in her nightie. I'd give you my next two paychecks for that picture."

Before I can formulate an adequate reply to Truman's preposterous suggestion, Angie opens the back door of Bubba's. I don't know what her job title is. She unlocks the place in the morning to let us in. All I ever see her do, other than that, is smoke cigarettes and drink coffee. She gives us a stern evil eye.

"Break time must be over," I say.

"Yeah, okay. We'll talk more about that picture, later."

"No we won't."

"Come on, Dylan. Don't be like that."

Angie cuts our conversation short. Which I'm thankful for, but I know will only provide me a brief reprieve.

"Stop goofing off, you two. Those vats don't clean themselves."

~14~

Hit me with your best shot

I'm excited about the rehearsal today with Josh, Truman and me. This will be the first time we get together with something solid to work on. If they like the song, and I think they will, it will be interesting to see what develops once our creative juices are flowing in the same direction.

I get home from work at 11:30 AM and head immediately to the bathroom to shower. Nikki is sitting slumped forward at the kitchen table eating something out of a bowl. Soup or cereal, perhaps. Her face is only inches from the bowl. She appears hungover, though I'm no expert.

"You don't look so good," I say, as I pass her.

"You should talk."

I keep walking.

"Don't be too long in the bathroom. I'm not feeling well. I may need to get in there."

I can't tell you how ridiculous that sounds coming from Nikki. Not the part about feeling sick. The other part about not being in the bathroom too long. Nikki is notorious for her two-hour bathroom marathons. I have no idea what she does in there for all that time.

"Did you hear me?!" she yells at me, right before I close the bathroom door.

"The whole neighborhood hears you, Nikki."

I'm in and out in fifteen minutes. Nikki is in the same spot as before when I pass by the kitchen with a towel wrapped around my waist. She doesn't bother to comment on my boney physique or lack of muscle tone. She really must be feeling bad.

"Truman and Josh will be here at one for rehearsal. Thought I'd give you a heads-up," I say.

"Not today."

It's only fifteen minutes of one. Too late for me to call it off.

"Sorry. They're on the way."

"Dylan, I really don't want them here, today. Okay? Will you do that for me? When they get here tell them something came up and you have to postpone the rehearsal until tomorrow. Alright?"

In the fifteen years I've lived in the same house as Nikki, I can count on one hand the number of times she's asked something of me rather than demanded it. I have no recollection of her ever pleading with me like she's doing now.

"If it's really that important to you."

"It is," she says, and glances at me.

It's brief. Her head turns to look up at me, then turns away a millisecond later. But it's long enough for me to see.

"What happened?" I ask.

"Nothing," she answers, curtly.

I sit down across the table from her. She turns her head to the left, to hide the bruising around her eye.

"Who hit you?" I ask.

"No one. It was an accident."

"You mean like your head bumping into their fist? That kind of accident?"

"Just leave it alone, Dylan."

I reach across the table to put my hand on top of hers. I can't remember the last time I touched her gently. Any other time she'd jerk away. This time she looks at me and gives me a weak smile. The bruising is worse than I previously thought.

"Talk to me, Nikki. What happened?"

"You can't say anything to momma."

"I won't if you don't want me to."

"I don't. And you sure as hell can't tell poppa."

I don't answer immediately. I'm imagining Isiah's reaction to learning a man struck his little girl.

"I mean it, Dylan. Not one word to my parents."

"Okay. Can I ask something?"

"What?"

"The guy who did this, was it someone you went out with?"

She nods to indicate it was.

"Will you be seeing him again?"

"I don't know."

"Nikki, I know we haven't been close, but I don't want to see something happen to you. If you're not going to tell Isiah and Chandra, then at least promise me you won't go out with this guy again."

"It's not that easy. He's not someone I can just say no to."

"Why not?"

"It's Damien Wilson. Do you know who he is?"

I do. He's some kind of leader in a gang faction. There are all kinds of rumors about him and the nature of his crimes and gang activities. I don't know how much of it is true. I just know he's not someone Nikki should be hanging around with.

"Wow," I say.

"Yeah. Tell me about it."

"What are you going to do?"

"I don't know."

"If there's anything I can do, I mean it, anything at all, just ask."

"There is one thing."

"What's that?"

"Go put some clothes on. And make damn sure that towel doesn't fall off your boney white ass before you do."

~15~

Where am I to go now that I've gone too far

Josh and Truman are okay with cancelling rehearsal. I meet them at the front door to explain. I don't tell them the truth about Nikki. I say she's come down with something and it could be contagious, but we won't know for twenty-four hours. I've never been any good at lying. Even with seemingly harmless white lies like this.

"Contagious?" Truman says, dubiously. "Like the measles or something. Does she have red spots all over her?"

"No. She feels really bad. That's all I know. I would have told you sooner, but I didn't find out until ten minutes ago."

"It's okay. We can still do this tomorrow, right?" Josh asks.

"Absolutely. Same time here, tomorrow."

I feel bad about deceiving them, but it's for the best. We say goodbye and I start to shut the door.

"Let's go over to SS&B," I hear Truman say to Josh, as they walk away.

"Hey, wait up. I'll come, too," I call to them.

For me it's just what the doctor ordered. SS&B is always fun. This is the first time for me since Maddie started working there.

"I am the master of the Stratocaster," Truman says as we enter.

He heads for the guitar display and Josh follows. I hesitate. Scanning the store, I don't see Maddie, anywhere. That's understandable. The store is stocked full of merchandise. Amplifiers are stacked floor to ceiling. Shelves holding keyboards and accessories rise to seven feet. Someone Maddie's height could be hidden for days in this place.

I walk down an aisle toward the far back corner of the store. There are PA systems with microphones set up and drum machines. It's where the hip-hoppers congregate. I seldom venture back here. It's like crossing a border into a foreign country where everyone speaks an unfamiliar language. Still no sign of Maddie.

Six guys and one girl are gathered around a pair of microphones. A drum machine puts out a steady background rhythm at 90 BPM while they trade off rapping lyrics. Have I mentioned my disgust for repetitive noise passed off as music? That isn't what has my hackles up, though.

At the center of the group is Damien Wilson. The guy who hit Nikki. I'll be the first to admit Nikki has a sharp tongue and is quick to provoke guys who don't respect her like she feels they should. But Damien is several inches taller and outweighs her by a good one hundred pounds. That's not a fair fight.

It's a good thing he's busy rapping and doesn't see me, because I'd have a tough time looking back at him without sneering. And since he's bigger than me and has five homeboys with him, it might be a problem. I listen to their jam for a minute.

"I been tryin' to find ya, I want to remind ya, I'm right behind ya. That ain't no reason, for you to go teasin' me, you should be pleasin' me."

I understand why Nikki would hang around someone like Damien. People look up to him. He's the center of attention. The party doesn't start until he arrives. Without question, that would appeal to Nikki.

Suddenly, he looks up to see me looking at him. Cold, hard eyes stare back at me until I look away. As much bitterness as I feel toward him, I won't confront him. Not here and now, anyway. Six to one, not counting the girl with six-inch fingernails. That's not just bad odds, it's suicidal. I wander back to the guitar section, where Truman and Josh are.

"I don't see Maddie anywhere," I tell them.

"I figured you were looking for her. She's right over there," says Josh.

He jerks his chin toward a line of glass display cases full of all kinds of guitar and drum accessories. Several people are leaning on the cases peering down at the items inside. I still haven't spotted Maddie.

"Where?" I ask.

"Behind that counter, there. She's squatting down."

I move closer. Sure enough, Maddie is bent over pulling trays of guitar picks from the lowest shelf and placing them on the counter for people to see. She's wearing tight-fitting jeans that stretch even tighter when she reaches for items on the lower shelves. This seems to interest the customers every bit as much as the picks.

She sees me when she raises up to set another tray on the counter. Her eyebrows bunch up. She comes over to me.

"What are you doing here? I thought you had rehearsal."

"We had to cancel for today."

"Why?" she asks, but before I can answer, a customer asks to see another tray of picks. "Sorry," she says.

I stand there feeling out of place for ten minutes. Then she returns.

"We're going to rehearse tomorrow, instead. I'll tell you about it later."

"That's probably best. We're so busy right now I can't stop to talk. Call me tonight. Okay?"

"Okay."

I take down a Jazz Bass and sit on an amp beside Truman and Josh to play. Truman gives me a look.

"Don't say it, man. Okay?" I tell him.

"Say what? That you suck on bass? Alright. I won't, but you do."

Josh laughs. I laugh too. I can't help myself. This place wouldn't be the same without Truman ribbing me. Before long Josh has to leave for work at the pizzeria. A while later, Truman decides to go.

"I guess you're going to hang around until Maddie gets off?"

"No. She's busy. It's probably better if I leave, too."

I wave at Maddie as we're walking out. She holds her hand to her ear with her little finger and thumb spread, like it's a phone. Most of the time when people do that, I think it looks stupid, but not so with Maddie.

She mouths, "Call me."

I mouth back, "I will."

"So, tell me about this song your mother gave you," Truman says, once we're outside the store.

It catches me off-guard. There's only one way he can know.

"Maddie told you I had a visit from my mother. Didn't she?"

"Yeah, she told me. Why wouldn't she? It's not like I'm going to call the National Enquirer on your ass. You know that."

"You didn't think I might be hallucinating?"

"Hell no. If you tell me something happened, then it did. End of story. And anybody who says different is going to answer to me."

"Thanks, Truman. I appreciate your support."

"Anytime and every time, brother. I've always got your back."

~16~

You are the sun, I am the moon
You are the words, I am the tune

When I get home Isiah and Chandra aren't there, yet. It's a little after five. Nikki is in her room. I stand outside her closed door listening and hear tapping on the keyboard of her laptop. I knock lightly.

"Nikki. Are you okay?"

"Yeah."

The reply is barely audible. Which means she's not okay. If she was, she'd scream at me to go away and leave her alone.

"If you need anything I'll be in my room."

"Okay. Thank you."

Thank you? Did she really say that? It's a lot worse than I thought.

Alone in the basement, I strap on my dad's Jazz Bass to pluck at the strings while I sing my mom's song. That's how I see it. Every time I pick up the bass I feel my father's presence. He watches over me while I play, probably grimacing at each sour note I strike. No doubt my mother feels the same about me singing off-key.

I pluck away and sing, trying to get the melody right, hoping mom will steer me in the right direction. My fingers move clumsily at first, but more smoothly after a few minutes. The page with the lyrics lays in front of me. I go through the first verse several times, then move on to the second. The chorus comes easier. In my head I hear it more clearly. I can even hear how it sounds with backup singers.

"Dylan," Isiah calls from the top of the stairs.

"Yes," I answer.

I've been concentrating so hard I don't realize he's home. His footfalls sound as he descends the wood stairs. The sight of me with the Jazz Bass puts a smile on his face when he comes into view.

"I'm sorry to interrupt."

"No problem."

"Do you know if anything happened to Nikki?"

I look at the fretboard because I'm about to tell a lie and I fear Isiah will see right through me.

"No, not that I know of. Why do you ask?"

"She's in her room with the door closed. I didn't hear anything so I peeked in on her. She's in bed with the covers pulled over her. Usually she'll be getting ready to go out with her friends around now."

"Maybe she's sick. You know how it is with Nikki and me. I'm the last person she'll tell anything to."

I can look him in the eyes as I say that because he knows it's the truth.

"Alright, then. I just thought you might know something."

He pauses, looks thoughtfully at the Jazz Bass, then at me and changes the subject.

"What are you working on?"

"Just a song."

"Is this for that contest?"

"I hope so. I guess it depends on whether the others like it."

"You want to try it out on me?"

I do. I respect Isiah's opinion above that of most other people.

"Umm, yeah. I would, but I have to warn you. It's pretty rough."

"That's okay. I'm sure I've heard rougher."

"Here goes then."

I sing the first verse. When I finish I look at Isiah. He looks stunned. He doesn't speak.

"What do you think?" I ask.

"You wrote that?"

"Sort of."

I'm not ready to tell him the whole story.

"I'll be right back," he says.

He gets up abruptly and ascends the stairs. *What's that all about?* It's twenty minutes before he reappears. He practically runs down the stairs carrying a sheet of paper.

"It took me a while to find it. Here. Read this."

"What is it?"

"Just read the whole thing first, then I'll tell you."

At a glance, I see it's lyrics to a song. I begin reading. Isiah is watching me intently, waiting for my reaction. I finish reading and I'm stupefied. It's almost word for word the same lyrics as the ones my mother sang the other night. Without knowing it, I've copied the lyrics from an existing song.

"Well, I guess I won't be entering it in the contest, after all."

"Why not? I think it's a great song. I always have."

"There's this thing called plagiarism. Stealing someone else's song and passing it off as mine will get me kicked out of the contest. And probably sued to boot."

"Nobody's going to know but you and me."

"The person who wrote it will know. So will their agent and record producer."

Isiah shakes his head at me like I'm a complete idiot.

"You don't know do you?"

The perplexed look on my face answers his question.

"I guess you don't. Tell me this, then. Where did you find a copy of the lyrics?"

"I didn't find a copy anywhere. I heard them and wrote them down from memory."

"The song was never recorded. I know that for a fact. Your mother wrote it while you were still in her womb. She sang it to you all the time. Before and after you were born. How the heck did you remember it? It's been at least fifteen years since you've heard it."

There's no easy way to work up to it, so I spit it out.

"My mother visited me the other night. Or maybe I should say her spirit came to visit. For that matter, it could have been nothing more than a dream. She sang it to me. The next day I wrote it down from memory."

I brace myself for what's coming.

"How's she doing?" he asks.

He's not poking fun at me. There's no hint of sarcasm, only sincerity.

"Dylan, I'm a firm believer in the hereafter. If you're looking for an explanation for your mother's visit, look no further than these lyrics. Love will transcend the worlds between us. If you ask me, that's exactly what happened. Grace brought you that song to use in the contest. You'd be foolish not to."

~17~

Call out the instigators,
Because there's something in the air

The next day when Josh, Truman and I get together for rehearsal, things really start to come together. I practiced the song for hours ahead of time and know the lyrics and melody by heart. I'm confident and more than ready to play it for them.

"So, that's basically how it goes," I say, after the first time through. "We still need to work out the intro and ending before we start trying to record it. I'm thinking we start it with a drum thing for two beats. Something like, bap-bap-ba-da-bap. Then one time through the same chord progression as the verse. Then start the vocals. What do you think?"

Truman and Josh trade a glance at one another, then Josh speaks.

"Who are you and what did you do with Dylan?"

"I think what he's trying to say is, you're moving a little fast for us," Truman explains. "We're having trouble keeping up."

"I'm sorry. I've been practicing the song. I'm more familiar with it. You have to hear it a few more times. I understand. But what do you think of it up to this point?"

"I like it a lot," Josh says.

"It has potential," Truman says. "That part where you sing, love will transcend. I think we could give that more punch. Like this."

I cringe because I know what's coming.

"Love-Will-Transcend," he sings, hip-hop style. "Then you repeat that, sort of like an echo in the background while the lead singer is doing the melody. See what I'm saying?"

"I like it a lot," Josh says.

After several rehearsals it's become apparent that Josh is the most agreeable member of our group. He likes everything. And usually a lot.

"I can't believe I'm saying this...,"

"Come on, Dylan. Don't shoot me down before you give it a chance. Remember what Maddie told you. You have to be more open-minded."

I do remember Maddie telling me that. I don't remember her saying it in front of Truman. I make a mental note to express my concerns to Maddie about her being such a blabbermouth. In a nice way, of course.

"What I was about to say before you interrupted me is, I think your idea is good. The song was written eighteen years ago. It could use some updating."

"Did you hear that, Josh? I think we have just witnessed a miracle. Dylan likes one of my ideas. I can't believe it."

Truman always keeps things light. It's what I like about him.

"I have an idea on the intro," Josh says.

"Praise the Lord," Truman says. "I think we are about to witness another miracle. Two of them within a minute of each other."

"What if we start it with saxophone? Something like this. Wah—wah-wah—du-du-du—du-du—. What about that?"

I glance at Truman for his opinion. He nods. I nod back. Josh smiles. It's a really productive session with plenty of enthusiasm and everyone participating.

"There's something we need to consider ahead of recording," I say. "I was reading over the contest rules, yesterday. The recording we submit can only be two-minutes long. The songs we hear on the radio are three minutes or more, on average."

"So we stop it at two minutes," Truman says. "I don't see a problem with that. Do you?"

"It will sound like someone pulled the plug on the jukebox," Josh says.

"What do you suggest?"

"We can time the song like it is now. That will give us a better idea of what we need to eliminate. Dylan, do you have a clock with a second hand we can use?"

"Sit tight. I'll see if I can find something."

I rummage through drawers until I find a kitchen timer. We time the complete song, each verse and the chorus. From start to finish it's about three minutes. And that's without an intro or fade out at the end.

"Well, as I see it, we can leave out the last verse and the second chorus, or we can speed the song up to 120 BPM," Truman states.

"That's almost twice as fast as we're playing it now. I don't think that will work."

"I'm sorry to do this to you, but I have to go to work," Josh says. "Maybe we can think about it for a day before we make a decision."

"We can do that. Go on to work. We'll talk again, tomorrow."

"Yeah, go on to work," Truman says. "We don't want people to have to wait for their pizzas. They might complain and get you fired."

"How long do you think it will take to record the song?" Truman asks, after Josh is gone.

"I've been wondering the same thing. I have no idea. There are too many things I know nothing about. Like how many takes before we get the one we want. I don't know about you, but I'll be nervous once the record button is pushed. I might freeze up."

"We better try and figure it out. July first is less than a week away, which means we have a month to record and submit the song."

The month since school let out has gone by quickly. If we're going to make the deadline we need to act soon. I do some calculations in my head.

"I think we should rent the equipment and begin recording the week after July Fourth," I say. "That should be enough time. The recording doesn't have to be professional quality, just reasonably clean."

"Alright. I agree with that. That brings us to the equipment. We need a basic recorder, microphones and instruments. How many microphones and which instruments?"

"Since we have limited funds we have to keep it to a minimum. We have my bass. We can get by with two mikes. We'll need a guitar."

"Preferably a Stratocaster."

"If we can afford it, I'd like to have a keyboard. One of those that can simulate a bunch of other instruments and has a drum machine included."

"Some of this stuff we might be able to get from SS&B. If they don't rent it, they can tell us who does. Let's have Maddie check into it."

"Okay. I'll call her tonight."

~18~

If you'll be my dixie chicken, I'll be your Tennessee lamb

These days at my house I never know what to expect when dinner time rolls around. I think it would be fair to say the timing of the evening meal, what we eat and who's in attendance has always revolved around Nikki. When she left for college, the importance of having a sit-down family meal left with her. Chandra, Isiah and I still eat together. Just not as often, and not on a specific schedule.

I know something about this evening is off as soon as Chandra gets home. From the basement I hear her walking quickly. There's a certain urgency to her steps. From the kitchen to the window in the front room, to her bedroom, to the bathroom, to Nikki's room. I sense a change in the air.

"Dylan," Nikki calls from the top of the stairs.

"Yes."

"Momma says dinner will be ready in fifteen minutes. She thought you might want to wash up beforehand. Isiah should be home any minute."

I don't reply because I'm busy attempting to decipher the true meaning of her words. The keywords are momma, dinner, beforehand and Isiah. I do the translation. Come upstairs before Isiah gets home.

"Did you hear me?" Nikki calls, a little louder, this time.

"I'm coming."

The dinner table is set. The aroma of fried chicken, mashed potatoes and string beans fresh from the stove fills the house. Isiah has just arrived. He's washing his hands in the bathroom. Chandra, Nikki and I are seated at the table. The empty chair waiting for Isiah is on Nikki's right, Chandra's left and across the table from me.

Nikki's eye looks worse today. She has makeup covering it, but it's not helping much. There's blood visible in the white of the eye and swelling around the cheek bone. I hate Damien Wilson more by the second.

"Dylan," Chandra whispers, in a slightly admonishing tone.

She catches me staring at Nikki's black eye. I understand what this means. Isiah doesn't know. Sometime during dinner he'll find out. The home-cooked meal and the family partaking in it together. It's all an elaborate ruse. In a minute he'll walk in here thinking all is right in the world and life has never been better. Then when he least expects it, they'll chop his legs right out from under him. Poor bastard.

"Mm-mm-mm. Something sure smells good. This is some surprise. What's the special occasion?"

On some level, I'm sure Isiah suspects an ulterior motive is at play, but why let it ruin a perfectly scrumptious meal. He beams at his wife and daughter. They beam back. I can't face him.

"Nikki, would you say grace, please?" Chandra asks.

It's a good thing I didn't have food in my mouth at that moment. I'd have choked to death right then and there.

"Thank you, Lord, for that we are about to receive. Amen."

Nikki raises her eyes and smiles, careful not to turn her head toward her father. Chandra passes the chicken to Isiah, he passes it to Nikki, who passes it to me. The potatoes and beans go around the table in the same fashion. We start eating.

"How was your day, Nikki?" Isiah asks.

"It was really good, poppa. I took it easy, caught up on some reading. How was your day?"

"Unremarkable for the most part. Thanks for asking. Anything new at work for you, hon?"

"Not really. I stayed busy all day. We have two girls out on maternity leave. They can't hire anyone to replace them, so the rest of us have to work harder."

"Did you have a rehearsal, today, Dylan?"

"Yes. Truman and Josh came over. Maddie had to work."

The notion of the conversation focusing on me appeals to Nikki.

"I could hear some of what you were playing. It sounded good."

"Thanks," I say.

"What were you playing? I didn't recognize it."

I don't believe for a second Nikki listened to us today, but I play along.

"It's a song we're working on for the contest."

"I know that much. What's it called?"

"I don't know. I mean, we haven't named it, yet."

"Love Transcends," Isiah says. "That's the title she gave it."

Chandra looks puzzled.

"The song was originally written by my mother," I say. "We're rewriting and updating it."

That probably invites more questions than it answers. And it threatens to lead the conversation in a more somber direction if Chandra decides to pursue it. She chooses not to.

"It sounds like this project is going well, Dylan. I'm happy for you."

I can see it pleases Isiah that Chandra is taking an interest in something I'm working on.

"Tell me again," Isiah says to me. "When is the deadline for contest submissions?"

"August first. I think we'll be ready."

"Is there anything I can do to help?"

"Not that I can think of, but thanks just the same."

Nikki is eager to keep the conversation on anything other than the inevitable discussion of the origin of her black eye.

"Poppa plays drums," she says, forgetting for the moment that's something I'm well aware of.

That's when she makes the mistake which changes the course of the evening. As she mentions him playing drums, she turns her head to face him full on. His smile flips upside down.

"What happened to your face?"

"Isiah, it's alright," Chandra consoles. "Nikki and I have already discussed this."

"Discussed what?"

Anger is seeping into his voice, now. In those few words Chandra informed him something unpleasant happened to Nikki and she doesn't want him to make a big deal of it. Fat chance of that working.

"Nikki," he says, more forcibly now. "What happened?"

"Uh…,"

He reaches out to grab her chin. She tries to pull away, but he holds firm and tilts her head for a better look at the damaged eye.

"Who did this?"

"It was an accident."

She tried that on me and it didn't play. I don't think it will work on Isiah, either.

"An accident? Girl I've seen enough black eyes in my time to know damn well how they get that way. Now, who did this?"

"Isiah," Chandra cautions. "Not in front of Dylan."

It comes out like I'm not a member of the family and therefore am not privy to their squabbles. I know she doesn't mean it that way. She's just grasping at straws. Anything to forestall the simmering pot from boiling over.

"I can't tell you, poppa. I'm sorry, but it's better if you don't know."

Isiah lets go of Nikki's chin. He turns his stare on Chandra.

"What do you know about this?"

She hesitates, debating with herself on how much to say.

"Isiah," she begins, speaking slowly. "Nikki is an adult. We have to trust that she can handle any situation she gets into. She went out with a man. They had an argument and he hit her. Nikki assures me it won't happen again, because she won't be seeing him anymore."

Honestly, I'm impressed with how Chandra handles that. Isiah's anger is diffused for the moment. We finish dinner with innocuous subjects like the weather and current news events dominating the conversation. Afterward Chandra and Nikki wash the dishes. Isiah retires to the front room to watch TV. I go to my room.

~19~

It's like trying to spin the world the other way

Shortly after dinner, I'm lying on the mattress in my room, thinking about Maddie when she calls.

"I was about to call you," I say.

"Great minds think alike. Meet me at Riverfront Park. At the same place as last time. I want to hear how it went today, and I have some good news for you."

"I can be there in forty-five minutes."

"I'll see you then."

She could tell me over the phone, but I like this way better. She sounds happy and I love seeing her happy. When I get to the bus stop at Orleans Street and Atwater, she's waiting for me. She's carrying a plastic bag.

"I made sandwiches for us," she says, raising the bag.

"That's really sweet of you, but I already ate."

"That's too bad. I make really good sandwiches. You might change your mind after you've had a bite."

I probably will change my mind. My stomach is a bottomless pit.

"Maybe later. Go ahead and eat yours if you want."

"I think I'll wait a while. Let's walk. Tell me what Josh and Truman thought of your song."

We walk along a path that runs parallel to the river. Dozens of joggers run by as we stroll along at a leisurely pace.

"They liked it. Or at least they said they did. They both had some ideas. Truman wants to add some background vocals. Josh thinks we could use a sax in the intro."

"That's great. It's finally coming together. That must make you happy."

"It does, except there's still a lot of work left to do. The deadline is a month away. I'm eager to start recording."

It's less than a week past summer solstice. There are still two hours of daylight left. We pass a group of people doing yoga.

"That has to hurt," I comment.

"Recording?"

"No. I was talking about that lady with her knee next to her ear. It looks painful."

"It's not really, once you've done it a few times. I can do it."

"This I've got to see."

"I'll show you some other time. I can't do it in jeans."

I imagine her in leotards bending her arms and legs in the shape of a pretzel.

"What are you smiling at?" she asks.

"You doing yoga."

"You don't think I can?"

"It's not that. I mean, who am I to doubt you?"

We walk in silence for a minute. The smile remains transfixed on my face. Maddie seems a little preoccupied.

"We want to ask you something. Truman and me. It has to do with SS&B."

"That reminds me. I have some good news. It has to do with SS&B, too. You go first."

"Alright. It's about the equipment we need for recording. Could you find out if SS&B rents stuff? And if they don't, who does. Also, we'd like to know how much it costs."

"I can't believe you're asking me that."

"I'm sorry. I don't mean to put you on the spot."

"No. That's not what I mean. I already found out about the equipment. That's the good news. I can't believe we were thinking the same thing at the same time."

"That is pretty cool. What did you find out?"

"I was talking to Troy, today. He's an assistant sales manager."

"I thought you were an assistant sales manager."

"No. I'm a sales assistant. There's a big difference. Anyway, let me finish what I was telling you. Troy says he'll arrange it so we can borrow whatever we need and it won't cost us anything. He'll sign it out for us."

I'll be the first to admit I'm young, with limited life experiences, but I've yet to receive anything free that didn't come with strings attached.

"What's the catch?"

"There's no catch. Troy's a nice guy and he's willing to help us. That's all there is to it."

I'm not convinced. And if I'm reading Maddie right she isn't either.

"Did Troy imply he might want something down the road?"

"Nope."

"He didn't say something like, maybe you can do him a favor sometime?"

"I told you already. No."

I don't pursue it further. It's probably nothing more than petty jealousy making me suspicious of Troy's intentions.

"He wants me to let him know when we decide what all we'll need. Then, we'll meet after work to discuss it."

"That's fine. Where does he want to meet us?"

"I don't think that's what he has in mind. He wants to get together with me to iron out all the details. That's how he put it."

"Just the two of you. Are you sure he doesn't have something more on his mind than discussing our equipment needs?"

There's a hint of irritation in her voice when she speaks next.

"No, I'm not sure. So what if he does? That doesn't mean I'm going to do anything with him I wouldn't do otherwise."

I don't know how to interpret that last sentence. She senses my discomfort.

"He's my boss. I have to maintain a friendly relationship with him. That's all I'm saying. You understand that, don't you?"

"Yes. Does he understand that's all you're doing?"

"Dylan, you're starting to annoy me. This is a huge break to have anything we need at no cost. I thought you'd be thrilled about this."

"I am. I'm really happy about it. I just don't want you to do anything with Troy you might feel bad about, later."

"I like being with you, but you don't own me. You have no right to question what I do with other men."

Her words sting and embarrass me. I don't want to look at her. Don't want to see the anger in her eyes or for her to see the hurt in mine.

"That didn't come out right," she says, attempting to soothe my feelings.

Too late. She can't unsay it.

"Look," I say, in what I think is a very reasonable tone of voice. "Maybe I'm acting jealous, and maybe I have no right to feel that way. But I don't think I'm out of line to worry about you. Nikki came home with a black eye the other day. Some guy hit her. I'm not saying she deserved it, but she can go too far with guys sometimes."

"I'm not Nikki, Dylan. Don't compare me to her."

"I wasn't comparing you to her. I'm saying even a girl like Nikki who has a lot of dating experience can misread a guy."

"That is comparing me to her. And not only are you comparing us, you're saying I'm not as smart or experienced as her."

The longer our conversation continues the madder she seems to become. And louder. People are stopping to stare. If I can't calm her, somebody might call the cops.

"Maddie, I think you're overreacting. Can't we discuss this like two rational adults?"

"How about we discuss it like one rational adult and one jealous juvenile? How would that be?"

"Come on Maddie. I'm sorry."

I don't think I did anything I need to apologize for, but right now I'll say whatever is necessary to get back in her good graces.

"Sorry isn't going to cut it. I'll see you later. Maybe."

She turns and walks away. I consider following her, but people are still staring. And besides, I can't think of another thing to say. I turn around and walk back to the bus stop.

~20~

It's love's illusions I recall

Maddie is no longer my girlfriend—if she ever really was. It was over before it ever started, might be stating it more accurately. My first attempt at romance ended poorly. I could spend the next ten years wondering where it went wrong and not get any closer to knowing. I tell myself it wasn't meant to be and I should get on with my life.

Ultimately, I gained more than I lost from the experience. Maddie is still my friend. In fact, I think our friendship is stronger now. She's still an active member of our songwriting group, as well. Thanks to her—or maybe I should say, thanks to Troy and because of her—we now have unlimited access to everything we need to record our song.

"Look at it this way, Dylan," Truman is quick to point out as we prepare for our first recording session. "You took one for the team. Letting her go allowed her to get close to Troy. If it wasn't for that, we wouldn't have all this stuff. And I would like to express my sincere gratitude to you for making the supreme sacrifice. Man, I love this Stratocaster."

My basement room is our studio. Isiah, Chandra and Nikki are really supportive. They give us the okay to record anytime day or evening. For the most part, my room won't require soundproofing, as I thought it might. All the instruments are plugged directly into an interface for a digital audio workstation, a DAW. That's a computer software program for recording.

The recording process is going to be a real learning experience for us. We have no idea what's involved, yet. Maddie will serve as our recording engineer. Because of that, our sessions will have to take place after she gets off work at SS&B. Troy has shown her the basics of using a DAW system. The rest she'll learn as we go.

"I'm going to start by recording a drum track," Maddie says. "That will set the tempo for all the other instruments."

It's 7:00 PM. We're all here. Truman, Josh, Maddie and me. Josh calls in sick to the pizzeria so he doesn't miss out on our first session. Tonight he's in charge of the keyboard workstation. It simulates a hundred different instruments, including drums. Maddie instructs Josh on what to do next.

"Listen to the metronome lead-in. Let it click off four beats. On the fifth beat push the button to start the drums."

Easier said than done Josh finds out after six attempts.

"There's nothing to be nervous about, Josh," Truman tells him. "It's a piece of cake. Relax and count along with the metronome. One, two, three, four, push start. Just like that."

"Maybe if you close your eyes," I suggest.

It's something I've heard people do to get past stage fright. The others look at me like it's an incredibly stupid idea.

"How's he going to find the button with his eyes closed?" Maddie asks, more sarcastically than is absolutely necessary. "Let's just keep trying until we get it right."

It takes almost an hour and twelve more attempts before we have a drum track to work from.

"We'll record the guitar track now," Maddie says. "Dylan, you sing along while Truman plays. We're only recording the guitar. It won't matter what you sound like. It will help Truman to keep his place."

Unlike the drum track, which needs to be continuous, the guitar can be recorded in parts. Anytime Truman makes a mistake, Maddie can edit it out and he can start at that point and go forward. Still it takes an hour to get down a satisfactory track.

"I think that's enough for one night," Maddie declares. "Same time tomorrow?"

She looks to me for an answer, since it's my room.

"That's good with me. Josh, Truman?"

"Tomorrow is my day off. I won't have to call in sick," Josh says.

Truman doesn't bother to answer. We all know he'll be here. It's one more opportunity to play the Stratocaster guitar before Maddie takes it back to SS&B. If he had his way, he'd take it home and sleep with it next to him.

"Alright then. I'll see you guys tomorrow," Maddie says.

"If you want, I'll see you home," Josh tells her.

"Thanks, Josh, but I have a ride. He's probably waiting for me out front right now."

It shouldn't bother me that Maddie is seeing another guy, or other guys if that's the case. But it does. Truman and Josh hang around after she leaves. Obviously, no one is waiting out front for them.

"Isn't anyone going to tell me how good I make that Stratocaster sound?" Truman asks.

"I've already told you at least three times. You did great," Josh says.

"Dylan?" Truman says.

"I think it sounds great, too. But after forty takes it should."

"It wasn't that many. More like thirty-five."

"Whatever. I'll probably do the bass track tomorrow. I'll be happy if I get it in less than forty takes."

"You will," Josh says. "I have confidence in you."

"Let me ask you both something," Truman says. "What do you plan to do with your share of the money if we win? No, strike that last part. Make it when we win."

"I'm going to buy a car," Josh says. "I'm tired of riding the bus."

"I hear that. What about you Dylan?"

"I'll probably use it to get my own place. Isiah and Chandra have taken care of me long enough. What about you? What will you do with the money you have left after you buy a new top-of-the-line Stratocaster?"

"I've been thinking about getting my own place, too. Maybe we could be roommates."

I get along with Truman better than anyone I know.

"Yeah, maybe we could. Do you like macaroni and cheese? I could eat that stuff every night."

"I can get into macaroni and cheese. Just don't bring home any catfish. I don't care if I never see a catfish again."

"No problem. No catfish."

"You think Nikki might come to visit occasionally?"

"I seriously doubt it."

~21~

Just push play, they're gonna bleep it anyway

I'm ready when it comes time to put down the bass guitar tracks. I've practiced it until my fingers are sore. The recording gear is still in place from the previous night. All we have to do is turn it on.

"You'll hear the drums begin. Give them one measure, then you come in," Maddie instructs.

"Can you play it through one time first, so I can get a feel for it before we start recording?"

She lets out a sigh, like it's an imposition, but does what I ask.

"Okay. I'm ready," I say, after that.

She hits record. The drums play. I come in perfectly. Maddie hits pause.

"Let's try it again," she says. "You were a little late."

"No I wasn't," I protest.

"Yes, Dylan. You were."

She says it slow and deliberately, which makes me want to debate the point that much more. I look to Truman and Josh. They look away. I realize it's futile to argue with Maddie. She can take her ball and go home.

"Are you ready?" she asks.

She doesn't wait for my answer. She hits record. Again, I come in at the precise millisecond I should. She hits pause.

"You were late, again," she says.

I may not be the fastest learner in the room, but I know arguing with her further is a waste of time.

"Oh well," I say. "We'll try again."

This goes on another four times before she lets the recording continue past the first measure. She doesn't pause until I'm done. I think it went well. I wait for her to decide.

"Let's listen to it all the way through once," she suggests. We do.

"That's good for now. I can clean it up some, later."

Clean it up? Someone needs to clean you up, I think, but don't say.

"Now we have the basic structure of the song. We can add the vocals and any other instruments to it in any order we choose. What do you guys think we should do next?"

I'm not convinced she wants our opinion. She might just be thinking out loud. I wait to see.

"I'd like to hear it with the vocals," Josh says. "I think the lyrics are what makes the song. No offense meant, but the music alone isn't enough to win a songwriting contest."

He makes a good point. I've been thinking the same thing.

"I feel the same," I say. "The vocals should come next."

"Who wants to go first?"

It's an easy call. Truman and I are the weakest singers and Maddie is manning the computer.

"Josh should do it," I say.

"Okay, then," Maddie says. "Here's what we'll do. Set up a microphone near the center of the room, so it's farther from the walls and doesn't pick up sound bouncing off them. Keep your mouth close to it. I'll turn the volume down to cut back on background noise. Attach the sheet of lyrics to something. If you're holding it in your hand, the microphone might pick up the sound of it rustling."

It takes a few minutes to set things up. Maddie and Josh put on headphones. Maddie switches the playback from speakers to headphones. This way the instrument tracks won't be in the background on the vocal tracks. Maddie hits record. The intro plays. Maddie cues Josh.

"The greatest force known to man…, hold on a minute," Josh says. "Can I do it over? I think it was a little flat."

"Take two," Maddie says.

"The greatest force known to man cannot compare with love."

He stops there.

"How does it sound?" he asks.

Truman and I don't have headphones on. We don't know.

"It sounds fine to me. You have to remember we're recording it dry and with minimal instruments. It will sound weak until we add the other instruments, vocals and reverb. Go ahead and sing it all the way through. We can go back and fix anything we need to."

Josh sings the song from start to finish while Maddie records it. It's evident he's not happy with it.

"There's not enough time left to do much more tonight," Maddie says.

"Before you go can you play it for us through the speakers?" Truman asks. "Dylan and I could only hear Josh while you were recording."

"Okay. And I'll add reverb to his voice, too."

"You can do that?" I ask.

"Yes. It's real easy. Just a couple of clicks of the mouse."

A minute later it's playing through the speakers. I'm impressed. Not only with the overall sound. Maddie is working the DAW system like a true professional. Already we have a recording of the song which with a little editing could be submitted. And we have three weeks to improve on it.

"We can stop there for tonight," Maddie says. "My ride is probably waiting for me out front."

"Is your ride Troy?" Truman asks.

I'm curious about that as well, but I'm glad it's Truman and not me who asks Maddie.

"Yes, it is. Why?"

"Tell him thanks for loaning us this stuff. Especially this fine Stratocaster guitar."

"I already have. I'll see you all tomorrow."

I watch her climb the stairs to leave. Then I turn to the others.

"Did you pick up a vibe when she said, 'I already have'?"

"What kind of vibe?" Josh asks.

"I can't put my finger on it, exactly. Like she's thanked Troy enough and doesn't want to do it anymore."

"Dylan," Truman says. "I know you don't want to hear this, but I'm going to tell you anyway. It's none of your concern. If she wants to know what you think, I'm sure she'll ask."

"You're wrong if you think it's just me being jealous. I'm concerned about Maddie our friend. She's not as tough as she thinks."

"Maybe the best way to help her is to finish recording the song as quickly as possible. Then we can return the stuff and she won't feel obligated to Troy. If that's what's happening."

"Josh is right, Dylan. Maddie may not be tough, but she's smart. She can think her way through this without your help. Let her be and concentrate on the song. Okay?"

"Okay," I agree, reluctantly. "I'm going to grab a soda. You guys want one?"

"No."

"I'm good."

I go up the stairs to the front door and look through the peephole. Maddie is standing near the curb. I can't make out her facial features in the dark. Her hands are in her pockets, shoulders slumped and head turned downward. It's reminiscent of the girl who stood alone outside the school. That sad and introverted girl I felt sorry for. Maddie before I knew her.

Her chin jerks up suddenly. She's lit by the headlights of a vehicle coming swiftly toward her. It stops at our house. The passenger door opens and the dome light comes on. The driver leans toward the open door, extends his arm and beckons to Maddie with his fingers. She seems to consider it for a long moment before getting in. The door closes and the car pulls away.

"What are you looking at?"

Nikki is standing behind me.

"I was checking to see if Maddie's ride had come. How long have you been standing there?"

"Not long. Are things okay with you and Maddie?"

Nikki says it as if she actually cares, which I find hard to believe.

"Everything's fine."

"She's seeing someone else?"

I answer with a shrug of my shoulders, like I couldn't care less. She shakes her head slowly, expressing her pity for me as she walks away. Over her shoulder she says, "Poor Dylan. You have so much to learn."

~22~

And you can tell everybody this is your song

In hindsight I feel we would have been better off had we rented the equipment at full price. It would have limited the time and resources available to us. We wouldn't have spent all the hours we did on recording, re-recording, editing, tweaking and re-recording again.

By my count we did upwards of thirty hours of recording to get the two-minute finished product—a 25.5 MB size MPEG file. The upside takeaway is this. We learned a heck of a lot about digital recording of music and bonded as friends in the process.

Five days before the contest deadline we gather around the computer to register the copyright and then log on to the official Songwriter of the Year contest website. On the screen is the entry submission form. The top line is for the title of the song.

"The original title is, 'Love Transcends'," I say.

"Type it in," Truman says.

No one objects, so I do. The next line is for the songwriter/s. Easy enough. I type in all four names. The third item is for genre. The choices are Hip-Hop, Pop, Rock, R & B, Latin and Country.

"What do you think?" I ask.

"We can eliminate four of those right off the bat," Maddie says. "It isn't hip-hop, r & b, Latin or country."

"It's not edgy enough for rock," Josh says.

I click on the box beside Pop.

The next section is for contact information. We discuss it for a minute and decide to use my phone number, email and house address, with Josh's as the alternate. There's one last thing to do.

"We're all in agreement?" I ask them. "This is the one we're going to submit in the contest?"

Maddie, Josh and Truman nod in unison. I click on the box that says, UPLOAD and hold my breath while the file containing our recording travels through cyberspace. A screen icon signals the uploading is completed.

"What now?" Josh asks.

"Now, we wait," Truman answers.

It isn't what Josh meant, but I think Truman knows that. Josh is wondering what happens to the friendships forged by the hours we spent working toward our common goal.

"Actually, we're a long way from being done," I say.

"What do you mean?" Maddie asks.

"Contest aside, we've learned a lot about songwriting. And it was a lot of fun. Maybe we can do something with that."

"If we could sell a few songs it would be great. Ten times better than delivering pizza."

"I don't mean to rain on anybody's parade, but we know only a little about writing songs and nothing about selling them," Truman says. "There's bound to be a lot of competition. And I'm talking about people who have been writing songs for thirty or forty years."

"Yeah, but even if we don't win this contest we might get some exposure from it. We could build on that. The point I'm trying to make is, there's no reason to stop working on songs together if we enjoy doing it."

"What do you think?" Josh asks Maddie.

She's been unusually quiet today. Actually, she's been a little withdrawn for the last week.

"I've really enjoyed it, but there's a problem going forward," Maddie replies. "Now that we've completed the song, the equipment has to go back to SS&B. That's the agreement."

She hasn't referred to it as an agreement before now. It's always been more of a casual thing between Troy and her. Agreement sounds too formal. I'd love to have been a fly on the wall when that deal was struck.

"The truck is scheduled to pick everything up tomorrow. I told them I'd give them a time after I spoke with Dylan."

"Oh man. They're going to take Ethel away. What am I going to do without my baby?" Truman says.

At some point, I'm not sure when it was, Truman named the borrowed Stratocaster Ethel. I told him it would only make it harder when it came time to say goodbye if he named it, but he wouldn't listen.

"I can't stand to think about all those strangers coming into that store and putting their slimy fingers on her fretboard. I just can't."

"I'm sorry, Truman," Maddie says. "You can come visit her, though. Anytime you want."

I don't think he hears her. He's preoccupied with looking forlornly at the case containing Ethel. Fender Stratocaster guitars start at around five hundred dollars, which Truman could manage to save out of his wages. But Ethel is a tricked-out upgrade. It sells for more than two thousand bucks. That's out of reach for him, unless we win the contest.

"Maddie," I say. "I think I speak for all of us when I say this. Arranging for us to use the equipment went above and beyond the call of duty. Thank you. Without that, I'm not sure we could have completed the song and entered the contest before the deadline. That said, the recording gear isn't essential to writing songs. We can still get together to collaborate on lyrics and music."

No one seems to be paying close attention to me. They've tuned me out and turned inward, self-reflecting it appears. If I was a psychiatrist I could attach a fancy name to the malaise they're experiencing. But I'm not. So I'm going with postpartum depression. We gave birth to a song.

We gave it everything we had. Poured every smidgen of our hearts and souls into it. The effort has drained our energy and left us physically and mentally exhausted. I can understand why giving birth to another song so soon after the first would hold no appeal.

~23~

Don't ask me no questions, I won't tell you no lies

I've known Isiah as long as I can remember and lived in the same house as him for most of my life. I've seen him sad and I've seen him angry. But I've never seen him stay that way for more than a few hours. Ever since Nikki came home with a black eye a month ago, he's been in a funk.

During that time I've focused so hard on getting the song ready to submit I've barely spoken to him. Most of the time when I pass by him on my way to the bathroom or kitchen, it's as if he doesn't see me. I worry about him. He doesn't have a close friend he can talk to when something is bothering him. Not since my dad.

"We finished the song, 'Love Transcends', and entered it in the contest," I tell him, one evening after dinner.

"That's good," he replies.

His response shows as much enthusiasm as he might display while sweeping the floor.

"I have a copy of it on a CD. You want to hear it? I have a CD player in my room."

I bought the CD player so I could listen to the song. I play it so often, I've almost worn it out.

"Alright."

Maybe a little more enthusiasm then. It's hard to say. We go to my room where I play the song for him.

"What do you think?" I ask, when it's done.

"Not bad," he says, without looking at me.

Instead, he's looking around my room distractedly like something's on his mind.

"Isiah, is everything alright? You don't seem yourself."

"I'm alright. I have things on my mind. That's all."

"Anything you want to talk about?"

"Actually, I would. I know you and Nikki don't always get along and I'm sure it's more her fault than yours. I wish it wasn't that way."

"She feels like I was forced on her. I guess I was."

"No one chose for things to happen the way they did. There's nothing to be done about that now."

He chews his bottom lip, working up to something. I wait.

"Do you know who hit Nikki?"

I owe him the truth, but to tell him would betray Chandra and Nikki.

"Isiah, it would be better if I don't say."

"Better for who?"

"For Nikki, Chandra and you."

"Dylan."

He pauses for a long moment before continuing.

"Did you hit Nikki?"

I feel like I've been gut-punched by a gorilla.

"No," I blurt out. "She can make me madder than anyone else in the world, but I'd never lay a hand on her."

I can tell from the set of his jaw he wants to ask if I'm lying, but he doesn't go there.

"I've been trying to understand why everyone keeps telling me it's better if I don't know who hit her. It's like they're protecting whoever did it."

"We're not protecting him. We're protecting ourselves."

"So you do know who it is."

"Isiah, you're the closest thing I have to a father. I hate lying to you, but I swore to Nikki I wouldn't tell you. Besides that, I agree with her. It's better if you don't know. The guy is a gangbanger. He doesn't go anywhere by himself. There are always other gang members around. You can't get to him without risking your life, as well as Nikki's. It does no good to report it to the police because they won't do anything. And again, he'll retaliate against you or Nikki."

"Now I understand. I don't know why someone didn't tell me this earlier."

"It's only a guess on my part, but I think Nikki is ashamed. She thinks of herself as this tough and independent young lady. It wouldn't be good for her image if it got out that she was slapped around by a gangbanger."

"What is this guy's name?"

"Isiah. I feel like I'm betraying Nikki if I tell you."

"Dylan. You and I are the men in this house. It's up to us to protect the women, whether they like it or not. This is just between you and me. Nikki won't find out. I won't confront him this time. But I need to know his name in case it happens again."

"Damien Wilson," I say.

"Damien Wilson," he says, committing it to memory. "You did right by telling me. Chandra and Nikki don't have to know you did."

"Good. I can do without another verbal beating from Nikki."

"I'm sorry I accused you of hurting Nikki."

He didn't really. But he came damn close.

"That's okay. I know you're worried about her."

"Yes, I am. You're song sounds real good. Trevor and Grace would be very proud. I wish they could be here to hear it. I don't say it enough, but I'm very proud of how you've turned out, Dylan."

As far as I can remember he's never said it. But that's Isiah. A man of few words.

~24~

I've been waiting a long time for this moment to come

Relatively speaking, I think I'm a patient person. I attribute this to the fact that few things in life have come to me swiftly or easily. That said, waiting through the entire month of August for the results of the Songwriter of the Year contest to be announced is excruciating.

During this period I'm checking my phone for messages and the contest website for postings every hour. I get a call from Truman, Josh or Maddie every fifteen minutes or so. Half the time I let it go to voicemail. They call me from other phones, thinking I won't know it's them and I'll answer. But I'm not fooled. Then they start calling each other to see if anyone has talked to me. In the messages they leave for me they sound desperate, and even a little threatening sometimes.

"Dylan. It's me, Josh. I know you're there. Answer your phone. Stop dodging me. I'm calling Maddie to see if she's talked to you."

"Dylan. It's Maddie. Call me back the second you get this. I'm worried something's happened to you. I'm calling Truman."

Truman is only ten feet away when his phone rings. We're in the middle of cleaning the frying vats at Bubba's. I hear his side of the conversation with Maddie.

"No, I haven't spoken to him since yesterday. He didn't come to work today. He said something about going out of town for a few days. Alright. Uh-huh. Okay. Yeah, I'll tell him. Bye, now."

"What'd she say?" I ask.

As I say it, my phone sounds again. It's Maddie.

"Ask her yourself," Truman says. "I'm tired of covering for you."

I put the phone to my mouth and say, "I haven't heard anything," and hang up.

I never thought the day would come when I dreaded a phone call from a close friend, but I was wrong. By Labor Day the tension between the four of us mounts to the point we're barely speaking to one another. I don't give up, though. I continue diligently checking the website.

Finally, on September 3rd, the day after Labor Day a notice appears on the home page of the website. The Songwriter of the Year contest finalists have been chosen and an announcement will be made this coming Friday at noon, Pacific Daylight Time. I immediately call Maddie to share the news.

"Yes, I saw it," she says, as soon as I tell her. "I told Truman and Josh, but they had seen it already."

Nice to know where I stand in order of importance.

There's other information posted on the website. Statistical data. More than forty thousand contest entries from all over the world. No wonder it's taken so long to sort through them. I had no idea there were so many or that the odds of our winning were so poor.

After the announcement about the finalists is posted my phone goes silent. Truman, Maddie and Josh are apparently satisfied I won't know more before Friday. I use the quiet time to self-reflect and try to think about anything other than the contest.

"Man, I can hardly sleep. I can't stop thinking about it," Truman says, during our coffee break at Bubba's. "You don't seem excited at all. What's up with you, Dylan?"

"I'm afraid to think about winning and what we're going to do with the money. It might jinx it," I say.

It sounds better than, the odds against us winning are astronomical and I don't believe we have a snowball's chance in hell.

"Josh told me if we don't win he's going to kill himself," Truman says.

"Really! He's not serious is he?"

"Of course not. That's just Josh being Josh. Gay guys are always melodramatic like that. They can't help themselves."

"You knew about that?"

"Maddie told me, a long time ago. I wouldn't have guessed it otherwise. But you know Maddie. She can't keep a secret."

Blabbermouth.

"Has she told you anything about me?"

"You mean like how you get jealous of any guy she talks to?"

"You're lying. She didn't say that."

"Yes she did. I'm not lying."

"Yeah, you are. Uh-oh. Angie's looking out the back door. We better get back to work."

"Now, you're lying. We haven't been out here for ten minutes."

"Fine sit here and get fired. I don't care. I'm going back to work."

He tosses his coffee out, gets up and turns to see Angie isn't there.

"Damn, Dylan. I can usually tell when you're lying, but not this time. This is a new development. I'm not sure I like it. And you owe me a cup of coffee. I wasn't finished with that one."

The banter with Truman takes my mind off the contest, but only until I get home. In my room where the rehearsals and recording took place, I can't think of anything else. Forty thousand to one. Those are the odds. I would give anything—absolutely anything—just to make it into the finals.

~25~

One step closer to knowing

The announcement isn't due to take place until 3:00 PM our time. Still, I'm up at 4:00 AM checking the website, just in case. No news. Today is a work day like any other. So I ready myself for the same old grind at Bubba's. After the announcement, whether we make it to the finals or not, I'm still going to need a job. Near the end of the shift I have an idea. I share it with Truman.

"We should all get together at my place at three for the announcement. What do you think?"

"That's a great idea. We should have some champagne on hand for the big celebration."

"Chandra won't like that. She'd probably throw us all out. Even me."

"It can be non-alcoholic champagne. She won't mind that, will she?"

"That should be okay with her. I'll call Josh and Maddie to tell them."

Everyone arrives early. I have snacks for us. Barbecue flavored potato chips, tortilla chips with salsa and sodas. We agree to save the champagne until after the announcement.

Isiah and Chandra aren't home from work, yet. Nikki's injuries inflicted by Damien Wilson are no longer visible. She's back to her normal routine of being who-knows-where doing who-knows-what.

I have a desktop computer I salvaged from the garbage after Nikki threw it away. It has two missing keys. Q and

Y. She broke them off so Chandra would buy her a new laptop. On the screen is the home page of the Songwriter of the Year contest website.

We glance at it while we snack and talk. We're having a great time. More fun than the four of us have ever had together. I'm not even going to think about it coming to an end if the news is bad.

"I don't know why we didn't do this before now," Truman says.

"We should do it more often," Josh adds.

At five minutes before 3:00 my phone goes off. The room goes quiet.

"Hello," I answer.

"Hello," the man on the line replies. "Is this Dylan Jones?"

My pulse quickens.

"Yes."

"I'm Franklin Aubrey with the accounting firm of Duncan and Beasley."

My pulse slows.

"Yes."

"We are the auditors for the Songwriter of the Year contest."

My pulse quickens. My mouth and eyes go wide. I look at the others. They're reading my reaction.

"Put it on speakerphone," Truman says, loudly enough for Franklin Aubrey to overhear.

"Is that one of the co-writers I hear in the background?" he asks.

"Yes."

"Go ahead and put it on speakerphone so they can hear, too."

I do.

"Now, can everyone hear me?"

"Yes," we say in unison.

"Good. Dylan Jones, Madeline Lee, Josh Martinez and Truman Dixon. I am pleased to inform you that, 'Love Transcends', has been chosen as one of the songs to be considered for the grand prize."

Whatever he says after that is drowned out by our squeals.

"This will be posted on the website in a short while. I wanted to give you a heads-up and explain what to do next."

"Thank you," I say. "I can't believe this is happening."

"I can assure you, it is. But the contest is not over, yet. There's still work to be done."

My pulse slows, again. I brace myself for bad news.

"The judges want you to submit a bio and recent photographs of yourselves. In your case, four bios. It should be concise. Approximately one hundred words. These bios and photos will be used to make the final decision. The winner will be expected to represent the sponsors and endorse their products. That's the reason for this personal information. Do you have any questions?"

"About a jillion," I say.

"Mr. Aubrey," Maddie says. "When do we have to submit the bio?"

"You have forty-eight hours. You'll receive an email confirming what I've just told you and instructions for the bio. Good luck to you all."

We come together all at once, wrapping our arms around each other, jumping up and down, spinning around and squealing at the top of our lungs. It's deafening, but we don't care. For the moment time seems to stop and the world outside our circle of four disappears.

"Is this really happening?" I ask.

"I think so," Maddie says.

"What if there is no Franklin Aubrey? What if somebody is playing a practical joke on us?"

"Don't be that way, Dylan. Enjoy the moment," Truman says.

"Let's check the website," Josh says. "Maybe they've posted the names of the finalists."

We do, and they have. We navigate to the page where the finalists are listed by category. Four finalists in each of six genres. The first song under pop music is 'Love Transcends', written by Dylan Jones, Madeline Lee, Josh Martinez and Truman Dixon. I pull up my email and find the one Franklin Aubrey said to expect. The others read along with me.

"I know we're going to win," Truman says. "I can feel it."

I wish I had his confidence. When you've been dealt a lousy hand as many times as I have you expect it's always going to be that way.

"Click on that link," Maddie says.

It takes us to a page for the amended contest rules.

"They can't change the rules in the middle of the contest, can they? Not after we've already submitted our song," she protests.

"Look at what it says," I tell her. "They're increasing the prize money. Instead of one overall winner, there will be six. The winner in each category will receive one hundred grand, not to mention a bunch of other stuff."

Our odds of winning just increased dramatically.

A loud pop sounds behind me as Truman uncorks the champagne.

"Shoot! We forgot to pick up some of those plastic champagne glasses. Oh, well. Ladies first," he says, and hands the bottle to Maddie.

She takes a swig and passes it to Josh, who passes it to Truman, who passes it to me. It's the best tasting grape juice I've ever had.

~26~

The story of my life is very plain to read

After our brief and exuberant celebration we go to work on our bios. I've never been one to talk about myself, let alone write an autobiography. Not even a short one like this.

"Why do you think they want these?" Josh asks.

It's an excellent question and one we should mull over at length before we proceed.

"It's like that Franklin dude was telling us," Truman says. "They want to know if we're the kind of people they want representing them. So in our bios we should mention how often we use their products and how well we like them."

"That's going to be difficult," Maddie says. "There are five or six major sponsors and twice that number of minor ones. They sell everything from musical instruments to computers."

"You write something like this. When I'm not playing my Fender Stratocaster through my Marshall amplifier while wearing my Skechers walking shoes, I'm usually lying around in my Calvin Klein boxers talking on my Samsung Galaxy and drinking Michelob Ultra."

Truman has a lot of imagination. And he never fails to make me laugh.

"I could be wrong, but it seems to me companies these days focus less on their product and more on their image."

"Uh-oh. Get ready everybody. Dylan is about to say something profound," Truman says. "I can tell. He's got that look in his eyes. Go ahead, Dylan. Tell us."

"I don't know that it's profound. I'm just pointing out that companies don't talk about how well-made their product is or how much better it is than their competitors'. Instead they brag about how much they've contributed to cancer research or some other worthy cause. You see what I'm saying?"

"Not really."

"Alright. I'll put it another way. If the sponsors are image conscious like I think they are, then our bios should take that into consideration. Instead of saying we use their products, we say we can't afford them, which also happens to be true. That way it makes them look good when they give a helping hand to poor underprivileged people like us."

"That's what I'm talking about. Right there," Truman says. "I knew you were going to say something profound."

"I don't know," Maddie says. "That sounds like we're asking them to feel sorry for us."

When my parents were gunned down in a botched robbery attempt and I became an orphan, everyone I came in contact with tried to console me. That charitable act toward a child in need of kind words and a tender touch made them feel better about themselves. I have to confess something. Throughout my life I've used this to my advantage. I haven't profited financially from their sympathy, but I've benefitted from it in other ways.

"I'm not suggesting we ask them to feel sorry for us. I'm saying we let them feel that way if they're so inclined. We don't need to make up anything. The truth about us is sad enough."

I can practically hear the gears grinding away as they consider what I've said. Making it to the finals in this contest might be the first break any of us has gotten in our entire lives. I'm sure they agree. The truth regarding our short lives will elicit plenty of sympathy. We decide to work on the bios individually and review them together before we submit them, tomorrow.

I'm eager to share the good news with Isiah and Chandra. Chandra arrives home first. I tell her.

"Oh, Dylan! That's wonderful! I'm so happy for you!" she replies, with more enthusiasm than I can remember seeing from her. "When will they announce the winner?"

"I'm not sure. Soon, I think."

I explain about the bio we have to submit.

"Isiah and Nikki will be so excited to hear the news."

She's right about Isiah. I never know with Nikki.

"I can't wait to tell them," I say.

Isiah comes in fifteen minutes later. I tell him. He's genuinely thrilled. He lets out a whoop and gives me a bear hug that nearly cracks my ribs. I wiggle loose.

"How do you feel?" he asks.

"I feel sort of numb, at the moment. It still hasn't sunk in. Besides that, we still have to beat out three other songs."

"If you ask me, you've already won. You had to beat out a thousand others to make it this far."

Actually, it was closer to forty thousand, but who's counting. I hear a door open and then shut. Nikki walks in. I can tell from her don't-mess-with-me expression she's in a foul mood.

"Why is everyone standing around in here looking like the cat that ate the canary?" she asks.

"You'll never guess," Chandra says.

"No I won't, because I'm not going to try."

"Dylan is a finalist in the songwriting contest."

"Finalist? What does that mean?"

"It means only a few songs were picked to be considered for the grand prize," Isiah explains.

Nikki thinks about that for all of five seconds, then turns to me and asks, "How much is the grand prize?"

"That's not important," Chandra says.

"Maybe it is and maybe it's not."

I tell her because I know she won't give up until she hears and I'm dying to see the look on her face when she does.

"One hundred thousand dollars," I say, enunciating each syllable clearly.

For the first time in as long as I can remember Nikki is speechless. She looks at Chandra and Isiah who are smiling at me. They're sincerely happy for me and I'm not sure how Nikki feels about that. This is unchartered territory for her. She's always the one in the spotlight. Not me. Then she surprises me. She takes my hand and gives it a squeeze.

"Good luck, Dylan," she says. "I'll be pulling for you."

~27~

And I wonder should I laugh or cry

In Josh's bio he writes about how he's suspected he was gay for several years. He goes on to say he's still learning to deal with it and he plans to tell his family as soon as he works up the courage to do so.

Maddie reveals she barely knows her father, hasn't seen him since she was a toddler. She recalls the time the police took him away after he and her mother got into a drunken brawl in the front yard. While he was in jail, Maddie and her mother moved away.

Truman's bio could be the basis for a sitcom script. In it he tells a story about the time one of his half-sisters called the cops on him. She'd seen him so infrequently, she didn't recognize him as he entered the house late one night.

I write about being orphaned at three. I bypass the gory details of my parents' deaths. It would have been laying it on too thick.

"If this stuff doesn't have them in tears, they haven't got a heart," Truman says.

I hope I've steered us right by suggesting we write our bios this way. We take selfies with our phones and email them along with the bios to the contest judges twenty-four hours ahead of the deadline and prepare to wait for who knows how long.

Monday it's business as usual. Truman and I go to work at Bubba's. Maddie and Josh plan to go to their respective jobs as well. Nearing the end of our shift, my phone sounds.

"Answer it Dylan," Truman shouts over the noise of the ventilation fan.

"I'm trying," I shout back.

I'm struggling to get my rubber gloves off. They're caked with grease and slippery as hell.

"Hold out your hands," Truman says.

He grabs the gloves and pulls until they come loose. I snatch my phone from my pocket.

"Hello, this is Dylan," I answer.

"Mr. Jones?" the caller inquires.

"Yes."

"I'm Julia Tremont with Multimedia Management," she says in a clipped voice.

"Yes."

"I'm in the process of making the travel arrangements for Madeline Lee, Josh Martinez, Truman Dixon and yourself. Do I have those names right?"

"Yes."

"I can put the four of you on a flight leaving Detroit Metro at ten-twenty Thursday morning. It's nonstop, arriving in LA at eleven-ten our time. Does that work for you?"

"Yes."

"A limousine will take you from the airport to your hotel. And the same limousine will take you from the hotel to the rehearsal and ceremony. Okay?"

"Yes."

"Mr. Jones. Do you speak English?"

"Si."

"You may want to expand your vocabulary a bit. Do you have any questions?"

"About a jillion."

"Ask them one at a time."

"What's this about? I mean, I get it that it concerns the contest. Does this mean we won?"

"I can't tell you. It's my job is to control what and when information is released to the press and social media outlets. Officially you're one of the finalists invited to the announcement ceremony. Didn't you get the email explaining this?"

"I guess not. When was it sent?"

"I sent it over ten minutes ago. I thought you'd have read it by now."

"Sorry. I'm at work, but we get off soon. I'll read the email as soon as I get home."

"Yes, please do. If you have other questions, my contact info is in the email. Good luck, Mr. Jones. Bye, now."

"Thanks, goodbye."

"Who was it and what'd they say?" Truman wants to know.

"I think she said her name is Julia. She talks fast. I didn't catch everything she said."

"Damn, Dylan. You need to start listening faster. Did you understand anything she said?"

"Enough. I know we're flying to LA on Thursday."

"This Thursday?"

"I think. She sent me an email. I'll read it when I get home."

"What'd she say when you asked her if we won?"

"She can't tell us, yet."

"What? She doesn't want to spoil the surprise?"

"Something like that. Right now we need to finish up here and get going. I think we're going to be pretty busy between now and Thursday."

"You got that right. I have to figure out what I'm wearing. We're going to California. That's a whole different world over there. It's summer all year round. I need me some sunshades and Bermuda shorts."

As usual, my mind and Truman's are going in opposite directions. His is already in California. Mine is still wondering how to get there. I've never flown. I've only been in an airport one time. Isiah took Nikki and me to watch the jets land and take off. That was several years ago.

When I get home Nikki is in the kitchen looking like she rolled out of bed a minute earlier.

"Hey," I say, as I pass by at a trot on my way to the bathroom.

"What's your hurry? Is someone chasing you?"

"Sorry. I can't talk now."

I'm in and out of the shower in three minutes and racing toward my room to scan the email from Julia.

"Dylan. What is with you?" Nikki asks, as I zip by.

I don't stop to answer. Then it dawns on her.

"Is this about that contest? Did you win?"

"We won't know until we get to LA."

I head down the stairs to my room with Nikki on my heels.

"Did you say LA, as in Los Angeles?"

"Yes. The ceremony where they announce the winners of each category takes place this Saturday in LA."

"How are you going to get there in time?"

"We fly from Detroit Metro on Thursday. A woman with some media company is booking our flight and hotel room."

"They're paying for everything?"

"I sure hope so, because we can't afford it."

While Nikki is trying to wrap her mind around my trip to LA, I check my inbox for the email from Julia.

"We're staying at the Sheraton in downtown LA. Our flight leaves Detroit at ten twenty, Thursday morning."

"Dylan, you know what this means, don't you?"

"What?"

"It means you won. They wouldn't be shelling out all this money to get you to LA if you lost."

"I hope you're right about that."

"I know I am. I can't wait to tell my friends."

"Hold on, Nikki. You can't tell anyone we won. Not yet. What if it doesn't turn out that way? Everybody here will think I lied to them. They'll wonder if there ever was a contest or if I made the whole thing up."

"Dylan, you better start getting used to being a celebrity. You're going to have to crawl out of that shell and deal with the world. I can't believe it. My little brother is going to be somebody."

"Your little brother? Nikki, are you hearing yourself? You've never thought of me as a brother. I remember the time you locked me out of the house. I was five. It was January and something like ten degrees with snow on the ground."

"That's how it is between brothers and sisters. They don't sit around hugging and kissing each other. They yell and argue. That's how they express love. Don't take it personally."

"Call me cynical, but I think this newfound sisterly love has more to do with me winning this contest than your true feelings about me."

"All I'm saying is we're both adults now. We'll be moving out and starting our own lives. Maybe getting married and having kids of our own. We need to remember where we came from. Stay in touch with one another. You know what I'm saying?"

"Yes, I do. And we will stay in touch. I promise."

Then, the unthinkable happens. She hugs me.

"I'm glad we had this talk," she says.

"Yeah, me too."

She climbs the stairs leaving the basement. I hear the front door open and realize she's outside getting the mail. I hurry up the stairs to lock her out. If I'd known that's how siblings show their love, I would have done it years ago.

Part II

~28~

Going to California with an aching in my heart

Isiah takes time off from his job to drop the four of us at the airport. I don't ask him to, he volunteers. It's a task done for his sake as much as for ours. Opportunity is knocking for Maddie, Josh, Truman and me. Isiah senses this. We're passing through a portal without knowing what's on the other side. Maybe he's been there himself. Or maybe it's a chance for him to experience this event vicariously through us.

He pulls to the curb at the airport. We all get out, Isiah too. People honk. Isiah ignores them. He wants to say something, but the words won't come.

"Thanks, Mr. Jones," Maddie, Josh and Truman say, before heading inside with their bags in tow.

"Isiah…," I start.

I choke up and can't finish. I throw my arms around him and we stand there for a moment while I pull myself together.

"Good luck, Dylan. You knock them dead in LA."

I grab my bags and go to catch up with the others. They're several yards ahead of me with a throng of people between us, but I have no trouble spotting them. The four of us are all wearing tropical shirts, shorts and sunshades. We look like a Beach Boys tribute band.

We check our bags and arrive at the departure gate with an hour to spare. From that point until we board Josh, Maddie and I barely speak. Truman is every bit as nervous as we are, he just handles it differently. He talks nonstop right up to the point where the plane accelerates for takeoff.

I had no idea something that big could travel that fast on land. I watch the buildings passing by through the window as our speed increases. The air inside the cabin is thick with anticipation. I close my eyes and lean back. A few minutes after that a flight attendant taps me on my shoulder.

"Would you care for a towel?" she asks.

She's holding what looks like a white wash cloth between tongs. I figure it's something I should want. Why else would she be passing them out? She eases it closer and I take it. It's wet and warm.

"Thank you," I say. "This is my first time to fly."

"Oh? I couldn't tell."

My palms are sort of sweaty, which probably happens a lot to people during takeoff. I wipe my hands and set it aside.

The contest people spared no expense with us. We're sitting at the front of the plane in first class. Maddie is in a window seat to my right looking out. Truman is across the aisle with Josh in the window seat to his left. Like Maddie, Josh is gazing at the countryside passing beneath us.

Truman's attention is focused on something up ahead. He glances at me and tilts his head toward the subject of his interest.

"Check this out," he whispers.

I lean into the aisle to see for myself. In a seat facing toward the rear of the plane a Latino woman peruses a magazine. Her legs are crossed, her dress is short and there's a fair amount of skin showing, which I'm sure is what Truman wants me to see. As we stare at her like a couple twelve-year-old boys with a Playboy magazine, she looks up to catch us in the act. We duck back behind the seats in front of us, out of her view.

"Cut it out, man. You're going to get us in trouble," I whisper to Truman.

"This is not high school. This is the real world, Dylan," he replies.

I don't know which is more forgiving of misbehaving juveniles, high school or the real world, and I don't want to find out. It isn't ten minutes before he's at it again.

"Psst! Dylan."

I can pretend I don't hear him, but he'll just get louder or wad up pieces of paper and throw them at me. I look at him. He tilts his head toward the Latino lady, again. I shake my head, no. He jerks his head toward her more vigorously. I'm afraid he'll sprain his neck, so I give in and look. She has what appears to be a glass of champagne.

"They gave it to her free. She didn't pay for it," he says.

I hold out my hands, palms up, to express my disinterest. He waves to the flight attendant. She comes over.

"I'd like a glass of champagne, please," he tells her.

"I'm sorry, young man. I can't serve anyone under twenty-one. Would you like coffee or a soft drink?"

He settles for a cola. Josh and Maddie overhear and ask for the same. The flight attendant returns with the drinks.

"I'm Carolyn," she says. "If you need anything else, please press the button there."

In other words, waving to get her attention is considered to be poor airplane etiquette.

An hour into the flight and we're soaring smoothly through the sky.

"This is not half as bad as I thought it would be," I say to Maddie.

"This is the easy part of the flight. Sometimes you hit turbulence that bounces the plane around. And landings can be dicey, too."

Thank you, Miss Sunshine.

Two hours into the flight and my bladder is reminding me it hasn't been emptied in way too long. There's a restroom near the cockpit designated for first class passengers. How cool is that? Our own restroom.

"I'll be right back," I say to Maddie. Not that she cares.

I'm not a big guy. There are people on this plane who would make three of me. They must hold it until we land, because I can't see anyone that big trying to squeeze into an airplane restroom. When I return to my seat, the flight attendant is passing out meals to everyone.

"Would you like teriyaki chicken or braised salmon?" she asks me.

I take the chicken. Salmon is too close to catfish. Truman and Josh chat while they eat. I turn to Maddie. She's having the salmon.

"How is it?"

"It's delicious. You want a bite?"

"No, thanks. Fish and I don't like each other that much. You want some chicken?"

"No. The salmon is plenty for me. Can I ask you something?"

"Sure."

"Are you nervous about the ceremony, Saturday?"

"I haven't thought about it. Everything happened so quickly I haven't had a chance to think about anything other than this flight."

"I can't stop thinking about it. There'll be news reporters, music producers and bigwigs from several companies. None of us has ever experienced anything remotely close to what will happen."

"Now, I'm nervous."

"Sorry, I didn't mean to do that to you."

"It's okay. Look, we're all going to be nervous come tomorrow. Like it or not. We're venturing way outside of our comfort zone. I think it will be a good experience, though. And whatever happens tomorrow, we'll still have each other. The four of us will still be a team."

"I hope you're right about that."

"You're saying, you have doubts?"

"We're four different types of people. This contest has brought us together. What's going to keep it that way after the contest is over?"

"The same thing that held us together long enough to finish the song. Something about it feels important to us."

~29~

I'm learning to fly, but I ain't got wings

It takes almost four hours before I begin to relax aboard the aircraft. Then the pilot tells everyone we're going to land soon, and the anxiety returns. I can feel the plane roll one way and then the other as he points out one famous landmark after another passing by on our left or right.

"Look at the hills everywhere," Maddie says.

I do. The terrain looks rugged and unforgiving.

"Do you see the runway up ahead?" I ask.

"Not yet. We're still pretty high above the ground."

That's reassuring. High above the ground with no runway in sight. I close my eyes.

"Look at the houses," Maddie says, a minute later.

Reluctantly I open my eyes to see. We're much lower now. Thousands of houses, maybe millions, all of similar size, shape and color are laid out on a grid pattern. Streets running perpendicular to one another form straight lines that seem to disappear beyond the north, west and south horizons.

"There are four times as many people here as in Detroit," Maddie says.

I can believe it. We pass over a highway with six lanes going in each direction, right before we land. The cars are bumper to bumper and seem to stretch for as far as I can see.

I feel the plane bump the tarmac, roll down the runway, then slow and turn toward the main building. It pulls up to a terminal, the doors open and we walk from the plane through some kind of tunnel to get inside. We're greeted by a sea of people scurrying in every direction.

"Which way do we go?" I ask, but the others are as confused as I am.

"Just follow everyone else," Truman says.

It's probably good advice and it beats trying to swim upstream. The bulk of the people end up in baggage claim. We see our flight number posted on a sign above one of the carousels.

The carousel starts up. One after another the bags come down a chute and onto the conveyor. The people crowd around the rotating baggage so tightly I can't see anything beyond them. Twenty minutes later it clears out enough for us to retrieve our bags.

"According to the email, a limousine is going to take us to the hotel," I tell the others.

A sign points us toward ground transportation. Taxis, shuttles and buses. We head that way.

"Look," Maddie says. "That must mean us."

There's a guy holding a piece of paper with our names on it.

"Songwriters?" he asks, as we approach. "My name is Matt. I'll drive you to your hotel. This way, please."

We follow him outside. A blast of hot air hits us full-on as we exit the building. He leads us to a black stretch limo and opens the door for us to get in. Then, he puts our bags in the trunk.

"I am liking this VIP treatment," Truman says, as we seat ourselves in the limo's cozy confines. "In my opinion it's long overdue."

"The hotel is about fifteen miles from here," Matt says, as he takes his place behind the steering wheel. "It should take anywhere from thirty minutes to an hour, depending on traffic. There are cold drinks in the refrigerator. Help yourselves and enjoy the ride."

If you can afford it or if someone else is footing the bill, as is the case with us, I highly recommend traveling by limousine when visiting LA. While our driver deals with the traffic, we take in the sights and sounds of the city in the cool comfort of the limo.

"We should see some of the city this afternoon," Maddie suggests. "Today may be the only one where we have free time. There's no telling what it will be like with the rehearsal tomorrow and the ceremony on Saturday."

"I'd love to," Josh says. "I've wanted to come to LA for as long as I can remember. There are so many things to see. Universal Studios, Venice Beach, Rodeo Drive and Hollywood."

"I don't think we can fit all those into one afternoon," I say.

"That's okay. Any of those is one more thing off my bucket list."

"We should go to the hotel first," Truman says. "There might be a message from the contest people."

"I agree. Let's check in first."

Matt drops us at the hotel. A bellboy puts our luggage on a cart and leads the way to the front desk.

"I'm Dylan Jones," I tell the clerk. "This is Maddie Lee, Truman Dixon and Josh Martinez."

She enters our names into her computer as I give them.

"We're supposed to stay here," I say.

"Yes, I know," she says.

She uses the same clipped tone as Julia Tremont used when I spoke with her. Maybe it's an LA thing. She gives each of a pass card for the room and has us sign a paper saying we won't trash the place. Probably another LA thing.

"The elevator is right over there. Take it to the twenty-second floor and go to your left. You're in room twenty-two-o-four. Your bags will be there shortly."

"That was easy," Josh says, as we get into the elevator.

"More of that VIP treatment. I can get used to this," Truman says.

"I didn't realize we'd be staying in the same room," Maddie says, sounding concerned.

It's one more detail of this trip that never crossed my mind beforehand. The only hotel room I've ever seen had a bed, a chair and TV in one room, and a bathroom with a door for privacy.

"The room probably has two beds that sleep two people each. We just need to decide who sleeps with who," I say.

I can see from their expressions no one likes that idea.

"Either we work out sleeping arrangements or we get separate rooms, and I bet they get a hundred a night for a room here."

"Try four hundred," Josh says. "I looked it up online."

"We can't afford that," I say. "I don't see why we can't work this out. Nikki and I used to sleep in the same room."

"Yeah, but how old were you?"

"What difference does it make? My point is we slept in the same room and nothing happened, aside from a few fights. You can sleep with me, Maddie. I'll be a perfect gentleman. You won't even know I'm there."

"You won't be there, Dylan. I'm not sleeping in the same bed with any of you guys."

"That hurts my feelings," Truman says. "I can understand why you don't want to be in the same bed with Dylan, but what did I ever do to deserve to be treated that way?"

"Truman, would you share a bed with me?" Josh asks.

It catches Truman completely off guard.

"Well…, uh…, I…, uh…,"

"See," Josh says. "Now you know how Maddie feels."

We arrive at the room with the matter unsettled. I insert my pass card in the slot, see the green light and open the door.

"Problem solved," I say.

The room is a suite with a sitting room and two bedrooms. Each bedroom has two queen-size beds.

"I'll take this bedroom," Maddie says. "You guys get that one."

I look at Truman and Josh. They look back at me. We're all thinking the same thing.

"I'll sleep on the couch," I say. "It's probably more comfortable than my bed at home."

"No. I'll take the couch," Josh says. "Trust me. It will work out better that way and I don't mind."

~30~

People are strange when you're a stranger

With the sleeping arrangements decided, everyone is eager to explore the city. The problem is we all want to go different places.

"Since we aren't familiar with the city, I think we should stick together. There are probably parts of LA we shouldn't wander around in. Not solo anyway," I say.

"Dylan's right," Maddie agrees. "Let's stay together, at least for today."

"Maybe we can find out what's nearby in the lobby downstairs. They probably have literature for out-of-towners like us."

In the hotel lobby we find a rack of pamphlets advertising guided tours of the city's most popular attractions.

"It's too late to arrange a tour today," I say. "If we had a bus schedule that might help."

"Not if we don't know where we're going," Truman says.

A man approaches. I saw him a minute earlier sitting nearby holding a newspaper as if reading it. Every so often he'd look our way. He's older than us, maybe mid-twenties, with a slight build and Asian features.

"I overheard you talking," he says. Is this your first trip to LA?"

He directs the question to Maddie. A stranger in an unfamiliar place. I'm wary. It doesn't seem to concern Maddie, though.

"Yes," she tells him. "We're here from Detroit."

"Detroit. That's a great city. I love Motown sounds and American automobiles. How long are you here for?"

"We're not really sure. At least a few days."

"I've lived in California all my life. What kind of things interest you? Outdoor stuff or museums or sports?"

"I think we just want to do some sightseeing, today," I tell him.

"I can show you around, if you like."

"You'd do that?" Maddie asks.

"Sure. I don't have a lot else to do. I know everything there is to know about LA. You couldn't find a better guide to show you around."

Normally I wouldn't consider it, but this guy seems about as threatening as a kitten. Maddie doesn't wait for us to decide.

"That's great."

"My name is Kevin," he says, and extends his hand to Maddie.

"I'm Maddie. This is Josh, Dylan and Truman."

"Great to meet you guys. My car is this way. Come on."

Maddie doesn't hesitate. I hope her instincts are right about this guy. Josh, Truman and I follow. His car is in a parking garage across from our hotel. It's a late model Audi convertible. He unlocks it with a remote key. Maddie takes the front passenger seat. Truman, Josh and I squeeze into the back. He puts the top down as he leaves the garage.

"You guys okay back there?" he asks.

"We're fine," I say, though we're pretty cramped.

We drive around for an hour, all the time he's pointing to things we're driving past and explaining what it is. There was the Grammy Museum, Staples Center, Union Station, several restaurants and a bunch of other things I'll never remember.

"What time is it in Detroit?" Truman asks.

"A little after four," I say.

"That explains why my stomach says I'm hungry."

"I know a great place where you can get almost anything you want. It's called Grand Central Market," Kevin says.

We park a block away. Maddie and Kevin walk ahead of us. They seem to be hitting it off, chatting between themselves as they go and pretty much ignoring us. I'm not jealous. Alright, maybe I'm a little jealous, but mostly I'm concerned for Maddie. She just met the guy. He could be a serial killer for all she knows.

Once inside the place I see it houses a variety of food venders. Each one offers something different. We have a discussion over what to eat, but can't come to a consensus, so we split up agreeing to meet later.

I look over the menu at each place. My left brain is telling me to try something new. My right brain is telling me I'll regret it. Finally, I settle on fried chicken with a biscuit and coleslaw. It's really good. Better than Chandra's, though I'd never tell her that.

Truman is waiting where we agreed to meet when I get there.

"What'd you have?" I ask.

"Sushi."

I make a face.

"Have you ever tried it?"

"No."

"Then don't knock it."

"Have you seen Maddie or Josh?"

"I've seen Maddie. She and Kevin had sushi, too. Here they come now. I haven't seen Josh."

"Hi Dylan," she says. "What did you have for lunch?"

"Fried chicken."

She makes a face.

"Dylan, out of all the great stuff they have here, you chose fried chicken? You really have to broaden your horizons."

"I'll work on it. Have you seen Josh?"

"No. I'll call him."

She steps away to find a quieter spot and dials his number. I can see her alternate between talking into the phone and listening with it pressed to her ear. Then, she disconnects and returns to us.

"He says he'll see us back at the hotel, later."

"What do you mean?" I ask.

"Just what I said," she answers, matter-of-factly.

"Did he say why?" Truman wants to know.

"He met someone."

"A guy?" I ask.

"I assume it's a guy. He didn't say and I didn't ask."

I look at Truman who simply shrugs his shoulders.

"Dylan, we're not in Detroit anymore," Maddie says.

"Thanks, Dorothy, but I'm not Toto and I know where we are."

"I'm just saying that Josh has more freedom now that he's away from his family. He can finally be himself. Don't be judgmental."

"Judgmental?! Me?! Are you kidding?"

She doesn't think that worthy of a response.

"You guys ready to see more of LA?" Kevin asks.

"I'm more than ready," Maddie says.

They head toward the Audi at a trot. Truman and I hurry to catch up.

~31~

Follow follow follow the yellow brick road

Maddie didn't fool me with her comments about Josh. He's not in Detroit anymore and neither is she. That's the message behind her words. He can finally be himself, so can she. Don't be judgmental. What she means is give him some space. And her too while I'm at it.

The longer we drive around seeing the city, the closer Maddie gets to Kevin and the more distant she becomes with Truman and me. I don't dwell on it because there's too much else going on. With the rehearsal tomorrow and the ceremony the next day and everything that follows I have plenty of concerns to occupy my thoughts without throwing Maddie and Josh into the mix.

Kevin takes us to Griffith Park which is at the edge of the Santa Monica Mountain Range. The park is huge and the terrain is hilly and rugged. There's an observatory and several scenic vistas. From one point we can see the famous Hollywood sign. From another we can see the downtown skyline of LA. Kevin parks the Audi at a hiking trailhead and we all get out.

"Would you guys like to get high?"

I assume he's asking if we want to smoke some pot. We're not taken aback by the question. I think we've been halfway expecting it since Kevin first approached us. Pot smoking is commonplace among people our age. I don't have any experience with it myself. That's because I could never afford it.

"I would," Maddie says.

"Great," says Kevin. "There's a lookout point a short ways down this trail. We can light up there."

He turns and begins walking toward the trailhead. Maddie falls in beside him. I wait on Truman.

"I'll wait here," he calls to Kevin.

Kevin turns his head without stopping and says, "You sure?"

"Yeah, I'm sure."

Kevin and Maddie start down the trail.

"Go ahead without me," I call to Maddie, but she and Kevin are already out of earshot.

"First Josh and now Maddie. If we keep losing partners like this someone is going to have to accept the award on our behalf at the ceremony. Because none of us will be there." Truman says.

"We worked pretty hard all summer. Maybe they need some time off. They won't miss the ceremony. There's too much at stake."

We wait around for Maddie and Kevin to return. Thirty minutes go by. Then an hour. Then two hours.

"I'm starting to worry," I say.

"I am too, but there's nothing we can do except wait. As big as this park is. All the trees and hills. We'd just get lost."

He's right. That doesn't make waiting any easier, though. Three hours after leaving us, Maddie and Kevin reappear. They're both really stoned and having trouble walking in a straight line. Maddie's hair and clothes look like she rolled down a hill.

"We were getting worried about you," I say.

She squints and tries to focus her vision. Either the pot was premium quality or they smoked a lot of it. It seems to have rendered her mute.

"We lost track of the time," Kevin says.

"If you don't mind, maybe we can go back to the hotel, now," Truman says. "I'm still on Detroit time."

Finding her voice, Maddie says, "Not yet. I'm having too much fun."

"Maddie, don't forget about the rehearsal tomorrow." Truman reminds her. "I know you don't want to miss it."

"I won't. That's tomorrow, a whole day from now."

"It's in the morning," Truman tells her, his irritation beginning show. "And right now we don't know how early we have to be there."

"Worry about yourself Truman, and I'll do the same."

I feel the same as Truman, but I know firsthand how stubborn Maddie can be. Jumping in on Truman's side would just make her dig her heels in deeper. Kevin is caught in the middle.

"The sunsets are gorgeous here," he offers, hoping it might influence us to stay longer.

"Thanks, but I've seen plenty of sunsets," Truman says.

Kevin looks at Maddie.

"I'm staying," she states.

"The bus runs every twenty or thirty minutes. It goes right by your hotel," Kevin says.

"Where do we catch it?" I ask.

"At the observatory. It's not far. I'll take you there."

We load back into the Audi for the short ten-minute ride. Neither Maddie, Truman nor I speak during the ride.

"Thanks," I tell Kevin before he drives away with Maddie, leaving us waiting for the bus.

"Yeah, thanks for nothing," Truman says under his breath.

It's not long until the bus comes, but it's two hours and three transfers before we get back to the hotel. We're hot, tired and short of patience. My phone sounds while we're waiting on the elevator.

141

"That's probably Maddie calling to apologize," I say to Truman.

I'm wrong. It's Julia Tremont.

"I wanted to make sure you received the email with instructions for the rehearsal, tomorrow. You didn't reply as I asked you to do."

"We've been running around all day. I'm sorry I haven't checked my email since I left home this morning."

"Dylan, it's essential that you check your phone and email frequently. I need to be able to contact you at all times. The ceremony is a multi-million dollar production. It has to come off without a hitch."

I could explain how I don't have a mobile device for my emails, but she seems stressed out enough as it is. That might push her over the edge.

"I'll do a better job of checking my emails," I say instead.

There's a business center located on the second floor where guests can use a computer. We stop there to read the email Julia sent.

"The limousine is going to pick us up at nine," I tell Truman. I'll call Maddie and Josh to let them know. Past that it's up to them."

I make the calls. Neither answers. I leave a voicemail for both.

"They better not screw this up for us," Truman says.

~32~

Boom shaka-laka-laka, boom shaka-laka-laka

As the elevator ascends to the twenty-second floor my worries rise with it. Not for Josh and Maddie. I'm way past that. My concern is strictly for myself, now. I feel like I've earned the right to have something good happen. Some small degree of success is due me. To be this close only to have it jeopardized by their selfish whims makes me wish I'd never met them. Truman is thinking along the same lines.

"I know you like Maddie, but you need to start thinking about yourself. If she doesn't get back here in time we need to have an explanation prepared. The same goes for Josh."

"I liked Maddie once. Now I'm not so sure. If they don't make it back in time, we can just tell the truth. They met someone, went to party and we haven't seen them since."

"That makes us look bad, too. Like no one is in charge. Everyone is going to think we're so disorganized it's a wonder we ever wrote this song."

The elevator reaches our floor. We get off and head to our suite.

"Maybe we're worrying about nothing," I say. "Maybe they got the message I sent and are on their way back here, now."

I unlock the door and we go inside. I see something on the couch in the sitting area and go to investigate. It's Josh's phone. On the table next to the couch is the remains of a joint on the end of a roach clip.

"He's been here," I say.

I pick up the phone. The display shows a missed call. Probably the one I made from downstairs. I scan the suite and see the door to Maddie's room is closed.

Three possibilities play out in my mind. Maddie and Josh. Not likely. Maddie and Kevin. Maybe, except the phone on the couch belongs to Josh, not Maddie or Kevin. The third possibility is Josh and his new friend, which is the most likely scenario.

"Josh," I call out loudly.

No response. I listen for a moment, but hear nothing. Truman puts his ear to the door and then knocks.

"I'm coming in," he warns.

He turns the knob. It's locked.

"Just a minute," comes a voice from inside the room.

I recognize it. It's Josh. An exchange of whispers can be heard behind the closed door. Then, it opens a crack. One eye peeks out.

"What?" Josh asks.

"We need to talk," Truman says.

"I'm kind of busy right now."

Truman stiffens. Josh probably doesn't feel Truman has any reason to be angry. But justified or not his anger is real and Josh needs to respect that.

"It's important Josh," I say. "Get dressed and come out here."

It's ten minutes before he does. Which gives Truman that much longer to work himself into a snit.

"What's wrong with you?" Truman barks, the second Josh comes into the room.

"What's wrong with you?" Josh retorts.

Josh is six inches taller than Truman, but I'll bet against him if a fight breaks out between them.

"There's nothing wrong with me. I'm not the one who's trying to kill our chances of winning this contest and getting the prizes."

"Neither am I. Besides, we've already won the contest, haven't we? Why else would they fly us here?"

"Let's not start the celebration, yet. We don't know we've won. Not for sure," I say. "And until we do, we need to be careful. Anything the contest people think might bring them bad publicity, we need to avoid."

"You're speaking about me being gay, aren't you?"

"That has nothing to do with it," Truman says. "You were smoking pot here, weren't you?"

"It's LA. Everybody does it."

"Remember what I said about bad publicity. Getting busted for drugs is right there at the top of the list of things we can't afford."

"It was just a joint. No one is going to bust me."

We're not getting through to Josh, the same as we didn't get through to Maddie. The talk with Josh is doing more damage than good. I soften.

"Alright. I'll concede it isn't likely one joint will get you busted, but consider this. How well do you know the guy you're with? Does he have more than pot on him? Does he have a criminal record? You don't know, do you? When you bring a stranger into our room it affects us all."

"What I'm trying to figure out is what happened to you and Maddie between Detroit and LA," Truman says. "We were all good friends while we worked on the song. Then it looks like we might win and it's so long Truman and Dylan. We don't need you anymore."

"It's not like that."

"Then, what's it like. Let me remind you of something. Dylan wrote the song we entered in the contest. The rest of us are along for the ride because of his generosity. I would think you'd be more grateful for that."

Josh's gaze is downcast. He seems contrite. I expect him to look at me and say he's sorry. He doesn't.

"Dylan didn't write the song. His mother did. I can't imagine what the contest people would do if they knew."

A thinly veiled threat. But an effective one, nonetheless.

"You'd be kissing the money and prizes goodbye," I say.

"I don't care."

I believe him.

"The limousine will pick us up in front of the hotel at nine in the morning to take us to the rehearsal. You're not going to pull a no-show on us, are you?"

"I'll be there."

I toss his phone to him.

"You might want to keep that handy, in case something changes."

"Is that everything?"

"Yeah, that's it."

He goes back into the bedroom and shuts the door behind him.

"Can you believe this guy?" Truman says. "I'm sorry I ever met him. He's been nothing but trouble since we got here."

"There's nothing we can do about him now. Or Maddie either, for that matter. Let's eat dinner and get some sleep. Tomorrow's a big day."

~33~

Gonna live while I'm alive, I'll sleep when I'm dead

I can't sleep. I lie awake listening for movement. Truman is in one bed. I'm in the other. The door to our room is closed. We're in downtown LA. The noise in the city is nonstop 24/7. Outside the hotel, cars honk like it's New Year's Eve. Inside people are coming and going at all hours.

Each time I think I hear a door shut or someone's footsteps I get up to see if it's Maddie. Around midnight I hear something and open the door to peek out. Josh's boyfriend is raiding the minibar. I return to my bed.

"Was that Maddie?" Truman whispers.

"No. It's Josh's boyfriend."

I doze off and on. The clock beside my bed reads four eighteen when a knocking sound rouses me. I get up to investigate. It's coming from the front door. I look through the peephole and see Maddie. I open the door.

"I couldn't get this to work," she says, referring to her pass card.

She brushes past me and goes into the room where Josh is. The door isn't locked as it was earlier. I expect to hear Maddie scream or make a sound like she's startled to find Josh and his boyfriend in the room. She doesn't. It occurs to me that she knew ahead of time what she'd find when she arrived. I go back to bed.

"Was that Maddie?" Truman asks.

"Yes."

"How does she look?"

"Like an extra from that movie, Night of the Living Dead."

"I hope she can pull herself together in time."

"Yeah, me too. She went into the other room where Josh and his boyfriend are. I didn't hear her make a sound like she was surprised to see them. What do you make of that?"

"It's strange. But we've seen a lot of strange behavior from those two since we got here."

"It's like she knew he was there. Like they've been talking to one another, but keeping it secret from us. Am I just being paranoid?"

"No. You're being smart. You don't know if you can trust them. I don't either. We have to watch out for each other, now."

Things aren't any better in the morning. If anything they're worse. Truman and I are showered and dressed in tropical shirts, shorts and sunshades at seven. I knock on the door of the other room. No response. I call Maddie's phone and leave a voicemail.

"Call me back. We need to be downstairs in the lobby no later than eight forty-five."

Truman and I order breakfast from room service. There's still no response from Maddie or Josh when we finish at eight.

"If it comes down to it we'll go without them," I say.

"Fine by me," Truman says.

Still nothing from Maddie or Josh when we leave the room at eight thirty-five. We see Matt, our chauffer from the day before, as we get off the elevator. He's sitting in the lobby sipping coffee from a go-cup.

With him is a pretty young woman dressed in casual business attire. A sleeveless blouse and knee-length skirt. She's preoccupied with something on her tablet. Matt nudges her when he sees us approaching. She hops up to greet us.

I'm six-foot tall and she comes eye to eye with me. But then, she's wearing six-inch heels. She has a slender build with plenty of curves, brunette hair reaching to the small of her back and dark penetrating eyes that seem to look right through me.

She's younger than I first thought. If I had to guess I'd put her at twenty-four. Older than me, but what difference does a few years make? She flashes a smile that causes me to trip over my own feet.

"I'm Natalie Randall, with Multimedia Management. And you are…,"

"I'm Dylan Jones. This is Truman Dixon."

She consults her tablet.

"And where is Josh Martinez and Madeline Lee?"

"I think they're on the way," I say.

"You think?"

"We told them to be downstairs at eight forty-five. Truman and I are a little early."

Without another word she puts her phone to her ear and starts for the elevator. She takes long swift strides that would leave me running to keep pace with her. Within seconds she's in the elevator. I watch her until the doors close and it starts its ascent. I glance at the time.

"Maddie who?" Truman says to me.

"What?"

"That's what a girl like that will make you say. I think you ought to get to know her. She'll make you forget about Maddie and every other girl you've ever known."

"I don't need Natalie for that. I've already forgotten about Maddie."

"Natalie? See, you're already on a first name basis with her."

Eight minutes later by my count, the elevator doors open and Natalie strides out, her phone still to her ear. She stops in front of Truman and me, and disconnects her call.

"Here's the deal," she says. "They have exactly two minutes to get themselves down here or you and your song are disqualified."

My heart sinks. I'm so angry with Josh and Maddie at this point I could throw them off the twenty-second-floor balcony.

"We can do it without them," Truman says.

"I'm sorry. Those are my instructions. This is a multi-million dollar ad campaign involving several clients. The contestants, like yourself are expendable. We have other songwriters waiting in the wings. Normally, in a situation like this you wouldn't even be given two minutes. You'd be out on your ass and on your way home on the next plane."

"If you don't mind me asking," I say. "Why are you giving us a break?"

"I'm not. I don't make those decisions. They come from someone above my pay grade. But to answer your question, you get the extra two minutes because it would take longer than that to replace you."

Now, I picture myself dragging Maddie and Josh to the roof to throw them off. Natalie glances at her watch.

"Times up," she says. "Sorry."

She punches a number on her phone and puts it to her ear. At that precise moment the elevator doors open. Josh and Maddie come out, frantically fastening snaps and buttons as they run toward us.

Natalie disconnects her call.

"You two sure cut that close. As I was just telling Dylan and Truman, very few people get a second chance in this town and absolutely no one gets a third. So don't blow it."

Matt rises and heads outside. We all follow. The limousine is parked at the curb. Matt opens the rear door. Truman slides into the seat facing forward. I get in next to him. Josh and Maddie sit across from us facing the rear. Natalie sits beside me. The door closes and Matt gets in.

"Fasten your seat belts, kids. Enjoy the ride," Natalie says.

She doesn't mean it literally. She isn't talking about the seat belts or ride in the limousine. She's talking about the rehearsal, ceremony and everything that follows. She shines her radiant smile on me.

"Don't be nervous," she says and pats my thigh. "You're going to do just fine."

"Maddie who?" I mutter under my breath.

~34~

I'll find my limo driver, mister take us to the show

On the ride from the hotel Truman and I sit facing Josh and Maddie. We glare at them. They glare back. Nobody wants to be the first to blink. Natalie is busily tapping away at her tablet, doing her best to ignore us.

It's only a fifteen-minute ride to get where we're going. Matt pulls the limousine to the curb in front of another downtown hotel. Natalie puts on sunshades. She glances at us to confirm ours are in place. They are.

"Here we go," she says.

A hotel valet opens the door and Natalie steps out of the limo followed by us. We're greeted by clicks and flashes of cameras.

"Dylan, how does it feel?" someone shouts.

"Great," I shout back.

"What about you, Madeline?" another cries out.

She looks toward the voice and is blinded by several flashes going off at once. Natalie herds us inside.

"That's all for now," she tells the crowd.

She walks quickly through the lobby, down a hallway past shops and into an auditorium. We struggle to keep up with her. Thirty or more workers are putting the final touches on things. A podium sits on stage in front of a backdrop covered with sponsors' logos. Hanging above the podium is a banner reading, Songwriter of the Year.

Natalie stops to scan the room. We do the same.

"Wow!" I say.

"This is just the beginning, Dylan," Natalie replies.

"Who were all those people outside?" I ask her.

"Paparazzi. They pay hotel employees to give them a heads-up when celebrities arrive."

"We're celebrities?"

Saying it pleases me.

"Not yet, but they don't know that."

"How did they know our names?" Maddie asks.

"Online chatter."

She taps on her phone, and then puts it to her ear.

"It's Natalie. We're here," she says, and listens to the reply. Then there's a series of yes and no responses from her with a pause in between each to listen. Right before she disconnects, she looks at us and says, "They'll be okay."

I'm glad she thinks so, but it does nothing to boost my confidence.

"This is where it all takes place," she says. "Let's go over here to the anteroom where I don't have to scream over the noise."

It's a small room, the size of a dressing room. Josh and Maddie sit side by side with their backs to one wall. Truman and I sit on the opposite wall, facing them. We glare at them. They glare back. Because it worked so well in the limousine.

"Alright, listen up. There's a lot to go over and I don't want to repeat myself any more than necessary."

"Say again," I joke.

"Real cute, Dylan."

She says it sarcastically, but there's a hint of a smile as she does.

"In a little while they're going to begin rehearsals for the show. It isn't being filmed, but pay attention. During the actual ceremony things might get pretty hectic. Today you'll be shown where your table is, where the cameras will be, which steps to use if you're called to the stage. You'll get some pointers on what to do and what not to do."

"Are the other contestants going to be here?"

"Yes. They should be arriving in the next few minutes, if they're not here already."

The thought of an auditorium full of songwriters who want to win every bit as much as we do makes me feel a little queasy.

"I'm going to find out how soon they'll start. While I'm gone I suggest you use the time to iron out your differences. You need to appear unified as a group. You could be booted from the contest if my boss thinks there might be a problem."

We continue glaring across the room at one another, even after Natalie has left. Finally, Maddie speaks.

"You two need to stop being so bossy."

"Yeah," Josh chimes in.

"You two need to stop being irresponsible," Truman fires back.

"We haven't bossed you around," I say. "We haven't tried to stop you from seeing your boyfriends or doing anything else."

"Have too," Josh says.

"When?" Truman challenges. "Anything Dylan or I have asked you to do has been for the purpose of keeping this group together."

"That's just it. You haven't asked us, you've told us, like you're in charge and we're nothing more than employees."

"After this contest is over, we don't ever have to speak again, if that's what you want," I tell Josh. "Until then, don't sabotage our chances just to spite me or Truman."

"I think you owe Maddie and me an apology for the things you said, yesterday," Josh says.

"Do you have any idea what he's talking about?" I ask Truman.

"I don't think Josh knows what he's talking about. He and Maddie were both too stoned to know what you or anyone else said, yesterday."

"See. That's what I mean. Talking about us like we don't deserve your respect. Like you're better than us."

The discussion is going in circles and not making any forward progress. We don't have much time, so I try to make peace.

"I'm sorry, Josh. You too, Maddie. I'm sorry if I've offended you or been disrespectful. In my defense, I've been under a lot of pressure. I never meant to take it out on either of you."

"That's not good enough," Maddie says.

I'm really confused now. I apologize, even though I don't think one is due, because Josh asks for it.

"Are you speaking for Josh or yourself?"

"Both."

"What is it the two of you want, then?"

She glances at Josh before answering. Obviously, they've discussed this before now and it's something more than respect they're looking for.

"We want a bigger share of the money if we win."

"What! You're joking, right?" Truman says. "Why do you think you deserve more money than Dylan and me?"

"I'm the one who got us the recording gear. Without that we couldn't have recorded the song and wouldn't even be in the contest."

I can argue that point. A high quality recording of the song wasn't necessary. We could have rented a cheap recorder and a guitar. Truman and I could have pulled it off without Josh and Maddie. But that's all water under the bridge, and not worth discussing now.

"What do you have in mind?" I ask.

"Wait a minute," Truman objects. "You're not seriously thinking about giving them more money than us, are you?"

"We can discuss it. Maddie, you seem to be the spokesperson for you and Josh. Give us a figure."

"Sixty, forty," she replies without hesitation. "Sixty percent of the one hundred thousand to Josh and me. You and Truman get the rest."

I act like I'm mulling it over.

"What do you think?" I ask Truman.

"You don't want to know what I'm thinking, right now."

Natalie sticks her head in.

"They're ready for you now. Are you guys good to go?"

"Are we?" Maddie asks me.

"Yeah," I answer. "We're good."

"Shake on it," Maddie says, and extends her hand.

I take it, remembering back to a time when her touch warmed and comforted me. Today her hand is just cold and clammy.

~35~

When you smile for the camera, I know I love you better

They begin the rehearsal by seating the four of us at a table. The other contestants, maybe forty in all, are seated all around us. We have drinks on the table in front of us. The auditorium lights are turned off. The set lights are adjusted to illuminate our faces just so. Our director, Sidney, tells us what to do and what to expect.

"During the actual ceremony there will be more people in the room. We'll have a live audience and some of you will have spouses or others with you. There will be several cameras shooting from different angles. At any time you might be on camera. My advice is to keep your hands on the table or in your lap and look happy."

So far it seems easy enough.

"I know you're songwriters, but for the ceremony tomorrow, I want you to do some acting. For instance. When the host on stage says, and the nominees for best songwriter in the pop music category are…, you act like you're straining to hear because this is really important to you. Remember the cameras are panning the room recording your reaction."

Easy enough again, because it is really important.

"Now, you hear him say your names. You look at one another and smile. Stay calm. No high fives or anything like that."

Maddie smiles at Truman and me like she means it. We know better.

"Now, he says the winner is, and calls someone else's name. You're disappointed, but good sports about it. You clap for the winner."

I didn't expect we'd act out this scenario. My disappointment is real.

"Don't overdo it," Sidney cautions.

"If the host says you're the winner. You're very happy. You kiss and hug each other. Everyone is clapping for you. You wave to them and mouth 'thank you'."

We follow his instructions. We hug, we wave, we smile like idiots.

"I have a list of all the contestants. I'm going to call the names and one at a time I want you to walk up the steps to the center of the stage, and then down the steps on the other side."

It turns out to be the hardest part of the rehearsal. I'm glad we're practicing this part. I'd hate to trip and fall on my face during the televised ceremony. After the rehearsal the songwriters hang around to meet and talk with each other. They're from all over the world. Japan, Germany, Canada, Brazil, Australia and Ireland, just to name a few.

Then, Natalie leads us to another part of the auditorium for more photos. They take a few shots of the four of us and a shot with a space in the middle, so they can Photoshop one of the sponsors or a celebrity into the picture, later.

"Get some individual shots, too," Natalie tells the photographer.

She says it as if it's an afterthought.

"That's it for you guys. Your limo is out front. It will take you back to your hotel. Keep your phone close and check your email often."

"I'll give you my phone number," Maddie says. "In case you can't reach Dylan."

"You won't have any trouble reaching me," I say. "Anytime day or night, 24/7."

"We'll use the contact information you originally submitted," Natalie says, putting the kibosh on Maddie's attempt at an end run.

We stick to the same seating arrangement in the limousine. We glare at each other for the first minute, but after that it starts to lose its appeal.

"Don't think you're going to back out of our agreement, Dylan. I'm going to hold you to it."

"I'm not thinking that at all. After today, I don't believe we have any chance of winning."

"Not after what you pulled," Truman adds. "Natalie knew something was wrong from the minute she arrived this morning. Multimedia isn't going to give you a chance to embarrass them and their clients. Sixty percent, eighty percent, one hundred percent. It doesn't matter because one hundred percent of zero is still zero."

"You're not fooling us, Dylan. Or you either, Truman. We still have a chance of winning, and I think we will."

She's nothing if not stubborn. I'll give her that much.

Josh's boyfriend is waiting in the hotel lobby when the limousine drops us off there. Maddie heads straight for the elevator.

"I don't really want to go up to the room, right now," I tell Truman.

"My stomach says it's lunchtime. What does yours say?"

"I can eat. I'm not doing sushi, though."

"That's cool. You pick the place. It can't be too expensive, though. If we don't win the contest I'll be broke in a couple of days."

"Same here. I've been counting on that money."

"We better come up with a plan B pretty soon. I have a bad feeling we're going to need one."

~36~

Turn it up, bring the noise

A guy at our hotel tells us about a food court. The food is supposed to be good and reasonably priced. It's quite a hike to get there. About six blocks. We get a couple of gyros and sodas, and take them to a bench under a shade tree.

"I'm going to miss this city," Truman says. "There's a whole bunch of stuff I wanted to see while I was here. It doesn't look like that will happen."

"Yeah. I wanted to spend some time on the beach. Maybe learn to surf. Wouldn't that be a kick?"

"I'd be happy just to lay around looking at all those fine-looking girls in their tiny bikinis."

"Yeah, I hear California girls are pretty hot."

"What do you want to do for the rest of today?"

"We passed by a music store, yesterday. It was near Grand Central Market where we ate. We could go there."

"I like that idea. I'm still in a funk over that stuff Maddie pulled on us. If there's one thing that will get me out of a funk, it's playing a Stratocaster. Especially if it looks and feels like Ethel."

It's an even longer hike to get to the music store. I'm not complaining. Except for the exhaust fumes, the traffic noise and heat radiating off the concrete, I enjoy walking in LA.

The store is called California Sounds. There's not much similarity to SS&B. This place sells mostly used instruments.

Lots of guitars, basses and keyboards. We're not in the store a full minute and Truman already has an Eric Johnson signature Stratocaster in his hands.

I don't know how he does it. I'd have to ask somebody behind the counter where they are. Not Truman. He can go in a store he's unfamiliar with and find a Stratocaster quicker than a pig finds truffles.

"I'm going to name this one Natalie, after the girl from Multimedia Management," Truman says.

"Don't you think you should look at the price tag first?"

"No. This is nothing permanent. It's just a fling."

Out of curiosity I take a look at the tag. Two thousand bucks.

"Alright, how much is it?" he asks.

"You don't want to know."

Truman digs into his pocket for a guitar pick. He takes Natalie into his hands as gently as he would his own daughter, seats himself on an amplifier and starts to play. As he does, a store employee comes from behind a counter heading in our direction.

It's a goth-looking person dressed in black with dark eye shadow and lipstick, and a spiked collar and wrist band to match. It could be a guy or a girl. It's impossible to tell.

"You've got great taste in axes, dude," he/she says.

The voice doesn't put me any closer to guessing its gender.

"That's the finest one in the store, bar none. Plug it into this Marshall Jubilee over here."

Truman does.

"Turn it up as loud as you want, man. Nobody here minds."

He/she really shouldn't have said that. I stand to the side of the amp and cover my ears as Truman twists the volume knob to the max.

With his index finger barring the first and second strings on the twelfth fret, Truman strikes down with his pick. Then he wiggles the tremolo bar to add vibrato. It rattles the window glass in the storefront.

People suddenly appear from the dark recesses of the store. They walk zombie-like toward the sound. Truman tugs harder on the tremolo bar. The zombies play along on their air guitars. I clasp my hands tighter over my ears.

He slides his index finger up to the fifteenth fret. He strikes down on the strings and then up, repeating the stroke over and over while jiggling the tremolo bar. The zombies seem mesmerized. He's never gotten this sort of reaction at SS&B. Nothing even close. I stick a finger in my ear, pull it out and check for blood.

Truman puts a chokehold on the neck of the Stratocaster, wrapping his thumb and four fingers across the fretboard. Then he slams the pick down on all six strings and lets the sound ring and echo off the walls. The zombies jump up and down, and fist pump the air.

The human ear has a built-in defense mechanism. When a noise is so loud it threatens to permanently damage one's hearing, the ears involuntarily shut down. It's like tripping an overload switch on machinery that's running too hot. The overload switch protects it from burning up. Once it cools sufficiently, the switch cuts off and the machinery can start back up.

That's the only explanation I can give for what occurs. I can see Truman striking the guitar and I can feel the wave of sound rocking me, but I can't hear a damn thing. I run for the door to get out of the building and into the relative quiet of the streets of LA.

On the sidewalk outside, people walk by talking on their phones. I see their lips move, but can't hear their voices. It's the same with the cars going by. I don't hear the roar of the engines, the tires on the pavement or the horns blaring. I take a wobbly step and stumble. My equilibrium is off due to my deafness.

Truman emerges from the store. I can't tell whether it's concern or irritation I see on his face. His lips and hands move. He's asking me a question. That much I get.

"I can't hear a thing," I shout.

"………," he says.

"I'm completely deaf," I scream, thinking he must be deaf, too.

"………," he says, next.

He/she comes out of the store holding the Eric Johnson signature Stratocaster and gestures for Truman to come back in. He/she wants Truman to either buy the guitar or play some more. I'm not sure which.

"I'm going back to the hotel," I say.

Truman gestures for me to wait and disappears back into the store with he/she. As I wait my hearing slowly returns. At first it's just a ringing in my ears. Then it's joined by a low rumble. After another minute I can make out some of the words people around me are saying. Truman comes out and joins me on the sidewalk. It's as I suspected. His hearing is shot.

"I took it to another level all together," he says.

"Warn me before you do that again," I say.

"Born to be the man? I like the sound of it, whatever it means."

"That's not what I said."

"What's wrong with my head?"

"Nothing, aside from the fact it's getting bigger."

"I thought you didn't use the N word. Did you see all those people getting down over what I was putting out?"

"You mean the zombies?"

"Yeah, wannabes. That's what they are. Wannabe just like me."

"Truman, I'm starting to tire of this."

"Hell yeah, I was on fire."

"I can't do this anymore."

"Find another music store. That's a great idea."

I give up. I point to my chest, and then down the street toward the hotel. I start walking that way.

"I don't know any sign language, Dylan. What does that mean?"

I wave goodbye without turning around and keep on walking.

~37~

You're a shining star, no matter who you are

I'm almost to the hotel before Truman manages to catch up with me.

"Didn't you hear me calling for you to wait up?" he asks.

"I heard lots of people yelling. I didn't know one of them was you."

"I didn't hear anyone else yelling."

That much isn't hard to believe. We continue to the hotel and inside to the business center where I check my email inbox. The schedule for the ceremony tomorrow is in an email from Julia Tremont.

"The limo picks us up at noon for the ceremony," I tell Truman. "The clothing they want us to wear will be delivered to us this afternoon."

"Clothing? Nobody said anything about that, did they?"

"Not to me. They probably want to make sure we wear something that looks okay on TV."

"I hope we don't have more problems with Josh and Maddie."

"They both want their money. That should be incentive enough."

I expect Maddie and Josh to be somewhere with their boyfriends, so I'm surprised when we open the door and find Maddie in the sitting room with some old man. Older than us anyway. Maybe even in his forties.

Maddie is sitting on the couch reading something that looks like a contract. The old guy is sitting across from her with his hands steepled and fingertips pressed to his lips. She glances at us as we enter, but says nothing.

After what we went through earlier in the day I feel like giving her a taste of her own medicine. I go over and sit beside her on the couch. Truman sits down on her other side.

"Hi, I'm Dylan," I say to the old guy.

"And I'm Truman."

"We're in the middle of a meeting here," Maddie says. "If you'll please excuse us."

"No need to apologize," I say. "Go right ahead. We won't interrupt."

She glares at me. She's getting better at it. But then, she's had a lot of practice of late. I glare back.

"You must be Miss Lee's songwriting assistants," old guy says. "I'm Hamilton Spence."

Truman looks at me and mouths, 'assistants'. Hamilton reaches over to shake our hands. Then he takes a couple of business cards from his shirt pocket and hands one to Truman and one to me.

It says, 'Spence Talent Agency'.

"I'll be representing Miss Lee in her future songwriting and entertainment endeavors."

"Really?" I say. "Are you sure you can handle a star of her caliber?"

Another glare from Maddie.

"Don't make light of her potential, Dylan. As one of her assistants, your wagon is hitched to her star, so to speak. What's good for her is good for you. If at some point you go out on your own, I might be interested in representing you as well. That goes for you too, Truman."

"Thanks. I'll keep that in mind."

"Dylan. Will you and Truman give Hamilton and me some privacy?"

I glance at Truman. He doesn't seem any more inclined to accommodate her than me.

"Go in your room and shut the door if you want to be alone with Hamilton," I say.

"We would except Josh is in there with a friend of his."

Truman snatches the paper Maddie has been reading out of her hand.

"What is it you don't want us to know about?"

"That's a private matter between Miss Lee and my agency," Hamilton declares.

He grabs for the paper, but Truman holds it out of reach. Maddie tries to get it back. Truman passes it to me.

"Talent Management Agreement," I read aloud.

"Give that back to me," Maddie says. "Stop behaving like children."

"Look who's talking about misbehaving," Truman says.

"I'm curious Mr. Spence," I say. "Why is my and Truman's name on this contract?"

"It's my understanding Miss Lee is the spokesperson for your group."

"You agreed I would receive a bigger share of the proceeds, which means I have more say in bookings," Maddie says.

"Bookings? Which of Maddie's many talents do you hope to exploit, Hamilton?"

"You two can have your fun now, but when the Songwriter of the Year award is handed out, Miss Lee will be a hot commodity."

"There's a guy or two who thinks she's a hot commodity, now. That aside, the contest is far from decided. Our chances of winning aren't great. Are you still interested in representing Maddie if we lose?"

"I'm happy to cross that bridge at the appropriate time."

"Another thing you should know. Maddie doesn't speak for me."

"Or me either," Truman says.

More intense glaring from Maddie.

"Maybe we should finish this another time," Hamilton says.

He gets up to leave.

"Here. Don't forget this," I say, handing him the papers.

He makes a hasty exit.

"Why do you have to be such an asshole, Dylan?" Maddie says.

"Why do you?" Truman asks.

"That's pay-back for what you tried to pull earlier. You have to admit you had it coming," I say.

"I'm only trying to get what's fair."

"That's all any of us wants. A fair shake, for once," I say. "The limousine picks us up at noon for the ceremony tomorrow. I'm not your alarm clock or Josh's babysitter. Be there on time and ready to go or you'll be left behind. I'm not bluffing."

~38~

Yes, you look wonderful tonight

For a very brief period I thought of Maddie as my girlfriend, even though she probably didn't feel the same about me. That's changed. I can honestly say I no longer harbor those feelings for her. That being said, when she came out of her room wearing the formal gown for the ceremony my heart did flip-flops.

It's a black off the shoulder, slit to the hip on one leg number. She took one look at it when it was delivered and ran out to get two tattoos. A rose for the exposed shoulder and barbed wire on the revealed leg. I don't know if they're permanent or temporary. I don't ask because I don't want her to think I care.

Truman catches me staring at her.

"Damn, Dylan. Show a little self-restraint. I don't want you falling in love with her all over again."

"You don't have to worry about that happening. I'm just looking."

"Famous last words."

The limousine drops us at a different spot than yesterday. It's the entrance to the auditorium, or Grand Ballroom as it's called. We step out of the limo onto a runner of red carpet. A banner over the entrance reads, 10th Annual Songwriter of the Year Awards.

Other limos are there and more are arriving. I see the songwriters getting out. The guys are wearing tuxedos, like

Truman, Josh and me. The girls are in formal wear similar to Maddie's.

The paparazzi are there, again. Only today there are twice as many. We're greeted by more cameras as we enter the building. Beside the cameramen are talking heads sticking microphones in the faces of the songwriters. One of them gestures for us to come over.

"Maddie, Josh, Truman, Dylan," she calls out. "This is your first appearance at the SOTY Awards, isn't it?"

She pronounces the acronym, 'sew tea'. Maddie fields the question.

"Yes, our first time. We're so excited to be here."

"Yeah, really pumped," Josh agrees.

He crowds in next to Maddie, blocking the camera's view of Truman and me. I feel like a fish out of water. Truman looks like he might bolt and run for the door any second. Josh and Maddie act like they do this every day of the week and twice on Sunday.

Out of the corner of my eye I see another songwriter going through the same thing with yet another talking head and cameraman. I turn for a better look as she turns to look at me. Our eyes lock on one another for a brief moment. She smiles at me. I smile back.

We're close in age to one another. That might be all we have in common. She's over-the-top, out of my league good-looking, and I'm not. She's poised and exudes self-confidence, and I don't. She could pass for a princess or a duchess. I couldn't pass for the duke's bootblack.

She turns her attention back to the woman holding the microphone. Truman elbows me in the ribs.

"That's what I'm talking about," he says.

It's one of Truman's expressions with several possible meanings. My reply is equally ambiguous.

"Uh-huh."

We move forward slowly, taking the time to talk to anyone with a camera or microphone, until we pass by the last one. I head toward our table taking everything in as I go.

"Remember what they said about the cameras constantly scanning the room," Truman says.

He says it for the sake of Maddie and Josh, but a minute too late to do any good. They've taken off in the direction of a table on one side of the room where songwriters and others are helping themselves to drinks. I see bottles of champagne and wine, as well as those containing clear and amber-colored liquids which I presume is the hard stuff.

"This could get pretty ugly before it's over," I say to Truman.

He looks at me and then at something behind me.

"I'll go keep an eye on them. You stay here," he tells me.

"Dylan," a voice behind me says.

I turn to see the princess smiling at me. She's even prettier up close.

"Uh…, hi," I manage to say.

"I've been wanting to introduce myself. I didn't get the chance, yesterday. I'm…,"

"Abigail," I finish for her.

It's not a guess on my part. And I'm not psychic. The names of the contest finalists and their pictures are posted on the contest website. Abigail Collier is one of the four finalists in the pop music category. The same category as us. She's probably the one most likely to beat us.

"That's a pretty name," I say.

A pretty name for a pretty girl, I want to tell her. But I'm not that smooth. Especially around a girl like Abigail.

"It's my stage name," she says, and then laughs like it's a silly idea to use one name on stage and another elsewhere.

"My parents named me Grace. Who wants a song written by someone named Grace, right?"

"I like Grace," I say. "It's my mother's name."

She gasps and puts her hand over her mouth.

"Omigod! I'm so embarrassed. I didn't mean anything by that."

"It's no big deal. Really. Don't worry about it."

"Please forgive me. I can't believe I stuck my foot in my mouth like that. I'm so sorry."

"Forget about it. Seriously."

"Don't tell your mother you met someone who hates that name."

"Don't worry. I won't."

The mention of my mother makes me sad. I look at my feet, then back at Abigail. She senses it.

"Oh no! I did it again, didn't I?" She smacks her forehead with her palm. "I am so stupid. Your mother is…,"

I nod. She apologizes twice more. We share an awkward silent moment.

"If you want to make it up to me, you could withdraw from the contest," I joke.

She smiles. I'm really starting to dig her smile. I smile back.

"No way. I'm not going to make it that easy for you. If you win, you're going to have to do it fair and square."

"I was afraid of that."

"It was good meeting you, Dylan."

She kisses my cheek, then brushes away the lipstick with her finger and says, "Good luck."

She's already walking away before I can untangle my tongue enough to reply.

"Thanks and good luck to you, Abigail."

~39~

The winner takes it all, the loser has to fall

The auditorium is abuzz with conversation and laughter. Truman and I are in our assigned seats. Josh and Maddie are MIA. Abigail is sitting two tables away with three other songwriters. I glance over at her every so often. I look at the other contestants, wondering what's going through their minds. And then I look at Abigail, some more.

"Maddie who?" Truman says. "Why don't you go over and talk to her, instead of sitting here staring at her like a lovesick puppy?"

"I wouldn't know what to say. I mean, look at her. Look at me."

"She came up to talk to you, didn't she?"

"She wanted to introduce herself. That's all."

"She didn't introduce herself to me. Or to Josh or Maddie."

I've been thinking the same thing, but it does nothing for my confidence.

Nikki would probably say something like, "What's a girl like that going to do with you? Clean her floor with your mop head?"

The room hushes as a voice comes over the loudspeakers asking all songwriters to take their seats because the filming is set to begin in ten minutes. I spot Josh and Maddie coming our way. Josh is holding onto Maddie's arm, either to steady her, himself or both.

They seem to be looking for their seats. I wave to them. They don't see. Truman stands and waves his hands in the air. Finally they see us. The lights dim in the auditorium as they sit.

Spotlights illuminate a circle in the center of the stage. A man and woman dressed in formal attire appear from the shadows. The host and hostess. They look like real-life Ken and Barbie dolls.

"Welcome to the Tenth Annual Songwriter of the Year Awards Gala," Ken says to officially kick things off.

Applause, hoots and whistles follow. Various sponsors of the event are mentioned. This takes about fifteen minutes to run through.

"Now, last year's winning song, 'Don't Hate My Weight', will be performed by Spunk Peabody. Give it up for Spunk Peabody."

The song sounds vaguely familiar. It's of the hip-hop genre and as I may have mentioned before, I've never understood its appeal. Spunk Peabody is a hip-hop artist, and not someone I'm familiar with. I clap politely once he's done.

"Each year at this time we present a lifetime achievement award for songwriting," Barbie says. "This year the award goes to John Patrick Olsen for his fifty plus years of songwriting success. During that period his songs have been recorded by artists such as…,"

She goes on to name a dozen or more performers.

"John's wife, Mrs. Elisabeth Olsen will be accepting on his behalf."

Mrs. Olsen is rolled onto the stage in a wheelchair. I'm guessing her to be north of eighty. When Barbie said his wife would be accepting on his behalf, I took that to mean he's not with us any longer.

Finally the announcing of winners begins.

"For Best Songwriter of the Year in the R & B category, the nominees are Blake Nelson...," Ken says, and pauses while the cameras find Blake.

He calls the names of the other three nominees, Kathleen Carter, Paul Esau and Judith Wright, pausing again between each name.

I take special interest in how each of them reacts when their name is called. They're graceful and subdued. A smile for the cameras. A wave to their fellow songwriters. I hope I can be so cool, calm and collected when my name is called.

"And the winner is...,"

Longer pause here.

"Paul Esau."

Paul makes his way to the stage, stopping for a hug or a handshake as he does. Even the losing nominees clap for him. Unlike the Emmys, there's no acceptance speech. He's given a trophy, a pretty girl escorts him off the stage and the show continues.

"For Best Songwriter of the Year in the Latin category, the nominees are...," Barbie says.

She names the four nominees, three men and one woman, pausing theatrically between each one.

The lone woman, Isabella Guiro is the winner. She covers her face with her hands. At first, I think it's an act. Then real tears spill from between her fingers and I see she's genuinely shocked.

She seems reluctant to rise, as if she doesn't trust her legs to support her. One by one all the female songwriters in the room, including Maddie, stand and applaud. Out of the thirty-two songwriters only five are female.

"Come on up here," Barbie calls from center stage.

She finds the strength to stand and walk. Maddie, Abigail and the two other female songwriters remain standing, shouting encouragement to Isabella as she makes her way to the stage.

The next category is Country. After that comes Rock, followed by Hip-hop. As the winning songwriter in the Hip-hop genre leaves the stage, I look at Truman, then Maddie, and then Josh. We know what's coming.

"For Best Songwriter of the Year in the Pop category, the nominees are…," Barbie says.

The pause feels longer than any that came before.

"Dylan Jones, Madeline Lee, Josh Martinez and Truman Dixon…,"

The mention of my name takes my anxiety level up a few notches. I can feel the adrenaline flowing through me and my heart pounding in my chest. It's making me light-headed.

"Abigail Collier…," Barbie says, next.

I glance over at Abigail. She has her eyes shut and head slightly bowed as if she's saying a silent prayer.

Barbie continues.

"Dennis Speck and Geoff Handel…,"

Until now, I haven't let myself even consider winning. Now, with the announcement only seconds away, I can't think of anything else.

Barbie calls the name of the last nominee.

"Stacy Bennett…,"

I look at my songwriting partners, from Truman, to Maddie, to Josh. They look back at me. I stretch my hands out toward them. Truman takes one hand. Josh takes the other. Maddie joins hands with them across the table from me, completing the circle. I close my eyes.

"And the winner is…,"

~40~

Because I'm falling down, with people standing round

I'm lying on my back in a bed staring at a white ceiling. My head hurts. My vision is blurry. There's a needle in my arm, attached to a tube which is attached to a drip bag. I have no idea where I am or how I got here. Somewhere nearby I hear people talking and their feet shuffling on a hard surface as they move about. I try to raise my head, but the pain is unbearable. So I ease it back down.

"Hello," I cry out as loud as I can.

No response. I take a deep breath and try again.

"Hello. Is anybody there?"

A woman appears beside me. A nurse, I think.

"How are we doing?" she asks, sympathetically.

She examines my head and face.

"We?" I ask.

She thinks I'm being a smart-ass.

"How are you doing?" she asks, less nicely.

"Where am I?"

"You're in the ER at St. Vincent Medical Center. You fell and hit your head. EMS brought you here. We've run a few tests. A doctor will be in to explain things to you. The last time I checked, you were still unconscious."

She takes the needle out of my arm and puts a bandage on.

"How long have I been out?"

"About an hour. I'll raise the bed a little. Just lie here and relax until the doctor sees you. Push that button if you need anything."

She raises one end of the bed enough for me to see my surroundings and leaves. I'm in a small space only big enough for the bed. A curtain serves as a barrier between me and everyone else in the ER.

"Dylan," Truman says, sticking his head through the curtain. "I've been looking all over for you. Nobody would tell me a damn thing. I was worried you died and they dumped your body in the trash. How are you feeling?"

"My head hurts when I move. The nurse said I fell and hit my head, but I can't remember anything. Help me up."

With Truman's help, I manage to rise to a sitting position on the bed.

"Were you there when it happened?" I ask.

"Of course I was there. You don't remember anything?"

"Nothing."

The curtain parts and a young man in hospital scrubs walks in.

"Dylan Jones," he says. "I'm Doctor Kirsh."

He has long hair, a full beard and doesn't look much older than me. He glances at Truman, who isn't supposed to be in the ER.

"I just came back here to check on Dylan. They wouldn't tell me nothing out front."

"That's cool, dude. This will only take a minute, anyway. Dylan, your tests all look good. You have a bump on the head and some swelling which might cause you some pain for a couple of days. You don't have a concussion or anything else to be concerned about. When they brought you in, your heart rate and blood pressure were really high. They're back to normal. I don't want you to overexert yourself, right now. Take aspirin for the pain if you need to. Do you have any questions?"

"About a jillion."

He ignores that. I guess he thinks I'm being a smart-ass, too.

"Someone will bring your clothes around. You're good to go."

It isn't until an orderly brings me the tuxedo I wore to the ceremony that my memory begins to return.

"They were about to announce the winner in the Pop category. That's the last thing I remember."

"That's when it happened."

"That's when what happened?"

"You fainted."

"What?"

"You fainted dead away as soon as they announced the winner. You hit your head on the table, and then on the floor. EMS came and took you away. I got in a taxi and followed them here."

There's blood on the tuxedo shirt. I reach up to feel bandages on my forehead and a golf ball-sized bump.

"I knew I was going to be disappointed over losing, but I didn't expect to faint. Who did win?"

"Uh..., the doctor said you shouldn't get yourself worked up. I don't want you to faint again."

"No, I don't want that either."

"Get dressed, man. Let's get you back to the hotel where you can lie down and put your feet up. I'll tell you all about the contest later. Okay?"

"Okay."

Putting the tuxedo on is an effort. Truman stands by to make sure I don't get my feet tangled in the pants and fall again.

"Thanks for looking out for me, Truman."

"I've always got your back, Dylan. You know that."

"Where are Josh and Maddie? Out drowning their sorrows over losing?"

"Actually, they're taking care of business for us. The contest folks had some papers to sign and other stuff. They're tending to that."

I finish dressing, leaving my shirttail out and the jacket slung over my shoulder.

"How do I look?"

"You look like crap, but it doesn't matter. We'll take a taxi back to the hotel. Nobody is going to see you."

We leave the curtained cubicle and head toward the exit. In the ER waiting lounge we find Natalie Randall of Multimedia Management.

"Dylan," she cries upon seeing me.

Her concern for me is genuine. I'm touched, and a little aroused, as well. She comes toward me. I hold out my arms, anticipating a hug. She stops an arm's length away. Apparently, she's not the touchy-feely type.

"How are you feeling?"

"Okay," I tell her.

"Good. We still have a lot to do. The limousine is waiting outside. I have a clean tuxedo in it. You can change on the way."

"On the way where?" I ask.

"Natalie," Truman interrupts. "He doesn't remember anything."

"He doesn't know he…,"

"No, he doesn't. And the doctor says he shouldn't get worked up over anything."

"Excuse me," I say. "I'm right here."

Truman and Natalie look at me, and then at each other.

"Dylan," Natalie says. "Sit down. I need to tell you something."

Once I'm comfortably seated she begins spitting it out, speaking even faster than her typical ten-words-per-second speed.

"The second the contest winners were announced, word spread across social media like wildfire. The sponsors want to milk the publicity for as long as possible. That's where the company I work for, Multimedia Management, comes in. We keep the story alive by releasing interesting side stories concerning the winners. Your trip to the hospital, for instance. It's an interesting side story. It has nothing to do with songwriting or the contest, but it gets the public's attention when they see a headline which reads, 'Songwriter of the Year rushed to the hospital'. They want to read further. And as they do, the sponsors are mentioned again and again. More publicity for them and more recognition for you. You see what I'm saying. While you're fulfilling your obligation to the sponsors by endorsing their products, you can be promoting yourself."

"Can we back up a second? When you said, 'Songwriter of the Year rushed to the hospital', were you speaking hypothetically?"

She looks at Truman. He looks at me. I look at Natalie. She looks at me. I look at Truman.

"We don't have time for this," Natalie says. "Dylan. You won. You, Truman, Maddie and Josh won Songwriter of the Year in the Pop category for the song, 'Love Transcends'."

My vision starts to blur and I feel light-headed, again. Natalie slaps me across the face. It hurts, but I'm not feeling queasy anymore.

"Snap out of it. We need to go. Right now."

I rise gingerly. Truman takes hold of my arm.

"I got you, man. Lean on me all you want."

Natalie looks me over once more.

"Hold the jacket to your side. There will be paparazzi outside. I want to make sure they get pictures of the blood on your shirt."

She heads out the exit. We follow.

~41~

This could be the start of something big

Right before exiting the ER Natalie puts on her sunshades. The paparazzi start snapping pictures as soon as we're out the door. We take our time getting into the limousine, giving them plenty of opportunity for shots from every angle. Natalie gets in facing rearward. Truman and I sit across from her facing forward. A clean tuxedo hangs on a hook beside me.

"Put it on," Natalie says. "We're going back to the Grand Ballroom. The party after is still going strong. You'll do several photo ops and interviews. It might go on until dark. There's free food and booze for the press. They'll hang around as long as it lasts."

I'm hesitant to undress in front of Natalie. I haven't taken my clothes off with a woman present since I was six.

"What are you waiting for?" she says. "Oh, I see. You're shy about taking your clothes off in front of me. Dylan. Get over it. We'll be at the ballroom in ten minutes. If you don't want to step out of the limousine with one leg on and one leg off, you'll start dressing."

She shifts her attention to her phone. I watch her as I take my shirt off. Then the pants. She peeks. I blush.

"Don't be embarrassed. I've seen a lot of guy's bodies," she says. "Yours is no better or worse than most."

Which to me sounds like another version of, 'you're not bad looking'. I don't bother to comment.

"Can I ask you something?" I say.

"You can ask. You won't necessarily get an answer."

"How old are you?"

"Nineteen. I bet you thought I was older, didn't you?"

"Yeah. A little older."

"It's all about perception. I act more mature and people think I'm older. You two need to start thinking about your own image."

"What do you mean?"

She puts her phone away to give us her full attention.

"You and Truman are both young, reasonably good-looking guys. You're naïve. But you can use that to your benefit. You've had a lucky break and won a songwriter's contest. You're probably not thinking about anything more than how you're going to spend the prize money. If so, that's a big mistake."

That pretty much sums it up. Dumb, naïve, but lucky nonetheless.

"I haven't had a chance to think about it. I just found out we won."

"This is LA, Dylan. You have to learn to think on your feet."

"Natalie," Truman says. "You're a smart person. I can see that. And I take it you've been in LA for a while. If you were in our shoes, what would you do?"

"The first thing I would do is hire a good agent. You'll be getting offers left and right. You have no idea what to charge for your time. That's what you need an agent for. He/she will negotiate the contracts, schedule appearances, handle your social media and drum up business."

"How do we go about finding an agent?"

"The same way you'd find a yardman, a mechanic or a realtor to sell your house. You talk to several. And you keep talking until you find one you like."

"A talent agent came to our hotel room to talk with Maddie. I don't know how or where she met him."

"What's his name?"

"Hamilton something," Truman says. He closes his eyes and tries to envision the guy's business card. "Spence Talent Agency. That was it."

"Never heard of him," Natalie says. "Probably a freelancer. As a general rule of thumb, if they approach you, you don't want them. The better agents are too busy to go out and find talent. Talent is referred to them. Typically by someone they already represent."

"That won't work for us. We don't know anyone with an agent."

"I know some people in the business. I'll ask around and see if I can come up with some recommendations. If I do, I'll call you tomorrow or the next day."

"We fly out of here, tomorrow," I say.

"Not anymore. You'll be here another week, at least. And that's just to fulfill your immediate obligations to the contest sponsors."

"That's fine by me," Truman says. "I'm in no rush to go back to Detroit."

"What about you, Dylan?" Natalie asks. "How do you feel about staying here longer?"

"I'm still trying to wrap my mind around winning the contest. If we're not flying back tomorrow, can we still stay at the hotel?"

"As long as the sponsors need you here, your hotel is taken care of. After that you'll have to pay your own expenses."

"Do you know when we get the prize money?" Truman asks. "I hope it comes before we're kicked out of the hotel."

"Sorry, I don't know. The auditors handle that. They'll be contacting you soon, either by phone or email."

It reminds me to go shopping for a mobile wireless device, so I can check my emails when I'm on the go. Which from the sound of things is going to be pretty much all the time.

"We're almost there. Dylan, zip up your pants and put your jacket on. You guys have a lot to be happy about. When you get out of the limousine laugh, smile and enjoy your time in the spotlight. You've earned it."

~42~

Got to give the people, give the people what they want

It's more than a little weird inside the Grand Ballroom. Men and women who wouldn't have given Truman or me the time of day before now are acting like long lost friends. They hug us, slap our backs and take selfies of us with our arm over their shoulders. Even Maddie acts as if all the grief she's given us over the last two days never happened.

"Dylan!" she screams upon seeing me. "Look everyone! Dylan's here! I'm so glad to see you're alright. We were worried sick."

I assume *we* means Josh and her. He comes over and wraps me in a bear hug. It's the manliest I've ever seen him behave. Then, he hugs Truman the same way.

"Thanks for looking after our guy," Josh tells Truman. "We wouldn't be here if it wasn't for him."

Truman looks at me like, *who is this guy*. I shrug like, *I don't know.*

Winning the contest is only part of the reason Josh and Maddie are so exuberant. It's been two hours since the announcement. During that time they've downed a lot of champagne. I'm guessing they've been treated to a little nose candy, as well.

"I have some great news to tell you about later," Maddie says. "I met this guy who wants to record our song. He's a record producer."

"Great," I say.

I'm skeptical about an offer from a stranger, but now is not the time to express my opinion to Maddie. Let her savor the victory, for now. In fact, I should be doing the same. Almost everyone in the place wants a minute with Josh, Truman, Maddie and me.

Truman is staring at something across the room. I follow his gaze. Isabella Guiro, the girl who won in the Latin category, is talking to Abigail Collier. I watch them for a minute along with Truman. Two really pretty girls made even more so by their smiles and dancing eyes.

"I'll see you guys later," Maddie says. "I'm going to circulate."

"Yeah, me too," Josh says.

"Are you thinking what I'm thinking?" Truman asks me.

I know he's going to tell me what he's thinking whether I tell him what I'm thinking or not. I wait him out.

"I'm thinking this," he continues. "Here we are. Two reasonably good-looking guys. According to Ms. Natalie, that is. We're single, unattached and we just won the Songwriter of the Year prize. Over there I see two lovely girls who I think would welcome the opportunity to chat with two guys like us. What are we waiting for?"

Off we go without another thought. Two reasonably good-looking guys who are also painfully shy and totally unprepared for the mission we've embarked upon. Truman walks a step ahead of me, glancing back often to make sure I haven't chickened out on him.

Not that I haven't considered it. I stick my hands in my pants pockets to hide the trembling. What if they shoot us down, I can't help but think. And we're left to slink away with our tails between our legs.

With just two more steps to go Abigail catches sight of us approaching. She says something to Isabella. They turn their radiant smiles on us. I feel weak in the knees.

"Congratulations, Isabella," Truman says.

A great ice breaker, if you ask me.

"And congratulations to you and Dylan," Isabella returns.

"We were just talking about you," Abigail says to me. "Are you alright? Your injury wasn't severe, was it?"

"I'm fine. I bumped my head. That's all. The doctor said I'll be as good as new in a few days."

"I'm glad to hear it."

"I'm sorry we beat you."

"No, you're not."

"I mean, I'm glad we won. I know how disappointed I would have been if we hadn't. I hate it that you might feel that way."

She gently places her hand against my cheek.

"That's sweet of you, but I'm holding up okay."

"Hey, Dylan," Truman says. "Did you hear that? Isabella plays guitar."

I didn't hear anything other than Abigail's voice.

"That's great," I reply. "You two have something in common. You should take her to California Sounds and let her play for the zombies."

Isabella looks puzzled by that.

"It's a music store," Truman explains. "It's sort of eclectic. I can show you where it is, if you like."

"We'll see," Isabella says. "I understand we might be pretty busy for the next few days."

"Yeah, that's what I've been told. Would you like something to drink? It's been two hours since we won. We should have a glass of champagne to celebrate our success. How does that sound?"

"You must have read my mind. I'd love some champagne."

"Dylan? Abigail?" Truman says.

I glance at Abigail. She seems content to let me decide. "You guys go ahead. We'll catch up in a minute."

"Alone at last," Abigail says to me, after they're gone.

I wish just once I could come up with a clever reply when a girl says something like that to me. In my defense, I don't get much practice since it doesn't happen often. Before I can even make an attempt, a lady taps me on the shoulder.

"Hi Dylan," she says. "I'm Sue Wesley with BMI."

BMI is one of the sponsors.

"Nice to meet you," I say. "This is Abigail Collier. She was another contestant."

"Yes, I remember. I wasn't a part of the decision making process, but I understand the judges had a difficult time narrowing it down because of so many fabulous entries. Better luck next time, Abigail."

"Thanks. That's kind of you."

"Abigail, would you mind if I borrow Dylan for a moment?"

"Uh…, I guess not."

I share Abigail's reluctance, but like everyone keeps telling us, we have an obligation to the contest sponsors.

"I'll see you later," I tell Abigail.

She looks a little sad as she walks away. Which makes me feel bad.

"Are you familiar with what we do at BMI?" Sue asks.

"No, I'm sorry. I'm not."

"There's nothing to be sorry about. We're not well known by the general public, but among songwriters we're a prominent and respected organization. Let me explain our purpose."

Before she can her phone sounds. She glances at the display.

"I need to take this. Give me just a minute."

While I wait, I scan the room for Abigail, but don't spot her. I see Truman speaking with someone. Not Isabella. Probably a sponsor. I see Maddie in conversation with someone. Again, it looks like a sponsor. Another tap on the shoulder.

"Hello, Dylan. I'm Jeffrey Cummings with Martin Guitars. Did you know more songs have been written with a Martin than any other guitar?"

"No, I didn't."

"Do you play guitar?"

"I play bass."

"That's great. Martin makes an acoustic bass. I can arrange for you to try one out. They sound good in live performances, but they sound even better in the studio."

"I've never played an acoustic bass. I'd like to try a Martin."

Sue ends her phone call. Jeffrey hands me his business card, excuses himself and disappears.

That's how the next three hours go. One sponsor after another subtly reminding each of the winning songwriters of their obligations. Have fun today because tomorrow you go to work paying us back. That seems to be their message to us.

During a lull between sponsors tapping me on the shoulder, I go in search of Abigail, to no avail. Several people have left in the last hour and I assume she was one of them. I see Truman and Isabella talking with a group of people. Same with Maddie and Josh.

My head is throbbing. I'd like an aspirin and a quiet place to sit down, but feel like I need permission to leave. Another tap on the shoulder.

"Congratulations, Dylan," they say.

I take a deep breath, smile and turn to meet the well-wisher.

~43~

Turn out the lights, the party's over

I thought the party after the awards ceremony would never end. Socializing with strangers, smiling at their witty remarks and laughing at their jokes is exhausting. Some people have a natural ability when it comes to that stuff. Not me. I couldn't make small talk if my life depended on it.

I've never been happier to get into a vehicle as when we load into the limousine to leave. Even Josh and Maddie have had their fill of partying by this time. On the ride back to the hotel, it's almost like the early days when the four of us would hang out at Sticks, Strings and Brass after school.

"I was having a great time, but I'm glad that's done," Maddie says.

"Me too," Josh says. "I'm all talked out."

"How are you feeling, Dylan?" Maddie inquires.

"Other than the throbbing pain in my head, I'm fine."

"I'm sorry I didn't come to the hospital," she says.

"Me too," Josh adds. "Somebody had to stay here to protect our interests. We thought it's what you'd want."

"You were right. It is what I wanted. You took care of business for the four of us. I'm grateful to you for that. I still can't believe we won."

"You better start believing it," Truman says. "I've got a feeling they're going to be working us to death for a while."

"We have a bunch of commitments to honor. That's for certain."

"While you were at the ER, Maddie and I were talking," Josh says, as if he has an announcement.

"And?" I prompt him.

"We owe you an apology for some of the things we said. You too, Truman."

Maddie takes it from there.

"There have been bad feelings between us for the last couple of days, and it's mostly my fault. I'm sorry."

"Things have been strained between us," I say. "I'm willing to put it behind us if you are."

"Thanks. I was hoping you'd say that."

"I'd love to see us getting along again," Truman says. "However there is the matter concerning the one hundred grand. Do you still expect to get a bigger share than Dylan and me?"

Maddie looks at Josh before answering.

"I just said that to irritate you."

"It worked."

"We were never going to do anything to hurt our chances in the contest. You two can get so bossy sometimes. I wanted you to stop and think before you give us orders."

"Bossy?!" Truman protests. "I'm not bossy."

"For a brief moment we had the hatchet buried. Do we really want to dig it up?" I ask.

"I'm sorry I called you bossy, Truman. If we have the hatchet buried, can we change the subject?"

"Fine by me," Truman says.

"I barely have enough money to make it through tomorrow. Has anyone told you when we get the prize money? I'll be broke soon."

"Me too," says Josh.

"Me three," says Truman.

"Me four," I say. "Natalie said the auditors will contact us about that. No one has called me. Maybe I'll have an email from them when we get back to the hotel."

We go straight from the limousine to the business center when we arrive. I log in to my inbox while the others hover over me. There's one from Nikki.

"Tell her I said hi," Truman says.

"I'll call her later."

There's one from Multimedia Management. It's our schedule of events for the next few days.

"I'll print out four copies," I say. "There's nothing from the auditors. At the risk of sounding bossy, I think we should go up to our room and have a group meeting to discuss things going forward."

Maddie slaps me on the shoulder, but she's smiling as she does.

We ride the elevator up. Other than my headache, I feel good. The tension between us has dissipated for now.

"Let's order dinner from room service," Truman suggests, when we arrive at our room. "They'll put it on our hotel bill. The one we don't have to pay, and therefore don't worry about. I think I'll have some prime rib."

No one objects. Why would they? We look over the menus and then place our orders. We grab sodas from the minibar.

"Let's start our discussion, while we wait," I say. "Maddie. Do you want to start?"

"You go ahead."

"Alright. On the subject of money. If we eat breakfast and dinner at the hotel and charge it to our room, we can get by for a few days on little or nothing. I'm hoping the limousine will take us to our scheduled appointments. If not, we can ride the bus."

"That makes sense," Josh says. "We're no strangers to getting around on the bus, if it comes to that."

"So we're all agreed?" I ask.

Nods all around.

"Natalie talked to Truman and me on our way back from the hospital. She seems like a smart person. She thinks we should get an agent as soon as we can. I agree. These endorsements for the sponsors don't pay anything. At least, I don't think they do. A good agent can show us how to use the freebies to promote ourselves."

"What about Hamilton Spence? He's an agent."

"We can consider him. Natalie said we should talk to a few different ones before we decide. If we sign a contract with one, and then find out we don't like them, we might be stuck with them. Did Hamilton say what he charged?"

"He charges a percentage of what we make."

"I figured out that much. Are we talking about ten percent, or fifteen, or twenty?"

"It said in the contract, but I didn't get that far before you and Truman interrupted us."

"We have more questions than answers where an agent is concerned," Truman says. "We should make a list of what we need to ask an agent before we start looking."

A knock on the door sounds. Josh gets up to let them in.

"That would be our dinner," Truman says. "I think we should postpone further discussion until after we've eaten."

"No argument here," Maddie agrees.

A hotel guy wheels the serving cart in and lays out the food and silverware on the table. Josh adds a tip onto the bill and signs it.

"Enjoy your meal, gentlemen. You too miss," he says, on his way out.

~44~

Taking care of business and working overtime

Apparently, songwriter contest winners don't get a day off. On Sunday we go to a recording studio, where we pretend to oversee the recording of our song taking place. We sit in a booth with headphones on acting like we're listening to something really good, while a photographer takes our picture. From there we go to a huge music store to have more pictures taken with us holding guitars or sitting at a piano.

For most of the day we're driven around the metropolitan LA area stopping off at one popular place or another just to be seen. Natalie is with us. We pose for photos. She posts them on Instagram, Twitter and on our very own Facebook page.

"You're up to thirty thousand followers on Twitter," Natalie says, without taking her eyes from her tablet. "That's not bad considering I set up your account less than twenty-four hours ago."

It boggles the mind how we can go from being virtually unknown and in one day have thirty thousand people wanting to learn more about us. Our faces are popping up everywhere online. Before long people begin to think we must have done something really good or really bad. Why else would they be seeing us everywhere?

Later, after we're done for the day, we use a computer in the business center. I google search Dylan Jones and get a hundred hits. Maddie, Truman and Josh do it with their names and get similar results. In our room we order dinner from room service, again. Afterward I call Nikki.

"Dylan! What took you so long to call me? Three days in California and suddenly you're too good for your own family."

The sound of her voice makes me homesick. She's a royal pain in the ass most of the time, but she's the closest thing to a sister I'll ever have.

"Sorry. I've been really busy. We won the contest."

"I know that. I'd have to be living on the North Pole not to know. All my friends have been asking about you."

"I don't know any of your friends."

"That's alright. They know you. How come you haven't called momma and poppa? They worry about you."

"I was going to call Isiah next," I lie.

"I'll save you the trouble. I'll hand him the phone when I'm through talking to you. What's it like there? Have you seen any movie stars? Did you receive the prize money yet?"

"LA is a huge city. People are always in a hurry. Everything is super expensive. I haven't seen anyone famous as far as I know. We haven't received the money yet, and I don't know when we will."

"They're going to pay you, aren't they? They wouldn't try to weasel out of the deal, would they?"

The thought has crossed my mind.

"I guess anything is possible. We should find out soon, one way or another. Is Isiah nearby?"

"Yeah, but I'm not through, yet. When are you coming back?"

"I really don't know. The contest people have us doing endorsements for all the sponsors. It's part of the deal and I don't know how long it will go on. Why do you ask?"

"I'm just curious. That's all. Would you bring me back something? You know, a souvenir. Maybe something from Rodeo Drive?"

That thought has crossed my mind, as well. Something for Isiah and Chandra, too.

"I'll try Nikki, but they've got us running all over with these endorsements. Now, let me talk to Isiah. Okay?"

"Alright, I'll hand the phone to him. You take care of yourself little brother. You hear? Here's poppa."

"Dylan. Congratulations. Chandra and I are so proud of you. How are you feeling? I bet you're on cloud nine."

"I still can't believe it's happening," I say.

It's my go-to line whenever anyone asks how I feel about winning.

"You've never been one to relish your time in the spotlight. How are you doing with all this attention?"

"To be honest, it's not easy for me. I'm not sure it's something I'll ever get used to."

"What about your friends, Maddie, Josh and Truman? How are they handling it?"

"Better than me, I think."

My phone beeps to let me know of an incoming call. I'm anxious to hear from the auditors about the prize money.

"I've got another call coming in, Isiah."

"That's okay. Go ahead and take it. It might be important. I'm real happy for you Dylan. Call me if you need anything. Alright?"

"Thanks, Isiah. I will. Bye now."

I switch callers.

"Hello."

"Hi Dylan. It's Abigail. I'm sorry we didn't get a chance to talk longer, yesterday. Are you busy?"

"No, I'm not at the moment. I'm glad you called. I looked around for you after we were interrupted by that sponsor. I meant to ask you for your phone number. How'd you get mine?"

"Maddie gave it to me. I hope you don't mind. I saw her as I was leaving the ballroom and asked her for it."

Strange she didn't mention it, I think to myself.

"I'm glad she did. I didn't want that to be the last I saw of you."

The line goes quiet for a long moment. I wonder if she's still there.

"Hello," I say.

"I'm still here," she says. "That was a sweet thing for you to say. I didn't know how you'd feel about me calling you. I felt like something sparked between us, but I didn't know if you felt the same."

"That's a sweet thing for you to say to me. I do feel the same."

"Are you real busy?'

"You mean, right now?"

"No, not now. During the next few days. Would you like to get together sometime?"

"I'd love to. The contest people have us pretty busy. Can I call you when I get free of them?"

"Sure, that'd be great."

"How long do I have? When are you flying home?"

"I'm already home, and I didn't fly. I live in Anaheim, about an hour south of LA. You have all the time you need. Just don't put it off too long. Okay?"

"Okay, then. I'll call you soon."

~45~

Money for nothin' and your chicks for free

Monday starts off with a bang. 'Bang Bang', actually. It's a song performed by Jessie J, Ariana Grande and Nicki Minaj. I use it as a ringtone for my phone. It sounds at seven in the morning. Even though that's ten o'clock in Detroit, I'm sound asleep. It's lucky I'm roused by the ringtone. I sit up, switch on the lamp beside the bed and answer it.

"Hello."

My voice sounds like I've been gargling with molasses. Thick and slow. The caller probably thinks I'm coming off a week-long bender.

"Is this Dylan Jones?" the caller asks.

He sounds familiar, but my mind is still in the process of waking.

"Yes," I answer.

"I'm sorry to call so early, but I wanted to be sure I caught you before you left for the day. You'll understand after I explain. I'm Franklin Aubrey with the accounting firm of Duncan and Beasley. Do you remember me?"

"Yes. I remember you."

I'm wide awake now. Truman is too. He senses something in my tone.

"First of all, congratulations to you, Truman, Madeline and Josh."

"Thank you," I say curtly, because I know there's more coming.

"A special courier will deliver your prize money directly to your hotel room between eight and eight thirty this morning. All four of you will need to sign the package receipt."

I let out a whoop. Truman hops to his feet in the middle of his bed and jumps up and down like it's a trampoline.

"Dylan. Are you still there?" Franklin asks.

"Yes, I am. And thank you. That's great news."

"The courier will deliver four packages. Inside each package is a debit card with your respective names on them. You'll find instructions on how to activate the cards. Each one has a balance of twenty-five thousand dollars. The cards expire automatically when the account balance drops to zero. If you have any questions feel free to call."

Truman is still jumping on the bed as I end the call. He sees the ear-to-ear smile on my face and adds spinning in circles to his repertoire. There's a knock on our bedroom door.

"Dylan. What's all the noise about?" Maddie asks.

Truman and I are in our underwear. Tighty-whities. I don't care. I throw open the door and give her the news. She's wearing a robe. I'm not sure what's underneath it. She starts jumping up and down. It must be contagious. I start doing it, too.

Josh comes from the other bedroom. He's in his underwear, too. Only his is fashionable. A sleeveless top and matching boxers. He starts jumping up and down. I wrap my arms around Maddie. She pushes me away.

"I'm not hugging you in your underwear," she says.

Josh wraps his arms around me. I push him away.

"Not in your underwear, dude," I say. "Even if it is really stylish."

I'm out of breath from all the jumping around and excitement of knowing we're getting the money in an hour.

The room phone rings. Maddie runs to pick it up, probably expecting more good news. I hear her side of the conversation.

"Hello. Yes. I'm sorry. Okay. We will. Okay. We're sorry."

She waves her arms at us. Then presses her palms downward, signaling for us to settle down.

"That was the front desk. Someone below us is complaining about the noise. I told them we'd be quiet."

We shower, dress and order breakfast from room service. I can hardly contain myself. It's not just the money or the fact that it's more than I've ever had in my entire life. I'm equally excited over how it came into our possession. We won it. We beat the odds and thousands of other songwriters. That makes us luckier than ninety-nine percent of the people on the planet.

There's a knock on the door at ten minutes after eight. We trip over each other getting to it. Sure enough, it's the special courier. We each sign for our package, slam the door on the courier and rip open the boxes. Inside each box is an envelope. Inside the envelope is a sheet with instructions and a smaller envelope. That one contains the debit card. We compare them.

"Mine's the prettiest of all," Maddie says. "Because it has my name printed on it."

"You may have the prettiest card, but an hour from now I'm going to have the prettiest Eric Johnson signature Stratocaster you've ever seen."

"You can't run out and get it now. The limousine is supposed to pick us up at nine," I say.

"There you go getting bossy again," he says, only half-kidding.

"Truman, Dylan's right," Maddie says. "We have to fulfill our obligations to the contest sponsors. Not only because they expect it. We can use the publicity to promote ourselves."

"This money is only the start," Josh says. "Once we hire an agent we'll get paid for endorsement deals. Who knows? We might make ten times this amount."

I heard someone say rich people are never satisfied with how much money they have. No matter how much it is, they always want more. I wonder if I'll feel that way when I'm rich.

~46~

Want you to sign your contract, want you to sign today

Finding an agent turns out to be easier than we anticipate. Natalie gets us started with a few names. We call them, listen to a recording and leave a message for each. The calls are returned within the hour. After brief conversations by phone we arrange to meet with three prospective agents. The three meetings take place thirty minutes apart, in our hotel room.

The first agent is a man, Leland Haley. I'd put him at mid-thirtyish, with neatly trimmed dark hair and mustache. He's wearing a tan sports coat, no tie, loafers and no socks. He's articulate, smooth, informative and listens patiently as we express our concerns.

Next comes a woman, Gina Young. She's close in age to Leland with long blonde hair, big blue eyes and the whitest teeth I've ever seen. She laughs at everything I say, though it isn't meant to be funny. Truman and I would choose her based on her body alone, but Maddie and Josh aren't as easily swayed by her looks.

The third and last agent we meet is Stella Rosenberg. Stella is north of fifty, with the build and demeanor of a bulldog. Judging by her voice, she chain smokes and gargles with tequila between cigarettes. She taps at her phone with one hand and a tablet with the other for the entire time she's speaking to us.

"What are they paying you for these appearances?"

"I don't think we get any money for them. It's part of the deal. The contest winners do promotional stuff for the sponsors," I say.

"That stops now," she says, matter-of-factly.

She taps her phone once to make a call.

"Leslie," she barks at her phone. "Get me a phone number for whoever is running the Songwriter of the Year Contest. See if you can put your hands on an entry form. I'm looking for any binding agreement the songwriters made when they entered the contest. Scan their website for any pertinent information. Okay."

She turns her attention back to the four of us.

"Tsk, tsk," she utters. "You should have come to me, earlier. You're babes in the woods. They'll tear you apart like a pack of wolves, if you let them. Never give anything for free. If you give it away, it's not worth anything. They'll keep on taking as long as you're willing to let them."

"Everything happened so quickly," Maddie says. "We didn't know we were coming to LA until two days before."

Stella receives a text message.

"It's the contact information for the contest people," she tells us. "I'll call them as soon as you tell me you want my representation."

We don't respond instantaneously. She gestures at her phone.

"Well, what's it going to be?"

"We didn't expect to have to make a decision this quickly," Truman says. "We need to talk about it, first."

"In my professional opinion, you don't have a lot of time to think this over. You're losing money every minute you don't have representation. If you don't want me, that's fine. We'll part company, no hard feelings. But hire an agent and do it soon."

"Ms. Rosenberg," Maddie says.

"Call me Stella."

"Alright. Stella, would you give us five minutes to talk this over?"

"Sure. I can do that. I'll go have a smoke and come back. How's that?"

"That woman scares me," Truman says, the second she's out the door.

"Me, too," Josh says.

"I liked Leland better," Maddie says.

"I liked Gina better," I say. "But neither Gina nor Leland are as tenacious as Stella. I think that's something we want in an agent. It takes someone tougher than us to make deals for lots of money. I'd hate to be the one sitting across the table from her when the negotiating begins."

"She still scares me, but I'll go along with Dylan on this," Truman says. "If he says he likes Stella for the job, that's good enough for me."

"I feel good about having her as our agent, but it has to be unanimous. Maddie. Josh. What do you say?"

A knock sounds. Truman let's Stella in. I look at Josh and Maddie. They glance at one another and then give me a nod.

"We'd be pleased to have you represent us," I tell Stella.

"Then it's settled."

She takes a one-page contract from her valise and sets it along with a pen before us.

"Read it over and sign it," she says. "While you're doing that I'll make some calls."

Legal papers intimidate me. Typically, they're written with a lot of big words that aren't used in casual conversation. Stella's contract is as simple as they come. I read it aloud to the others. Afterward we sign it without hesitation.

"Now what?" I ask Stella.

"Now," she says theatrically. "I start earning my commissions. The first thing I want each of you to do is go buy yourself a wireless smartphone. I need to be able to contact you twenty-four seven wherever you are. I'm going to put you in touch with a real estate agent I know. She'll help you find a place to live."

"We're okay here, for now," Maddie says. "Besides, we're not sure how long we'll be in LA."

"It'd be better for you to stay close. At least for the next few months. This way I can schedule local appearances. Say for instance a talk show has to fill a spot at the last minute. There's not time enough to fly you here. You may only get two hours' notice."

I think about Abigail living in Anaheim, an hour south of LA. If things work out between us, I can see her often.

"I'm okay with staying here in LA for a while, if you guys are," I say.

"I wasn't planning on leaving, anyway," Josh says. "I love it here."

"The realtor's name is Constance Rivera. You'll be hearing from her. Make sure I have your new phone numbers as soon as you get them activated. If you have any issues with the contest people call me. Do you have any questions?"

"About a jillion," I say.

~47~

I'll light the fire,
You put the flowers in the vase that you bought today

I have only a vague recollection of the first home I lived in with my parents, Trevor and Grace. It was a rented space. I'm guessing two bedrooms and one bathroom, no larger than Isiah and Chandra's house. I remember the rooms as being big with high ceilings. But in truth, that was probably just my perception as a toddler.

Truman, Maddie, Josh and I discuss where we want to live.

"I think it would be best if we each had our own apartment," Maddie says. "So we have our privacy when we want it."

"I agree," Josh says.

"Let's see what the realtor has to say before we decide on anything," Truman says. "I hear there are some dangerous areas. If we live together in one house, we can look out for one another, at least until we're more familiar with LA."

"If we can get a house with four bedrooms, we'd have ample privacy and we wouldn't share a wall with a neighbor who likes hip-hop," I say.

"Yeah," Truman agrees. "Or country western."

We make arrangements to meet the realtor in front of our hotel at a quarter past one in the afternoon. We don't know what she looks like, only that she'll be in a gray Dodge Caravan. She spots us standing on the sidewalk before we see her. She waves and pulls to the curb. The passenger side window comes down. I bend to address the driver.

"Constance Rivera?" I ask.

"Call me Connie," she says. "Get in."

Call me Connie is a large woman with a big platinum-blonde hairdo. She's wearing a bright yellow tent dress and enough makeup for three. Her perfume is overpowering in the confines of her minivan. Maddie rides in front, next to Connie. Truman, Josh and I sit side by side in the center seat. I crack the window an inch and breathe in what passes for fresh air in LA.

"I have a place to show you that meets your needs according to what Stella tells me. It's west of here, close to Beverly Hills, West Hollywood and Bel Air. You'll love the location."

I have no idea why being close to those places might be beneficial and I don't ask. We're putting ourselves in Connie's hands, the same way we put ourselves in Stella's, and hoping for the best.

"This is Sunset Boulevard," she says, as she turns onto the street. "The house is seventy-five hundred square feet with seven bedrooms and nine baths. It sits on one-point-seven acres. It's fully furnished and the yard and pool maintenance is included in the rent."

She turns off the boulevard onto a gravel drive leading into a wooded area. I'm thinking it's some kind of joke. Then this huge mansion comes into view and I'm thinking Connie has a sick sense of humor.

"What are we doing here?" Truman asks.

"What do you think?" Connie shoots back. "We're looking at this place. What's the problem? It's not big enough?"

"Oh, it's plenty big enough."

"How much is the rent?" I ask.

"Don't worry about that," she replies. "Let's go in and look around."

She gains access by punching a code into a keypad by a side door. I expect a squad of police cars to come barreling up the drive at any second.

"This is the service entrance," she says.

"This house comes with servants?" I wonder aloud.

"I said service, not servants," she corrects.

I feel stupid, but I'm no stranger to stupid.

We follow her through the entrance and into the kitchen, beyond which is this massive living/entertaining area. There's a dining table big enough for twenty people and tables outside on the veranda, as well. The four of us could seat every member of our families here and have room to spare.

We walk out onto the veranda which overlooks the lushly landscaped grounds. Steps lead down from the veranda to a flagstone patio with a swimming pool and cabana.

"This is incredible," Maddie says.

"You like?" Connie asks.

"Do I ever," Maddie replies.

She goes to the edge of the pool to dip her toes into the water.

"The temperature is perfect. You guys want to go for a swim?"

"Not now," Connie says. "You'll have plenty of time for that later, if you choose this house."

We go back inside.

"Upstairs are bedrooms, a library and an office. Down that way there's a gym and a rec room with a pool table. Go ahead and have a look around. I'll wait here."

We climb the winding stairs to the next level and go in the first room we come to. It has a poster bed, walk-in closet, bath with shower and soaking tub, and a sitting area. Maddie runs and dives onto the bed, landing on her back.

"This room is mine," she says.

"Don't you want to see the others?" Josh asks.

"I don't see how they could be any nicer than this."

We come to an office next. It has wood-paneled walls, a fireplace, leather furniture, an oak desk and a bar.

"This would be the perfect room for my Stratocaster and Marshall amplifier," Truman declares.

"Don't get your heart set on that," I warn. "I don't know why Connie brought us here, but I'm sure we can't afford this place."

We continue on through the house. I can't deny it's really impressive and I'm having fun dreaming of living here, even if it's not even remotely possible. After our tour of the upstairs we catch up with Connie.

"Can you see yourselves coming home to this house after a hard day?" she asks. "Soaking in the spa or cooling off in the pool while shish kabob cooks on the outdoor grill."

"Not in my wildest dreams," I mutter under my breath.

"There's an electric car charging station in the garage," Connie says.

"A what?" Truman asks.

"You know. A charging station for an electric car."

Maybe Stella didn't tell her we're from Detroit, the gas guzzler capital of the world.

"It's a California thing," she explains.

Connie is still naming off the finer points of the house when I get a text from Stella.

It reads: How's the house hunt going

I text back: Looking at a mansion we can't afford. What gives?

Next my phone sounds a call coming in from Stella. She begins talking before I say hello.

"We don't have time to text back and forth. Where are you?"

"At a huge mansion on Sunset Boulevard," I say.

"That should work well for what I have in mind. I told Connie what I wanted. A place like the one Jed, Granny, Ellie and Jethro had."

"Who?"

"The Beverly Hillbillies. You know," she says, and sings, "*So they loaded up the truck and they moved to Beverly.*"

"Uh…," I say. "That may have been before my time."

"It was before your time, but the reruns go on forever. No matter. It was a TV show about this poor hillbilly who strikes oil on his property and becomes a millionaire overnight. That's what brought it to mind. The story is similar to yours. Four kids who were struggling to get by until they win a lot of money in a contest. It's an irresistible feel-good story. Don't you think? And with my help, you're going to cash in on it."

"I'm sorry, Stella. I'm not following you. What does this hillbilly have to do with a place for us to live?"

"You want a place that will look good on TV. It opens up a lot of possibilities. Your own reality TV show, for instance."

"TV show! Are you kidding?"

"Not for a second. Look. I know this is coming at you faster than you can make sense of it. That's alright. You have to trust me. I've been doing this a long time. I know how to get the most out of this situation."

"We do trust you. It's just that this house looks like more than we can afford, and I haven't even been told the price. I'm afraid of running out of money before we can make more."

"You're looking at this wrong. You're no longer Dylan Jones the person, you're Dylan Jones the business. You have enough earning potential to live wherever you want. Choose a place that motivates you to work harder to keep it. What do you think of the house?"

"I love it. I think the others do, too."

"Then, sign the lease and be done with it."

"I don't even know what it rents for."

"You're not listening. It doesn't matter. You're not buying the place. You may get tired of it after a month and move."

"I doubt we'd get tired of it."

"I'm going to set you up with a money manager. I do this for all my clients. He'll handle paying the rent, your credit cards and other bills. You'll still have full access to your money. This will free you up to concentrate on your career and allow you to stop worrying about your expenses."

"That sounds great," I say.

But, what I'm really thinking is it sounds scary.

"If Maddie, Josh and Truman like the house, tell Connie you'll take it. And tell her to take you back to your hotel. I've set up a meeting for you at seven this evening with Ha Yoon Ghim."

"Who's that?"

"She's a new singing sensation from South Korea. I'm negotiating a deal for her to sing and record your song, 'Love Transcends'. It's tentatively scheduled to be released worldwide next month."

~48~

I need it, you know I'm a fiend,
Getting freaky in my Limousine

We sign the lease for the house on Sunset Boulevard on a Wednesday. It takes two days for the approval. That's okay. We're too busy to worry about moving in before then, anyway. We still have some commitments to sponsors to fulfill during the day and things scheduled each evening.

We meet with the singer, Ha Yoon Ghim, and her representatives on Wednesday evening at the restaurant in our hotel. She's a waif of a thing. Not a day over sixteen or a pound over eighty-five. She speaks to us through a translator.

"I am Min," the interpreter says. "This is Ha Yoon Ghim."

"It's nice to meet you, Ha," Maddie says, on behalf of our group.

Min translates. Ha says what sounds to me like two words.

"Ha Yoon is honored to meet the great songwriters she has heard so much about. She is looking forward to working together."

"That's very kind of her. We're looking forward to it, also."

"Can I ask you something?" I say. "Is Ha going to record our song in English or South Korean?"

Min relays the question and receives a one word reply.

"Both," Min says to me.

"Cool," I say. "I can't wait to hear it in a foreign language."

Thursday morning the limousine picks us up at 9:00 AM. Natalie is focused on her tablet as Matt opens the door for us. I slide in next to her. She doesn't look up. I don't know if she's heard about the recording deal with Ha Yoon Ghim. I'm pretty sure she doesn't know about the house we've rented on Sunset Boulevard.

"Good morning," I say. "How are you this fine morning?"

She glances up from her tablet briefly. Her expression is one of annoyance. Although I've never discussed it with her, I don't think Natalie is a morning person.

"What are you grinning about?" she asks.

"Ha Yoon Ghim is going to record our song," I say.

"Seems I heard something about that. Good for you."

"She's going to sing it in English and South Korean," I say, next.

"Who wants to hear it in South Korean?"

"South Koreans, I assume."

"That's nice. I'm very happy for all of you. Now, if you don't mind I need to tweet a couple of things."

"Sure. Go ahead."

She shifts her attention back to the tablet.

"Dylan," Truman says. "What's the address of the house we rented? I need to have something delivered there."

"It's 10105 West Sunset Boulevard," I say, casually.

Natalie's head jerks up.

"Get out of here," she says. "You guys are renting a house on Sunset Boulevard? I don't believe it."

"It's true," Maddie says. "We're moving in this weekend."

"Those places rent for ten thousand a month and up. You'll blow through your winnings in a matter of weeks."

"Our agent doesn't seem to think so," I say.

"By the way," Truman says. "Thanks for recommending her. Stella Rosenberg is a workaholic. And I'm glad she's working for us."

"You're welcome. I'm glad it worked out for you," she says, but not with much feeling.

The rest of the day as we make our scheduled appearances, I notice Natalie looking at me when she thinks my attention is elsewhere. It's not my imagination. Out of the corner of my eye I see her sizing me up.

When the limousine drops us back at the hotel, as Maddie, Truman and Josh are getting out, Natalie places her hand on my arm to stop me.

"We need to talk," she says. "Close the door Matt."

He does. Natalie hits a button to raise the tinted glass partition between the driver's compartment and passenger's. We're alone in the limousine, sitting side by side, our hips touching. I feel sweat beading on my forehead.

"Do I make you nervous, Dylan?"

"No," I lie.

I feel the beads of sweat sliding down my face.

"Let's stop pretending there's nothing going on here."

"I'm not pretending," I lie, again.

"You don't feel a certain sexual tension between us?"

"I wouldn't call it tension."

"What would you call it, then?"

"I don't know. Do we have to give it a name? I like you. I've enjoyed being around you. I haven't considered anything past that because …, well because it isn't going to happen. You're out of my league."

"Is that what you think? You're not good enough for me? If that was the case, would I be putting moves on you in the back of this limousine?"

"Are you?"

A simple yes would have sufficed. Instead, she puts her hands on the back of my neck and pulls our faces together. Her tongue goes so far in I almost gag. When our lips finally separate, I feel something in my mouth.

"Were you chewing gum?" I ask.

"Oh, sorry," she says, and kisses me again.

This time, when we separate, the gum is back in her mouth.

"You're a good kisser, Dylan."

I don't know why she thinks that. I didn't do anything but sit still. A mannequin could have kissed better than me.

With one hand she undoes the top two buttons on my shirt. Then she drags her long nails across my bare chest. The same chest Nikki refers to as being devoid of muscle tone. If she could only see me now.

"Have you ever had sex in the back of a limousine?" Natalie asks.

I'm not about to tell her I've never had sex anywhere.

"No," I say. "Have you?"

She doesn't reply. She begins undressing. I'm awestruck by her body as she strips off her top, skirt, bra and black lace panties.

"What are you waiting on?" she asks me.

I've never shucked my clothes so quickly in my entire life. It's over in under three minutes. I know this because there's a clock in the passenger compartment of the limousine. We dress, we kiss and she pushes me out.

"Sorry. I have to be across town in thirty minutes," she says. "See you later lover boy."

She blows me a kiss, shuts the door and the limousine speeds away.

So many times I've wondered what it would be like to rid myself of the stigma that comes with being a virgin. Now I know. I feel euphoria, liberation and exuberance all at the same time. I also feel a little guilty. Maybe it's my feminine side talking—if such a thing exists—but it seems like love should play a bigger part in the process.

I think that's what I'm feeling guilty about. Natalie is beautiful. Actually, she's drop-dead gorgeous. But, she's not special to me. Nor me to her. I won't dwell on it, though. It probably won't happen again, anyway. Whatever came over her has already passed, I'm sure.

I head up to the room. Truman greets me with a high five as I enter. Maddie and Josh are on the couch watching us and snickering.

"My man, Dylan. I am so proud of you. And I'm jealous, too. Popping your cherry in the limousine. What a stud. And with sweet Natalie, no less.

I consider saying nothing happened, but Truman seems certain it did.

"What are you talking about?" I say, instead.

"Listen to that. He's not the sort to kiss and tell."

"Don't be modest, Dylan," Maddie says. "We hung around to see what would happen. We saw two sets of feet pressed against the window. One pointing up and one pointing down. Are you still going to deny it?"

"No comment," I say.

"Come on, Dylan," Truman pleads. "Give us something. What's she like? Does she scratch your back with those long nails? Is she a screamer?"

"I have nothing more to say on the subject."

And that was that.

~49~

You go back Jack, do it again

At breakfast the next morning no one says anything about what happened between Natalie and me. I'm certainly not going to broach the subject. I breathe a sigh of relief that it's already old news. As soon as we're inside the limousine though, Truman, Maddie and Josh begin to snicker.

Natalie glares at me. I give her my best *I-didn't-do-it* look. She gives me her *you're-going-to-pay-for-this* look. That sets the tone for the rest of the day. Midafternoon we're done for the day and back at the hotel.

"You've fulfilled your immediate commitments to the sponsors," Natalie tells us, before we get out of the limousine.

We already knew this because Stella told us last night.

"Maybe we'll work together again. Whether we do or not, I wish you good luck and much success in the future."

Maddie shakes her hand. So does Josh.

"It's been a real pleasure," Truman says, and kisses her cheek.

Maddie, Josh and Truman slide out. I start to follow.

"Not yet, Dylan," Natalie says.

Truman turns to give me a thumbs-up. The door shuts. It's just Natalie and me. Alone again in the limousine.

"I'm sorry about the snickering earlier. I didn't say anything to them. They figured it out on their own," I tell her.

"That doesn't bother me. What bothers me is that we won't be seeing as much of each other and you don't seem to care."

I don't know how to explain that I lack the self-esteem and confidence necessary to say the things she wants to hear. I make an attempt.

"Natalie. What happened yesterday was incredible."

"But, that was yesterday. Is that what you're going to say?"

"That's not what I was going to say. What I started to say is, you're LA. You're always busy. You go a hundred miles an hour all day long. You're the kind of girl who will squeeze me in between appointments. Five minutes on Tuesday and three on the following Friday. Bottom line. You'll break my heart and be down the road before you realize you did."

She turns her face away. I study her profile, trying to read her mind. Her eyes glisten. She rummages through her purse. I'm thinking she's looking for a tissue to dab her eyes, but I'm wrong about that. Her hand comes out with a tube of Super Glue.

"Here," she says, stuffing it in my pocket. "If I ever break your heart, you can mend it with that Super Glue."

"I'm no cardiologist, but I don't think it works that way."

"Dylan," she says, taking a more serious tone. "I don't know what's going to happen, tomorrow. I'll admit I run around like a chicken with its head cut off most of the time. You're going to be busy, too. I'm asking you to squeeze me in when you have free time. What do you say?"

"Yeah. Sure, I'm up for that. Especially the part about squeezing you."

Her interest in me boosts my confidence. I'm feeling bold. I lean in to kiss her. While our tongues wrestle, my hands explore her body. I touch the bare skin of her leg, find her knee and then, venture northward. She pulls back, suddenly.

"Sorry," she says. "I don't have time for that, now. I'm meeting my fiancé in Santa Monica in an hour."

I don't know which disappoints me more. The fact that she has a fiancé or that I can't make whoopee with her before she goes to see him. I feel like I'm due an explanation.

"Your fiancé?" I inquire.

"Yes. His name is Richard. He's a plastic surgeon. He did my boobs. That's how we met."

I wait for her to go on. She doesn't.

"You're getting married? A minute ago you wanted me to find time for you. Now, you're telling me you have a fiancé. Doesn't that pretty much guarantee you'll dump me and break my heart at some point?"

"Not necessarily. He's my fiancé. We're not married. I mean, things change. You never know." She glances at the clock. "Look, I really do have to go. Can we talk about this later?"

"Later, tonight or later, another day?" I ask.

"Another day," she replies.

I try hard to keep a stiff upper lip and pretend it doesn't bother me, but I'm doing a lousy job of it.

"Dylan," she starts, then stops. She sighs and begins undressing. "Be quick about it. Richard doesn't like it when I keep him waiting."

I don't know if I can be beat my previous land speed record set the day before, but I give it my best effort.

~50~

My friends all drive Porsches, I must make amends

Having fewer material possessions than the average homeless person makes moving simple and easy. We walk out of our hotel with our luggage, hail a taxi to take us to Sunset Boulevard and we're lounging around the pool at our house by noon on Saturday. It's the first full day off for us since we arrived in LA.

"We should get a car," Josh suggests. "We won't have the limousine to take us around anymore. We can't depend on the bus if we have to be somewhere in a hurry. Taxis might be too expensive in the long run."

"We should each get a car," Maddie says. "So there's no argument over who gets to use it and when."

"That'd be too expensive, even for rich folks like us. We can compromise and get two cars. What do you think, Dylan?"

"Huh?" I utter.

My mind is drifting back in time to yesterday. The mention of not having the limousine anymore reminds me of what won't happen in the back of it anymore.

"Dylan, snap out of it. You're doing that lovesick puppy dog thing again. Josh and Maddie are talking about getting a car, or maybe four cars. I asked what you think."

"I think getting a car is a good idea. I don't know about four, though. We can run it by the money manager Stella set us up with."

"Boyd Proctor, that's his name," Maddie says. "I'll call him."

Boyd arranges for us to lease two Toyota Highlander Hybrids from a dealership in North Hollywood and have them delivered to our house that same afternoon. They're practical, not sporty. Big enough to comfortably carry all four of us at one time. But small enough to maneuver in LA traffic.

"I'm dying to drive it around," Maddie says. "Who wants to go with me?"

"I'll go with you," Truman says. "If we can go by California Sounds while we're riding around."

"Say hello to the zombies for me," I say.

"I don't know if I'll see them. I'm only going to be there long enough to pick up my Eric Johnson signature Stratocaster and Marshall Jubilee."

"You and I can take the other Highlander, Dylan," Josh says.

"I'm looking forward to quiet time and getting acquainted with the new place. You go on without me."

After they leave, I take a walk around the house sliding my hand across slick surfaces, turning faucets on and off, switching lights on and off and flushing toilets. I go in the room I've chosen as mine and sit on the bed. The mattress feels luxurious in comparison to the one I have in Detroit. I lie back and close my eyes.

A vision of Natalie pushes its way to the front of my mind. Beautiful Natalie, smiling at me. Kissing me. Pushing me onto the seat of the limousine and mounting me.

The irony of losing my virginity is it only happens once. You can have sex millions of times. Speaking theoretically, of course. But once you've passed through the portal, and gone from innocent and naïve to experienced and knowing, there's no going back.

Another thing I've learned about sex is that it's highly addictive. When you're having sex, nothing else matters. And when you're not having it, you can't stop thinking about it. I take out my phone and punch in Natalie's number. It goes directly to voicemail. I disconnect.

I scroll through my call log and find Abigail's number. I hesitate. It's not like I'm cheating on Natalie if I see Abigail. Natalie's engaged to Richard. And Abigail might be just what I need. Someone to make me stop thinking about Natalie every single minute. I dial the number.

"Hi Dylan," she answers. "I was just thinking about you. I'm glad you called. Tell me what you've been up to since we last talked."

I don't have to see her face to know she's smiling. I love her smile.

"Hi Abigail. It's great to hear your voice. I've been thinking about you all week. We've been really busy. I'm sorry I haven't called before now."

"That's okay. I understand. I take it things are going well?"

"Yeah. Really well. We rented a house and moved out of the hotel."

"A house in LA?"

"Yeah. It's on West Sunset Boulevard."

"Really. That sounds like a nice neighborhood. Expensive, too."

"It is a nice neighborhood, and the house is not too shabby, either. It was our agent's idea. She has something planned."

"A fancy house and an agent with plans for you. You are moving up in the world, Dylan. I'm happy for you. Are you going to invite me over to see you sometime?"

"You must have read my mind. Are you busy, tonight?"

"Nothing I can't get out of. Give me the address."

I do.

"I'll see you around seven, if that's okay."

"Perfect. I'll see you then."

A month ago I couldn't have made that call. I'd have been too shy and intimidated by a good-looking girl like Abigail. The self-doubt hasn't completely disappeared, but it is slowly fading away. I wonder if Natalie knows what she's done. She's created a whole new Dylan Jones.

~51~

Time goes by so slowly and time can do so much

At seven o' clock I'm alone in the house. I'm freshly showered and shaved and wearing my new hibiscus print Hawaiian shirt waiting for Abigail to arrive. Josh, Maddie and Truman haven't returned since leaving here six hours earlier. I'm not going to worry about them. They can take care of themselves. I imagine they're having fun. Seeing new things.

I'm still alone in the house at seven fifteen. I start to wonder if Abigail has changed her mind. I check my phone to be sure I haven't missed a call. Nothing. I look out the window toward Sunset Boulevard. The house is hidden from view to passersby by dense shrubs and foliage. Anyone unfamiliar with this place could drive by and never know it's here.

I take out my phone and begin punching in Abigail's number. Before I finish, a car turns into our driveway. The glare on the windshield prevents me from identifying the driver. Then another car appears in the driveway. The two vehicles park side by side in front of the house. I watch from the window as Abigail gets out of one and Natalie gets out of the other. This could be a problem.

The two girls stand beside their cars looking at one another. Natalie in short shorts and sleeveless tank top. Abigail in shorter shorts and cropped top. From where I am, I can't read their expressions.

Natalie says something. Abigail replies. Natalie smiles. Abigail smiles. Natalie walks around her car to be closer to Abigail. There's more talking. They hug. Then, they start up the steps toward the front door.

Nothing I've experienced in my eighteen years has in any way prepared me for this moment. Part of me wants to run and hide. The rest of me is dying to know what happens next. The doorbell sounds. I start that way, but the door opens before I get there.

"Anybody home?" Natalie calls. "Dylan. It's me, Natalie."

"Right here," I say, as I round the corner into the foyer.

I've had thirty seconds to think of how to handle this. I should act glad to see both of them. Which shouldn't be hard to do because I am glad to see them.

"You made it," I say to Abigail.

I spread my arms, inviting a hug. She throws a lip-lock on me that lasts for most of a minute. She glances at Natalie. "Take that," her eyes say.

"Natalie," I say, once our lips separate. "Do you know Abigail?"

"I know who she is from the contest. We introduced ourselves outside a minute ago. I didn't know you two were seeing one another."

"We're not," I say, a little too quickly. "I mean we haven't been."

"He's been so busy we haven't had a chance until now," Abigail explains.

"I guess I'm partially to blame for that," Natalie says to Abigail. To me she says, "I see I missed your call earlier. I just came by to bring you a housewarming gift."

Since she's not holding a package in her hands, I have to assume the gift is in a pocket or hidden beneath her clothing. I'm betting it's the latter.

"I'm not interrupting anything, am I?" Natalie asks, next.

The question is addressed to me, but Abigail takes it.

"We don't have anything special planned," she says, nonchalantly. "Stick around if you like."

"Thanks, I will. Dylan, be a good host and show us around your house. Where are the others, by the way?"

"We leased two vehicles today. They're out seeing LA. I don't know when they'll be back."

I take them upstairs first.

"I haven't seen the whole house, yet. Our bedrooms are on this level."

"Which one is yours?" Abigail asks.

"The second door on the left," I say.

A look passes between the girls. I half expect them to race for my room and stake a claim on it, but they don't. We go downstairs and I show them the gym, kitchen and great room. They do a lot of oohing and ahhing to show they're appropriately impressed.

We step out onto the veranda, descend the stairs and cross the patio. The tall trees on the property cast shadows across it. The photocell controlled underwater lights illuminate the pool. It's an intimate setting. Romantic even.

"This is nice, Dylan. Can we sit out here for a while?" Abigail asks.

"Sure. Wherever you want."

We sit at a glass top table with Abigail on one side of me and Natalie on the other.

"I have one already rolled if you're interested," Abigail says.

I'm slow to catch on.

"Fire it up," Natalie says.

"It's pretty good stuff. Don't you think?" Abigail says, after the joint has made two laps around the table.

As I've mentioned before, I haven't had any experience with pot because I could never afford it.

"It's kicking my butt," I say.

"Do you have any wine or beer, Dylan?" Natalie asks.

"Sorry. We haven't done any shopping yet. And then, there's the thing about not being twenty-one."

She makes a call to a nearby package store and orders a case of beer and chilled wine to be delivered. An hour later we're still sitting at the table as the sun is setting. There's an empty bottle of wine on the table and an empty glass in front of each of us.

There's beer and more wine a short distance away in the cabana refrigerator. I don't ask the girls if they want anything because I'm afraid of what might happen if I try to stand. Abigail picks up on this.

"Do you want more wine?" she asks me.

"I'd love some, thank you," Natalie answers.

While Abigail makes her way to the cabana refrigerator, Natalie reaches under the table and rakes her fingernails up my thigh.

"Pot always makes me horny," she whispers. "Does it you?"

The mere sight of Natalie does it for me, but now is not the time to confess this to her. Abigail returns with a fresh bottle of wine and a corkscrew. Natalie's hand is resting high on my thigh beneath the glass table top. It's clearly visible to Abigail. She sets the wine and corkscrew on the table in front of Natalie.

"You do this part, Natalie. I don't think I can."

"I'm too stoned to even try. Dylan, you do it."

I make an attempt to uncork the wine, but fail miserably. The combination of wine and weed has me too messed up.

"You know what would help?" Natalie says. "A dip in the pool would sober us right up."

I know what her response will be before I say it. Shame on me. I say it anyway.

"We don't have swim suits."

"No we don't," is her predictable reply.

She begins shucking her clothes. Not to be outdone, Abigail begins undressing as well. I'm frozen in place, mesmerized by the sight of these two gorgeous females, as naked as the day they were born. They casually examine one another. Either admiring or comparing, I'm not sure which.

"Who did your boobs," Natalie asks Abigail.

"No one did. They're all mine."

"Really! They're almost perfect. My fiancé did mine."

"Nice job. I'd have sworn they were real."

"Dylan, are you just going to sit there and watch?" Natalie asks, as she and Abigail slip into the water.

I fully believe I would be content to spend the rest of my life doing just that.

~52~

You can't fake it when you're naked

I undress slowly and clumsily, because I'm shy and stoned. Abigail and Natalie are in the pool treading water and wolf-whistling each time an article of clothing hits the ground. With each stroke of their hands, they drift farther apart.

"Come here, Dylan," Natalie says.

"No, come to me, Dylan," Abigail says.

I don't want to be put in the position of choosing between them. Abigail and Natalie are both exceptionally beautiful girls. Both are fun to be with. I feel blessed to be with either one, much less both. Proper etiquette dictates that as an invited guest Abigail should get preferential treatment over Natalie, the drop-by guest. But I'm afraid primal urge is going to trump decorum in this case.

"Eeny, meeny, miny, moe," I begin.

"Quit being silly, Dylan."

I consider running and diving into the pool with my eyes shut, letting their sexual magnetism draw me toward one or the other. But in my current condition I'm liable to do a belly flop onto the concrete deck. The girls begin playing rock-paper-scissors to decide which one gets me. I could get a big head if I thought this was about me, but it's not. This is all about the thrill of competing with one another.

I go to a point at the side of the pool equidistant from each girl and jump in. The water is colder than I expected.

It takes my breath away. I break the surface and sling my hair back out of my face.

"You were right, Natalie," I say. "This is invigorating. I feel wide awake, now."

"Me, too," Abigail says, as she floats toward me.

Treading water in the middle of the pool, I rotate to face her. Her hands come out of the water and over my shoulders. Another pair of hands come from behind to cover my eyes.

"Guess who," Natalie says.

Three might be a crowd for some, but in this case it's a wet dream come true. Her hands come away from my eyes. I see Abigail's beautiful face sporting a mischievous grin. Then, the girls pull me under.

They let me up long enough to catch a breath, then I go under again. This goes on several more times. It's more fun for them than me, but not by much. Each time I surface they giggle and squeal. Each time I go under I use the opportunity to pinch and grope while I'm flailing away.

Finally, they pause. Together we float to the shallow end where our feet touch. We stand with our backs to the pool's edge. A phone sounds. Natalie recognizes the ringtone.

"Crap," she utters. "I have to get that."

She climbs the steps out of the pool. Abigail presses herself against me and tilts her head back, inviting me to kiss her. I do. In the background we can hear Natalie's side of her phone conversation.

"I'm with a client." Pause to listen. "It's no one you know." Pause. "I'm sorry, I lost track of the time." Pause. "I'm not sure how much longer I'll be." Pause. "I said I'm sorry." Pause. "Don't be that way." Pause. "Maybe we should cancel for tonight." Pause. "What?! You don't mean that. Richard! Hello! Richard!"

She disconnects, sits down at the table and begins to weep.

"Richard is her fiancé," I tell Abigail.

"Aww. You should go console her," she tells me.

I do as she suggests. Natalie is covering her face with her hands, sobbing away when I reach her. I kneel beside her and gently place my hand on her shoulder.

"Are you okay?"

A stupid question to ask someone who is visibly upset, isn't it?

"No, I'm not. Richard just dumped me."

"I'm so sorry, Nat," I say, but inside I'm calculating what Richard being out of her life means to me. "Is there anything I can do? Anything at all?"

"That's so sweet of you."

We embrace. I pat her back. She presses closer. I stop patting her back. I squeeze tighter. I feel another set of arms as Abigail joins our hugging party.

This goes on for a while, and as far as I'm concerned could go on much longer, except lights come on in the house.

"Someone's here," I say.

We separate and look at the house where more lights go on and people can be seen walking around.

"Let's get dressed," Natalie says. "I don't feel like putting on a show for anyone, right now."

I find some towels in the cabana. We dry off and redress ourselves. As soon as that's done a motion detector is tripped and the path leading from the veranda is lit. Truman appears.

"I thought that was you, Natalie. It looks like you all have been swimming."

"This is Abigail, Truman," I say.

"I remember her from the contest. Good to see you, again."

He glances from Abigail to Natalie to me. He's having trouble understanding what's going on. I am too.

"Who else is home?" I ask.

"Maddie is here with a guy she met. And Josh is here with a couple of new friends. We were talking about having Chinese delivered. Have you eaten, yet?"

"Actually, I'm starving," Abigail says.

"I could eat something," Natalie says.

"Alright, then. We'll order a variety of stuff and plenty for everyone. When it comes I'll spread it out on that big dining table so everyone can help themselves. I'll holler down at you when it gets here."

He starts toward the house. I catch up and walk with him until we're out of earshot of the girls.

"Did you get the guitar and amp?" I ask.

"Oh yeah. I already have it set up and ready to play."

"You do? How long have you been home?"

"We've been here for a couple of hours. We saw you down by the pool and we didn't want to disturb you. Then we saw the three of you in the pool, and we really didn't want to disturb you, then."

"Really? You saw us…,"

"Yes, I did. Dylan, my man, you have truly outdone yourself this time. I have never been more proud or humbled by you than I am at this moment. You are without a doubt my hero."

He continues on into the house, laughing as he goes. I return to the poolside. Abigail and Natalie are talking conspiratorially among themselves. They end their conversation as I approach.

"What was Truman laughing about?" Natalie asks.

"He saw us in the pool," I confess to her.

"Well that little peeping Tom pervert," she says, but not derisively. "What about the others? Have they all been watching us?"

That question is answered twenty minutes later when we go inside to eat. While we scoop our food out of to-go containers we're bombarded with comments about my white ass and the girls' absence of tan lines. Abigail and I take the ribbing in good humor. Natalie is still in a funk over Richard breaking it off. We take our food out onto the veranda.

"I've enjoyed being here with you and Abigail," Natalie tells me, as we eat. "You make a lovely couple. I hope I haven't spoiled your evening by showing up unannounced."

"You haven't spoiled anything," Abigail says. "Has she Dylan?"

"I wouldn't change a thing that's happened today," I say. "And as far as this evening is concerned, it's not over, yet. Stay as long as you like."

"Strange you should put it like that," Natalie says. "Because Abigail and I were talking earlier."

She glances at Abigail. A sly smile plays on her lips.

"Dylan," Abigail says. "I don't think Natalie should be alone tonight. Not after what happened with Richard."

"Oh," I say.

"And Abigail has too far to drive after the wine and weed," Natalie says. "She should stay, too."

"Oh," I say, again.

I know what the girls are hinting at. I'm not that stupid. I just don't know if I'm up to the challenge.

"There's plenty of room for everyone. We have three bedrooms that aren't being used."

They look at me, then at one another.

"Isn't he cute when he plays dumb, like that?" Natalie says to Abigail.

"Oh, yeah. Just adorable."

~53~

You just keep on using me until you use me up

There is no word in the English language to adequately describe that night with Abigail and Natalie. I won't even try. Fifty years from now I'll look back on it as the best night of my life by a wide margin, regardless of what happens between now and then. Of this I have no doubt.

We sleep in until late morning—if you can call it sleeping. We shower and dress. Then, I walk them to their cars with one arm around Natalie and the other around Abigail. I kiss Natalie goodbye. It's a long lingering kiss. Next, I kiss Abigail goodbye the same way. Then the girls kiss each other goodbye before getting into their cars and driving away.

I walk back in the house. Maddie is standing in the foyer with her arms crossed over her chest and a look of disapproval on her face. She's been watching us, I presume.

"What happened to the old Dylan Jones? The one I knew in Detroit. I liked him a lot better."

"If you liked me so much then, why'd you dump me?"

"I didn't dump you. We were meant to be friends, not lovers. That's all. Is that why you're acting this way?"

"Acting what way?"

"Making an ass of yourself with those girls. What are you trying to prove, Dylan?"

"Nothing. I'm not trying to prove anything. Where do you get off calling me an ass? You've done your fair share of misbehaving."

"You can't see it, can you? You're so naïve. Those girls are using you and you don't even know it."

"Why do you have to cut me down this way? What'd I ever do to you to deserve your criticism?"

A guy I don't know comes from the next room over and into the foyer where Maddie and I are having this discussion. It startles me. He's sort of rough looking. Mid-twenties, paunchy with a receding hairline and hasn't shaved for three days.

"Is everything alright?" he asks Maddie.

"Yes. We're just talking about last night."

She raises her eyebrows and emphasizes "last night", like it's something they've already discussed at length. The guy extends his hand to me.

"I'm Jimmy. You must be Dylan."

What'd I tell you? They've been talking about me.

"Nice meeting you, Jimmy."

"We're going down the street for a late breakfast," Jimmy says to me. "You want to come?"

He says it like we're buddies or soon could be. We can hang together sometimes. Jimmy, Abigail, Natalie and me. Maddie who?

"Thanks, I'll pass. Eat a burrito for me, Maddie. I'll see you kids later."

I go into the kitchen wishing I'd found time the day before to go shopping for groceries. A cup of coffee and a bagel with peanut butter would be great, right now. I open the refrigerator. Nothing but a bunch of to-go containers with Chinese food in them. I take one out and find a fork in a drawer.

"Yuck," I utter, after one bite.

Back in the refrigerator it goes. I go to a window overlooking the patio and look forlornly at the pool. Josh and two friends of his are lying on chaise lounges working on their tans.

Josh is here and Maddie has one of the Highlanders. Unless Truman has the other, I can use it to grocery shop. I start for the garage to see if the other vehicle is there. I'm halfway down the stairs to the garage when I hear the first few notes of Jimi Hendrix's rendition of the national anthem being struck on a Stratocaster guitar.

Upstairs I find Truman in the study picking the final note and letting it ring out while he jerks up on the tremolo bar. Fortunately for me, the volume on the amp is set below ear-bleed level. He's waited a long time to have his very own Stratocaster. It's a big moment in his life and I couldn't be happier for him.

"That is one beautiful guitar, Truman."

"And it sounds even better than it looks. Wouldn't you agree?"

"I would. It's undoubtedly the best I've ever heard."

"Undoubtedly, indeed."

"I'm going to the grocery store to pick up a few things. Do you want to come with me?"

"Sure, I'll come along with you. I can use a few things myself."

"You want to drive?" I ask, when we get to the garage.

"You go ahead."

I don't have a lot of driving experience and what I have took place in Detroit. LA is an entirely different story. Luckily there's a store a few blocks away. Truman is quiet on the drive there. Which isn't like him.

"Are you okay?" I ask.

"Yeah. I'm fine."

"Maddie was ticked off at me this morning. She unloaded on me not long after I got up."

"You know Maddie. She blows hot and cold. It won't last long. I think she's jealous."

"Jealous of Natalie and Abigail?"

"No jealous of you. You have good-looking girls chasing after you. She's hooking up with whoever will have her. Did you see the guy she brought home?"

"Yes. I met him."

"She dropped me at the music store yesterday and said she'd be back in ten minutes. When she comes back, Jimmy is with her. It's like she picked up the first guy she saw."

"I didn't plan the thing with Abigail and Natalie, yesterday. It just happened. And I sure didn't do it to make anyone jealous."

"I know that. I don't think it makes any difference to Maddie, though."

We reach the store, find a parking spot and get out. Truman is still not his usual self. I see several young girls going in and coming out of the store. Any other day his head would be pivoting left and right checking them out. Not today.

"Are you sure there's nothing bothering you. You're not upset with me over hooking up with Abigail and Natalie, are you?"

We're walking into the store. He stops dead in his tracks.

"Hell no, I'm not upset with you. I'm happy for you. I love to see you having fun. I think it's long overdue. I'll admit I'm envious. I wish I could have as much fun as you. But I'm not jealous and I'm sure not upset."

I understand now what's eating at Truman. Just because my love life has been on something of a roll recently, it doesn't mean I can't remember when it wasn't. A really cute girl in shorts and a tank top is in the produce department with a tomato in each hand comparing the two.

"Check it out," I say to Truman. "Nice set of tomatoes, aren't they?"

That kind of comment always used to crack him up, but not today.

"Yeah, nice."

He goes quiet again and I let him be, figuring he'll come out of it when he's ready. We continue through the store picking up the things on my list. Finally, he breaks the silence.

"Dylan, you're always honest with me, even when I don't want you to be. So tell me the truth. What's wrong with me?"

He doesn't have to explain. I've been there. Every guy has been. You hit a streak where no girl will give you the time of day. It will send your self-esteem into a downward spiral that you can't stop.

"There's nothing wrong with you, Truman. There's no rhyme or reason to why a girl chooses one guy over another. She'll talk a lot about what a guy looks like, his hair, smile, intellect or how much money he makes. In the end it's none of that. Instead it's an intangible no one can put their finger on that influences her decision."

"There you go again, Dylan. Saying something profound at the appropriate moment. Thank you, brother. I needed that."

"Any time, Truman. I'll always have your back."

~54~

And all I gotta do is act naturally

Sunday afternoon as Truman and I are putting the groceries away I receive a call from our agent.

"Dylan," she says. "It's Stella. I'm working on a TV deal for you guys. The producer wants to come by your place to get a feel for things."

"A TV deal. Really?" I say.

"Yes, really. I don't kid about things like that."

I know this to be true. Stella is all business, all the time. I don't think she's capable of telling a joke. I don't think she even has a sense of humor.

"What kind of TV deal? Are we talking about an appearance on a talk show or a sitcom?"

"No. It's something far bigger and better. A reality TV series. The sort of thing the Kardashians do. If the deal is struck, each of you will get about ten thousand an episode for the first season. If the show is a hit, there's no limit to what you can make."

Truman is catching my end of the conversation and eager to know what's going on. I raise a finger to hush him.

"When does the producer want to come by?"

"Late this afternoon or early evening, between six and nine."

I think about Josh and his friends, Maddie and Jimmie, Natalie and Abigail should they drop by.

"That doesn't give us much time to prepare. I'd hate to make a bad first impression with so much at stake."

"Dylan. You can tell me anything. Think of me the same as you would your doctor or your defense attorney. Everything stays between us. What is it you don't want the producer to see? Are you worried about dirty socks or drugs and booze?"

I'm uncertain about telling her everything, even with her assurance that I can. But I decide to trust her. It's worked well so far.

"At the moment Josh is down at the pool skinny dipping with his gay friends. Maddie is somewhere around here with a guy she just met, probably getting high. Truman is talking about cranking his amplifier all the way up and blowing the roof off. Both of my girlfriends might drop by to spend the night with me. Other than that, not much worries me."

"Do you watch reality TV?"

"Not really."

"You've just described a great episode on a hit show. If anything you might want to work on spicing it up some. Orgies and drunken brawls are big this year."

"I'm not sure how the others will feel about that," I say.

"Talk it over with them. Tell them I said this TV deal has unlimited potential. Let the producer look around the place. He might have some questions for you. You might have some for him. He'll get back to me in a few days. We'll see what he says and go from there."

"We might become TV stars," I tell Truman, after I disconnect. "Stella says we can make a lot of money."

"Nothing wrong with that."

"The TV show's producer is coming by in a few hours. We should tell Maddie and Josh."

Truman looks down at Josh and his friends in the pool.

"I'll tell Maddie if you tell Josh," he says.

"I'll send them both a text so we don't interrupt anything."

Later, while we're waiting around I call Isiah.

"Hello Dylan," he answers. "How's everything in LA?"

"Unreal is the only way to put it. We hired an agent to represent us and she has us hopping. We're renting this big house for the four of us. We just moved in, yesterday. And get this. We might be doing our own TV show."

"That's really good. I'm glad to hear things are going so well for you."

"How's everyone there?"

"We're getting by. They cut back my hours at work. Nikki is going to the community college this year to live at home and avoid the dorm expenses. She's not happy about it, but she'll be okay."

I'm embarrassed about gloating over my success after hearing things aren't going so well for Isiah, Chandra and Nikki.

"I can send some money to help out."

"Don't even think about that. We'll get by. Just have to tighten our belts some. That's all."

I should have known he'd be too proud to accept my help.

"You took care of me for all these years. I'd love to do something for you, if you'll let me."

"I said no, Dylan. That's the end of the discussion on the matter."

Now I've gone and angered him on top of insulting him.

"Say Dylan. Nikki is right here. She's anxious to speak to you. You take care of yourself. I'm handing the phone to her, now."

"Hey little brother. What's new in California?"

"Plenty."

I go on to tell her about the house, the TV show, my two girlfriends, the vehicles we're leasing and our agent.

"I wish I could be there. Detroit gets worse every day. Most of my friends—or those that matter—are away at college or married and moved out of town."

"Yeah, Isiah said you're going to the community college this year to save money. I told him I could send something to help out. He said no."

"Poppa doesn't accept charity. That won't ever change. It's good of you to offer, Dylan, but I'm not planning on going off to college even if we could afford it, right now. I'm ready to get out of this town. Maybe find a job in New York. I don't know, I'm just really bored, here."

Nikki seems to be fishing for an invitation and this might be an opportunity to leverage a favor out of her.

"Nikki. If you want to get out of Detroit, we're renting a big house here in LA. There's more than enough room."

"You mean it?"

"Yes, of course I do. I'll take care of your airfare and your expenses here in LA. Just tell me when you want to come."

"I'm so excited. This is exactly what I need. You are the best little brother in the whole world. I'm ready to leave tonight."

"You're not even packed, yet. How about if we set it up for Tuesday, two days from now?"

"I'll be ready. Oh, I am so excited. This is great."

"I'm looking forward to seeing you. I know Truman will be happy to see you, too."

"He will? I barely know Truman. Why would he be happy to see me?" she asks, warily.

"He's always had a crush on you. He's too shy to tell you himself."

"He can crush on me all he wants. That doesn't mean I'm going to feel anything for him. He's not my type."

The old Nikki has reared her prima donna head.

"I was hoping you might be nice to Truman. He's been feeling blue these last couple of days. Consider it a favor to me."

"I don't want him to start thinking I'm his girlfriend or anything like that. I don't need nobody calling me night and day, or following me around to see who I'm with when I'm not with him."

"It won't be like that with Truman. I promise. He's one of the nicest guys I know. Give him half a chance. Who knows, he might grow on you."

"Yeah. So will a fungus. I'll tell you what I'll do. As a favor to you, my little brother, I'll make nice with Truman. We can talk. As long as he doesn't try anything with me, we can be casual acquaintances. How's that?"

"It's a start. Thanks, Nikki. I really appreciate it. I'll go to work on your plane ticket right away."

"You're welcome, little brother. I'll see you Tuesday."

~55~

You gotta stomp, whistle and scream
You gotta wake right up in your dreams

Sunday evening the TV show producer, Alfred Lehman drops by to introduce himself and look things over. Alfred's an odd-looking man. Almost as big around as he is tall, unshaven, sloppily dressed and bald. He brought the director with him, Nancy Hodges. Nancy is a tall broad-shouldered woman who seems to always wear a stern expression.

We put on the dog for them the whole time they're here. Josh and his friends splash around in the pool wearing little or nothing. Maddie ditches Jimmy and picks up some other guy with a body full of tattoos and a thousand-yard stare. Truman plays guitar loud enough to rattle the windows. Abigail and Natalie come over to provide additional scenery.

Alfred and Nancy walk around looking bored. Every now and again, Alfred holds his hands out in front of him and forms a square with his thumbs and forefingers, like he's framing an imaginary scene. They don't say much as they're leaving.

Afterward, we're really bummed. We were all looking forward to being on TV. Our disappointment doesn't last long, though. Stella calls Monday morning with the news.

"Alfred Lehman likes what he saw," she tells me. "He wants to start filming in three days. His people will be in touch."

Even though things seem to be going our way, Truman is still down in the mouth. Nikki is due to arrive in LA on Tuesday. I'm really hoping she'll raise his spirits. I miss the Truman of old. The one who always could make light of a bad situation. I don't tell him she's coming until the morning of.

"You want to go to the airport with me to pick up Nikki?"

"Your sister, Nikki? Oh, I'm sorry. I forgot. She's not your sister."

"That's okay. She's been calling me little brother, lately. Things have improved between us. It started when we won the contest."

"And she's coming here to LA?"

"Yes. I invited her to stay with us. You don't mind, do you?"

"How do you think she's going to feel about the new you? The one who's driving all the girls in LA crazy."

"There have only been two by my count. But I think she'll be cool with whatever happens here. She seems genuinely happy for me. You too. She'll want to see as much of California as she can while she's here. Maybe you can help show her around. You'd be doing me a favor. I mean, I like Nikki, but I don't want to spend every spare minute I have with her."

"Of course you don't. That wouldn't leave you any time for Natalie, Abigail and whoever else is on your radar. I'll be glad to help you out because I wouldn't mind one bit spending time with Nikki."

I'll never get used to LA traffic, no matter how long I stay here. We leave from the house two hours ahead of Nikki's scheduled arrival at the airport. By the time we park and make it to baggage claim, Nikki is slouched in a chair looking small, like a child who wandered away from her parents and can't find her way back.

"Nikki," I call to her, as we approach. "I'm sorry we're late. You wouldn't believe the traffic in this city."

She throws her arms around me and squeezes me tight. She's trembling and on the verge of tears.

"I thought you'd forgotten about me. There are so many people in this airport and they're all running around like the place in on fire."

"We're here now. Don't worry. We're going to watch out for you while you're here in LA. Isiah and Chandra would never forgive me if I let something happen to you."

I ease out of her grip and attempt to gently steer her toward Truman. She resists. I push harder.

"You remember Truman," I say.

"Good to see you again, Nikki," he says. "I really like what you've done with your hair."

She has a pixie cut with swooping bangs partially covering one eye.

"Thank you."

Her resistance wanes, slightly. Truman spreads his arms, inviting her to embrace him. She takes itty-bitty baby steps toward him. It would help if she'd lose the grimace, but that probably won't happen.

Finally, Truman takes a step in her direction to close the gap. He wraps her in a bear hug. Her arms are trapped between her boobs and his chest. She squirms and wiggles, and manages to free herself.

"It's good to see you too, Truman," she says.

"Come on, Nikki. Let's go to the house. You're going to love it."

I grab one of her bags, Truman gets the other two and we head for the exit. Nikki is wearing a waist-length faux leather jacket and slacks. It's thirty-five degrees warmer here, than it was when she left Detroit.

"Wait a minute," she says, as soon as we're outside. "I need to take this jacket off."

No one can turn heads like Nikki when she wants to. And she usually wants to. She unzips and slips out of the jacket as smoothly as a runway model. Underneath is a form-fitting tube top, off the shoulders and cropped above her navel. Which is sporting a gold hoop matching the ones dangling from her ears.

Truman drops her bags. Wolf-whistles come from the direction of the taxis lined up along the curb. Nikki smiles and strikes a pose. I worry jets are going to come crashing down because the pilots are distracted by her.

"Come on, Nikki. We don't have time for this, now."

"Oh alright, Dylan."

She smiles and waves to her admirers. Truman picks up her bags. We make our way to short-term parking where the Highlander is.

~56~

Everybody just have a good time

The filming of our reality TV show begins. I don't know who is more excited about it. Maddie, Josh, Truman and me or our growing group of friends and hangers-on. There are so many people coming and going as the filming progresses, I stick a sign on our front door that reads, 'It's open, come in'.

I knew in advance the filming process would be intrusive, but I didn't know how bad it would get. Our house has nine bathrooms. It seems like every time I need to use one it's occupied. It would be one thing if they were being used for the intended purpose, but they're not. People lock themselves inside the bathrooms so they're not interrupted or filmed while they're doing drugs, conversing on their phone or who knows what else.

After waiting almost an hour for a bathroom to become available, I have to go so bad I forget to lock the door. I no sooner drop my pants and sit down on the toilet when the door flies open and a cameraman barges in.

"Whoa, dude. A little privacy, please," I say.

Everything filmed is supposed to be impromptu. Like the cameraman just happens to be at the right place at the right time to capture a significant moment. The truth is most of it is scripted by Alfred with input from Stella or the director, Nancy Hodges. And none of it is very significant.

The show will appeal to a wide audience due to the diversity of our little group. That's according to Alfred. We represent youth, gay, female, black and white. The scripts are written with that in mind. Here's a sampling from some of the episodes.

Josh is sitting on the couch watching a big screen TV. A flaming gay guy steps between Josh and the TV. He holds out a phone which supposedly belongs to Josh.

He shouts at Josh, "Who the (bleep) is Ryan?"

Josh says, "He's nobody important. Just a friend."

Flaming replies, "You better not be (bleep)ing around on me."

Josh says, "I would never cheat on you, Lenny. You know that, don't you? Come here. Sit down beside me."

Josh pats the couch. Lenny sits. They kiss. On to the next scene.

In another, a yoga instructor comes to the house to conduct a class for Nikki, Abigail and Natalie. Any one of them could be a finalist for Miss Universe. The sight of the three of them stretching in spandex and twisting around like pretzels should send the ratings through the roof.

Ha Yoon Ghim comes to our house in one episode, ostensibly to discuss the recording of our song. The recording has been completed prior to the filming, but TV viewers won't know that. Stella wants the first airing of the TV show to coincide with the release of 'Love Transcends'.

Reading from the teleprompter, I say to Ha, "We'd love to hear what it sounds like so far."

Her translator relays the request and Ha begins to sing in English. We've already heard the final recording. With the full orchestration accompanying her vocals it could be the soundtrack for a movie about heaven. I'm thinking there's no way she can achieve anything close to that singing a cappella. I'm wrong.

The instrumentation on the recording enhances the overall effect, but at the same time, it masks the delicate nuances of Ha's angelic voice. She starts out singing the verse soft and melodic. Then the volume and intensity build going into the chorus. If we had any fine glassware it would be shattered into small bits by her high notes.

I'm standing and applauding before I realize it.

"That was incredible," I tell her.

Apparently, incredible is one of the few words of English she comprehends.

She smiles at me and says, "Thank you."

We do a lot of scenes depicting us during our down time. There's Josh and his gay entourage prancing around the pool in Speedos. Maddie getting a tattoo on her ass. Truman playing his Stratocaster for a live audience of zombies. Abigail kissing Natalie. Natalie kissing me. Me kissing Abigail. Nikki being Nikki posing for the cameras in every outfit she owns. And those are just the highlights.

At the end of the first few days with three cameramen filming during the daytime and unmanned cameras mounted on the ceiling filming at night, they have more than two hundred hours of uncut footage. I only saw a small portion of it being filmed. Much of it I'll view for the first time when our television audience does.

"Did you tell poppa about this TV show?" Nikki asks me, a few days into the filming.

"I think I mentioned something about it to him. Why do you ask?"

"Some of the stuff is kind of racy for primetime. I don't know how he and momma will feel about it."

"I think Isiah and Chandra are open-minded people. They'll understand this is how I make a living."

"They might understand when it comes to you. When it comes to their little girl, that's another matter."

"What specifically are you worried about them seeing?"

"I might have been caught using profanity."

I've heard Isiah use language which could singe my ears when he's out of earshot of Nikki and Chandra.

"Don't worry. They'll bleep that stuff."

~57~

Where are the clowns, there ought to be clowns

The road to success for Truman, Maddie, Josh and me is paved with BS and hyperbole. I'm not complaining. Just stating a fact. Less than a month ago, we were completely unknown to anyone outside of our own homes. With the simultaneous release of 'Love Transcends' and our reality TV show our celebrity status skyrockets.

Last night I celebrated. Along with Truman, Maddie, Josh, Nikki, Abigail, Natalie and thirty uninvited guests. I'm trying to sleep it off when my phone sounds a distinctive ringtone at eight this morning. It's Stella calling. I put it on speakerphone and listen.

"I don't want to burst your bubble, but in this town you can be forgotten as quickly as you became famous," Stella tells me. "Now is not the time to sit back and enjoy your time in the spotlight. You can do that when you're old and decrepit."

"Have you considered beginning with an anecdote?" I say. "You know. Something to lighten the mood before delivering bad news."

"I'm serious, Dylan."

"You always are, Stella. Why is that?"

"I'm serious because that's who I am. I'm your agent, not your buddy. If you want funny, rent a clown. Have you and the others begun working on your next song?"

"We haven't even thought about it. Where would we find the time?"

"You make time. Otherwise this will all be over before you know it."

"Do you have any good news to share with me before I hang up?"

"Yes, as a matter of fact, I do. 'Love Transcends' just topped ten million sold and it's still climbing."

I'm speechless.

"You're welcome," Stella says. "Now get your ass out of bed and go to work writing another hit."

She disconnects. I crawl back under the sheets to spoon with Abigail. It's just the two of us. Natalie is attempting to reconcile with Richard for the time being. Abigail rolls over to face me.

"That was our agent," I explain.

"So I gathered. Will you be starting work on another song?"

I've been asking myself that same question since we arrived in LA. It remains unanswered.

"To hear Stella tell it, we are."

"Hmm," she utters, as if considering something.

"What?"

"I've been thinking about something. An idea I've been kicking around. I want to run it by you."

"Alright, shoot."

"What if you and I did a collaboration?"

"I thought we collaborated pretty well, last night," I say, as I attempt to nuzzle her neck.

She shoves me away.

"You know what I mean. I'm a good songwriter. You could do a lot worse. Think of it. Written by Dylan Jones and Abigail Collier. Don't you like the sound of that?"

"Uh…, yeah. It has a nice ring, but I'm kind of committed to the others, right now."

"That doesn't have to change. You can do both. In fact, I'll do most of the work on our song. You contribute what you can, when you can. Your name and celebrity status will be enough in itself to guarantee its success."

Her blues eyes grow wider with excitement as she attempts to sell me on the idea. I have ideas of my own that don't involve songwriting.

"What do you think?" she asks.

"I think you're beautiful."

"Would you be serious for a second? Do you want to collaborate on a song or not?"

"Honestly, I don't think I can find the time."

"While you're doing whatever else, you can think of our song. It can be like background music. You go over the ideas in your head. Now and then you write the lyrics down. At night when we're together we collaborate on our song during our playtime. How does that sound?"

"Like an unnecessary distraction," I say.

"What?!"

"The song collaboration part, I mean. It would distract us while we're…, uh…, you know."

"Dylan, my songwriting is more important to me than anything else. It comes first. Eating, breathing and loving are after that. Sex is further down the line. I thought you felt the same."

I don't want to tell her how I really feel. That sex is equally as important to me as songwriting. That if I had to choose between them, songwriting would have to go by the wayside.

"Our playtime, as you call it, is just that. Recreational. A break from work. Songwriting is work. It's what we do for a living," I say.

She refuses to give up on the idea.

"When you and the others were writing 'Love Transcends', did you have fun? Did you cut up and joke around? Or was it strictly business?"

"We did both. We joked around sometimes and sometimes we got down to business, but it was only productive when we were serious."

"I don't believe that."

"It's true," I say.

"When I write it's so much fun I don't want to do anything else. I start with one line that I really like and build off of that. How do you do it? When you wrote 'Love Transcends', what method did you use?"

"We didn't know a thing about writing a song, starting out. It didn't go well. We might not have made the contest deadline if we hadn't caught a lucky break."

"What was the lucky break?"

"This is going to sound weird, but my mother who died fifteen years ago brought me the song. I had a dream she appeared in. She sang the song to me. The next day I wrote it down as I remembered it."

"You're right. That does sound weird. You dreamed a song, woke up and wrote it down. I'm having trouble believing that really happened."

"You're calling me a liar?"

"That's a little strong. I'm saying you're leaving out something."

"No, I'm not. I told you pretty much everything."

"Pretty much?" she echoes.

She slides closer and nibbles at my earlobe.

"What are you not telling me, Dylan?"

"Nothing. I've told you everything."

She drags her fingernails across my chest and slowly migrates south.

"Are you sure?" she asks.

I'm putty in her hands. She'll get it out of me sooner or later, anyway.

"There is one thing I left out. My mother wrote a song a lot like ours years ago. I'm told she sang it to me when I was a baby."

Abigail pulls away from me.

"It's not an original song?"

"Not completely, but what song is. Every song starts with something you've heard before. Ours is no different. I probably remember parts of what my mother sang when I was a baby. We took the idea and arranged it into what it is now."

She gets out of bed, picks her clothes off the floor and goes into the bathroom. I hear the water running and the toilet flush. After a few minutes she comes out dressed to leave.

"Did I say something wrong?" I ask.

She seems flustered and unable to look at me.

"No. I mean, I don't know. I have to go. I didn't realize it was so late."

"Will you come back tonight?"

"I can't tonight. There's a coffee bar and brew pub in Long Beach. They have open mike tonight. I like to test my songs on a live audience. I'd ask you to come, but it's not really your kind of place."

"That's cool. Maybe I'll see you tomorrow, then."

"Yeah, maybe. Don't get up. I'll let myself out."

I watch her walk out feeling like something significant occurred just now. But for the life of me, I can't put my finger on it.

~58~

When the moon is in the seventh house,
and Jupiter aligns with Mars

I don't put much stock in astrology and horoscopes. It's highly unlikely the position of the stars in relation to earth has any bearing on what happens to us on a particular day. What's the upside to knowing what the future holds for us, anyway? I'm not troubled by the possibility nothing in our lives is predictable. This might sound like a cliché, but stuff happens.

I'm good with that. I prefer random. I'd choose it over meticulously planned and structured every time. It's like having Christmas every day of the year and getting up each morning to see what's waiting for you under the tree.

That pretty much describes my approach to songwriting. The ideas for the melodies and lyrics should appear as if they simply dropped out of the sky like a meteorite. No formula. No outline. No predetermined direction. Just random ideas coming at me in no particular order or sequence.

After the call from Stella early this morning, I had every intention of speaking to Truman, Josh and Maddie about working on another song. Truman went shopping with Nikki. Josh and Maddie went somewhere before that. I haven't seen a one of them since. And the text messages I've sent haven't been answered. Stella calls again at 5:00 PM.

"How's the songwriting coming along?"

"Nothing's come to me, yet," I say.

"What? You're having it delivered? What does that mean, nothing's come to you, yet?"

I could try to explain the creative process as I see it, but Stella is more of a talker than a listener.

"Josh, Maddie and Truman have been gone all day. We haven't had a chance to put our heads together."

"When do you think that will occur? Tonight sometime?"

"I hope so, but I can't say for sure."

"I don't mean to be pushy…,"

"Really? You could have fooled me."

"Look, smart-ass. I'm working my butt off for you. I already have three record producers bidding on your next song. How long do you think they'll stick around if I tell them you're waiting for a song to magically pop into your head? About two seconds. That's how long."

"Wow! There are three producers who want a song from us? That's terrific. I can't wait to tell the others."

"Don't wait to tell them. Do it now. They need to learn how this business works. You should be spending sixteen hours a day, seven days a week working, right now. Take time off when nobody wants you anymore."

I leave a second text message for Truman, Josh and Maddie. There's no immediate response. I do the only thing I know to do and begin the process of writing a song all by myself.

The first step is to find some place where the noise of the traffic on Sunset Boulevard and jets overhead is muffled sufficiently. Somewhere I can tune out the world and open up my sensory receptors. Switch my brain over from transmit to receive. Silence the ringtone on my phone.

I go to my room, shut and lock the door, lie on my back in the bed and place a pillow over my face. It's not perfect, but it's quieter. I relax my muscles until they slowly unwind and tension I didn't even know was there begins to ease. I haven't slept more than a few hours a night over the past several days. It's catching up with me.

I try to meditate by imagining my inner self leaving my body and floating away. It ascends upward into the sky. Nothing but blue sky and puffy white clouds all around me. I rise higher. The blue sky turns darker. The earth is a thousand miles below. Above the stars twinkle so brightly I feel like I could reach out and touch them.

Suddenly the stars and the earth disappear. I'm immersed in total darkness. I'm falling asleep and unable to stop myself. Images come at me out of the darkness. Abigail, Nikki, Truman, Natalie, Maddie, Josh, Stella, Isiah and Chandra. They fade away and other images appear.

"Hi Dylan," my mother says. "I brought someone to see you."

"Hi son," my father says. "You're a young man, now. I'm so proud of you. I'm sorry we couldn't stick around to watch you grow up."

"Me too," I say. "But I understand. I know it wasn't your fault. Mom. I entered your song in a contest."

"I know. I gave it to you for that reason."

"We know all about what goes on in your life," my dad explains. "We see it through your eyes. We're right here." I feel his hand touch my heart. "That's where we exist."

"You know all about us winning the contest and everything that's happened since?" I ask.

"Yes, Dylan. Everything you know, we know. Everything you see, we see. Everything you feel, we feel. That's the best I can explain it."

It's reassuring to know my parents are always there for me. At the same time it's a little unsettling to realize they've been watching while I'm doing what I do with Abigail and Natalie.

"I don't really understand how this works, but I'm glad you're here," I tell them. "Even if it's only in spirit."

"I'm afraid we don't understand it any better than you do, Dylan. Take care of yourself, son."

His image starts to fade.

"Goodbye, Dad," I say.

I can't stop the tears. They trickle down my face. I feel my mother's warm embrace as she pulls me to her bosom.

"There's no need to be sad, Dylan. Your father is still here. So am I. And we'll always be here if you need us."

"That's why you came. You somehow realized I needed help. It's true. I'm being pressured by people to write another song and I don't think I can. I don't know where to start."

"Don't give in to the pressure, Dylan. It impedes your creativity. Relax and let it flow from your mind to your mouth. Then simply sing what you're feeling."

"It sounds so easy when you say it, but it's not working for me. Can you give me something to help me get started?"

"You don't need my help with that, Dylan. You were born a songwriter. It's in your DNA. All you have to do is trust yourself. The words and music will come to you, the same way I come to you. It's all right there inside you. Just let it out."

There's loud knocking on my door. My mother is gone. From the other side of the door comes Maddie's voice.

"Dylan! Are you alright?"

I remove the pillow. It's dark outside.

"Hang on. I'm coming," I shout back.

I unlock and open the door.

"I've been texting and calling you for the last hour. Why didn't you reply? I thought something happened to you."

I explain everything. How Stella wants us to write another song. How I couldn't get in touch with her, Josh or

Truman. How I tried to work on the song myself. Why I silenced my phone and how I fell asleep.

"Is anyone else here?" I ask.

"Just Larry."

"Who's Larry?"

"A guy I met."

"What about Truman and Josh?"

"I don't know where they are. Check your phone. Maybe they've been calling you while it's been off."

I do and they have. Truman and Nikki will be here after dinner. Josh says he'll be here sometime later.

"Stella is really putting the pressure on us to start writing songs," I say to Maddie.

"What have you got so far?"

"Nothing really. I'm hoping something will come to me, soon."

"Let's get together then. Set a time. I'll be there. I can text Josh and Truman to let them know."

"Let's do it tomorrow at one. There's something I want to do first thing in the morning."

~59~

Son can you play me a memory,
I'm not really sure how it goes

Being famous affords me certain privileges a regular Joe only dreams about. Having plenty of money to spread around doesn't hurt, either. I arrange to rent a Steinway grand piano and have it delivered to the house on Sunset Boulevard at eleven in the morning. Three burly guys wrestle it up the front steps and haul it into the house.

"Put it in this room," I tell them.

Josh, Maddie and Truman hear the ruckus and come to investigate.

"What do you think?" I ask.

"It's a beautiful piano," Maddie says. "Who's it for?"

"I thought we could use it to write songs with."

"None of us play," Josh says.

The piano movers have stopped to rest. They're panting and sweating from the effort involved in unloading the heavy beast. They cock an ear upon hearing the piano is nothing more than expensive décor to us.

"I can play some," Maddie says. "Not well, but I had a toy piano when I was a kid."

"And I know the notes on the keyboard," I say.

We move aside so the workers can set the piano up and fine-tune it.

"Aside from Truman's guitar, we don't have anything to create a melody with," I say. "Once you hear how big and full the notes sound on this grand piano, I think you'll agree it's perfect for our purposes."

"Well, I can't wait to hear it," Truman says. "I'll see everyone at one."

My phone sounds. It's Stella.

"Good morning, Dylan. I'm going to start the conversation on a brighter note, today. As of midnight, California time, 'Love Transcends' has sold thirty million downloadable copies worldwide."

I'm completely blown away. I can't wait to tell the others at the beginning of our one o'clock session.

"Also, I'm happy to report the TV show is a huge success. Alfred Lehman wants to begin filming for the second season as soon as possible."

"He does? When is that going to take place?"

"Probably not for another week or so. We're still in negotiations. You guys are going to get a lot more per episode this time around. The show is so popular with the younger crowd, I had to hire another person to handle your social media activity."

"More money is always good."

"You bet your ass it is. I have so many requests for personal appearances, I could book you every day of the week for the next year. I'm holding off on that until you finish the next song. Is there any progress to report on that front?"

"Yes, as a matter of fact, there is. There is a grand piano being readied for our session as we speak. We're all anxious to get started."

"Super. I won't bother you anymore today. I'll check back with you tomorrow. Keep up the good work."

"You keep up the good work, Stella. You're making superstars out of us. This is above and beyond my wildest dreams."

The piano guys finish with the Steinway. They gather up the moving pads, straps and dolly to leave. Before the last one out can shut the door, some girl runs in and starts snapping pictures. Paparazzi, I'm guessing. I have to be careful how I handle this.

"Can I help you?" I politely ask.

She evidently hadn't noticed me standing here before now.

"Omigod! It's you. I can't believe it. Dylan, omigod. I'm a huge fan. I didn't realize anyone was here. The tour guide said this is where the show is filmed. Are we on camera?"

She rotates three hundred sixty degrees, looking high and low.

"We're not filming today," I assure her.

"Oh darn," she replies. "That would have been so cool."

She's standing at the edge of the foyer, showing no inclination to turn around and leave. I'm between her and the rest of the home's interior wishing she would go. She looks up. I follow her line of sight.

It's an old trick. I shouldn't have fallen for it. She attempts to ease around me. I reach out to block her. She takes my hand in both of hers.

"Sorry," she says. "I'm Bridget."

"Dylan," I say.

She giggles and says, "I know."

I retrieve my hand from her grip.

"Bridget, I'm really busy, right now…,"

"Don't worry. I won't say anything. You won't even know I'm here."

She does that thing where she pretends to zip her mouth shut.

"I'm pretty sure I'll know you're here."

She sees something behind me. I'm not falling for that one, again.

"Omigod! It's her. Maddie!" she shouts.

Got me. I turn to look and she darts around me. Maddie watches Bridget running toward her and quickly sizes up the situation.

"I'm a huge fan," she says to Maddie.

"I'm so glad to hear that, but this is a private residence. We're not open to the general public."

She takes Bridget by the arm, guides her to the door, shoves her out and slams the door behind her.

"Why'd you let her in?" Maddie asks me.

"I didn't. She snuck past the piano guys as they were leaving. We might need to hire a private security company to watch this place. It's probably going to get worse around here. I just got off the phone with Stella. 'Love Transcends' has sold thirty million copies and our TV show is a hit."

"Have you told Truman and Josh?"

"No. I figure I'll tell them at our one o'clock session."

The doorbell chimes.

"It's probably Bridget, again," I say. "I'll get rid of her."

"Are you sure you can handle her? I'd better come with you, in case she slips past you, again."

I glance through the peephole before opening the door. It isn't Bridget. It's a middle-aged man holding a manila envelope.

"Who is it?" I yell loud enough to be heard.

"Special courier service," he shouts back.

"Be careful," Maddie whispers. "It might be a trick."

I crack the door open an inch.

"I have a special delivery for Dylan Jones, Josh Martinez, Truman Dixon and Madeline Lee. It requires a signature."

"Who's it from?" I ask warily.

"It says 'S O T Y'."

I open the door wider. He holds out a pad for me to electronically sign my name on. Then gives me a sealed package and leaves. Inside the package is a letter from the Songwriter of the Year contest organizers. Maddie looks over my shoulder as I read it.

"This can't be happening," I say. "Not now. Not when everything is going our way. They're reviewing the decision to name us as the winner. They might strip us of our title if they determine we did something wrong."

"Wrong? We didn't do anything wrong."

"Not that we know of."

"It must be some kind of mistake. Why would they do that? Omigod! Does this mean we might have to give back the money?"

"I don't know. This is too much to try and process. They want to meet with us Friday morning at nine. I guess we'll find out then."

Part III

~60~

All the time they want to take your place, the back-stabbers

Speculation feeds on itself. Guessing why the SOTY organization wants to review our win invites more questions than it answers. And each question requires further speculation. See what I mean? I feel like a dog chasing its tail. I'm running in circles and not getting anywhere.

At one o'clock, when we gather around the piano to begin working on our next song, I tell Josh and Truman about the letter from SOTY.

"They're not taking my Stratocaster," Truman says. "They can take everything else, but I'm keeping my guitar."

"What about the amplifier?" Josh asks.

"I'm keeping that too. They can't have it either."

"I've spent all the money from the contest," Maddie says. "There's nothing left to give back."

"Same here," Josh says. "What about you, Dylan?"

"I have some money left. Worst case scenario, if they want the hundred grand back, we can probably pay them from what me make on song sales, personal appearances and the TV show. I don't think paying them back is the worst problem we'll have if our song is disqualified."

"What else are you worried about?" Truman asks.

"Winning the contest was the beginning of everything. Losing it after the fact might start everything unraveling."

"Maybe we should hire an attorney to sue SOTY," Maddie says.

"It's too early to think about that," I say. "We just received the letter an hour ago. Until we meet with them on Friday, we still don't know what this is all about."

"Are we going to work on the new song?" Maddie asks. "Because if we are I don't think I'm going to be much help."

"Me either," Josh says.

"I'm sure Stella wants us to, but I can't concentrate, right now," I say.

At that same moment my phone sounds.

"Speaking of," I say. "That's her now."

"Your ears must be burning. We were just talking about you. If you're calling to see how the songwriting is going, we're just starting."

"You are? After what happened?" she asks.

"Are you talking about the SOTY thing?"

"Of course I am. Is there something else?"

"We just heard about it. A special courier delivered a letter about an hour ago. We have a meeting with SOTY on Friday. They plan to review our winning song. That's pretty much all the letter said. Where'd you find out about it? Did you get a letter, too?"

"The online news services have picked it up. It's all over the internet. They're saying the contest people disqualified you."

"We haven't been told that, yet. Do any of these news services give the reason we've been disqualified?"

"Most of what I've read is vague about that. One article implies the song was written by someone else. There's no truth to that, is there?"

"None," I say.

She's not convinced. I can't blame her. I'm not either.

"Hey, if there's something I should know, now's the time. I need to begin damage control. It helps to know what I'm trying to keep out of the news or what I need to spin should it become news."

Truman, Josh and Maddie are listening closely to my side of the conversation. I don't want to say anything that might jeopardize our futures. But I hate to leave Stella in the dark.

"The four of us wrote the song a few months ago. That's the truth. We used an idea my mother came up with to help us get started."

"What was the idea? Are we talking about a line in the lyrics or what?"

"Some of the lyrics and some of the melody," I say.

"Hmm," she utters. "Who all knows this?"

"The four of us and my family."

I glance at the others not knowing what if anything they've said to anyone outside our circle.

"Maybe a couple of other people. I'm not sure."

"Let's assume for the moment, this is what the contest people are concerned with. I'm going to do a little research on the subject. I'll call back after I've looked into it further."

She disconnects.

"What did she say?" Truman asks me.

"It's going around the internet that we might have the SOTY award taken away from us. As least one article implies we didn't write the song."

"Is someone out there saying they wrote it for us?" Truman asks, next.

"Not that I know of. I'm only telling you what Stella told me. I guess it's possible it got out that we had my mother's help with it."

Truman gives Josh a hard stare.

"Don't look at me. I didn't say anything to anyone," Josh says.

"You're sure?" Truman asks.

"Positive. I know I made a comment about telling the contest people, but I was bluffing. I'd never do something like that."

Truman turns his stare on Maddie.

"Don't even ask," she warns him.

"I damn sure haven't told anyone," Truman states.

All eyes turn to me.

"What?" I ask. "You think I'm the leak?"

"Dylan," Maddie says. "You haven't had a lot of experience with girls. You can be pretty naïve and easily manipulated."

She should know. She has first-hand knowledge of how easily I can be manipulated.

"Is it possible you said something you shouldn't have in a moment of weakness? As in *pillow talk*."

"Not that I recall."

The hard cold glare says she doesn't believe me.

"Listen everyone," I say. "It's not helpful to try and put the blame on someone. Especially since we don't know for sure what it is SOTY is bothered about."

"What did you say and who'd you say it to?" Maddie asks.

"I might have mentioned something to Abigail," I say. "We were talking about our songwriting methods and how we come up with the ideas. I told her my mother wrote a song similar to ours."

I can feel their disappointment as much as I can see it.

"Dylan. She lost to us in the contest," Josh reminds me. "She has more to gain than anyone else by getting us eliminated."

It wouldn't be the first time I misread someone and paid a price for doing so. That doesn't make it hurt any less.

"Abigail wouldn't do that," I say, but in truth, I don't really know what she's capable of doing.

"Why don't you call her?" Truman says.

"Abigail?" I ask.

"Yes Abigail. Who have we been talking about? Call her up. Make small talk. Tell her you've been thinking about her. Ask her what she's been doing. See if you can get a feel for what she's thinking. Maybe she'll drop a hint that she said something to the contest people."

"Okay, I can do that."

I punch in her number.

"Hi," she answers in a flat tone.

Not good. I try to sound upbeat.

"I've been thinking about you. How have you been?"

"Fine. You?"

"I'm doing okay. You want to come over tonight?"

"I can't. I'm busy."

"Some other night, then," I say.

No reply.

"The strangest thing happened," I say. "We have to meet with the SOTY people tomorrow about something."

"I know."

"Where'd you hear about it? Did you see it online?"

"No. Listen, I can't talk right now. I have to go."

"Abigail, wait. What's your rush? I don't understand what's going on with you. Why are you being so cold? Don't you like me anymore?"

"I can't see you anymore, Dylan. It's over between us. After you told me you didn't write the song everything changed. I lost all respect for you. I'll see you at the SOTY office on Friday. I filed a complaint with them to have 'Love Transcends' disqualified. I have to be there to testify against you and the others."

"I can't believe I'm hearing this. I don't know what to say."

"There's nothing you can say that will make any difference, anyway. Goodbye, Dylan."

~61~

'Cause I can't make you love me if you don't

I lie awake most of the night thinking about Abigail. I'm a lousy judge of people. I've always been. So it shouldn't be difficult to believe she'd do something like this. But it is.

Sleeping with Abigail and Natalie was kind of wild and crazy. It's one of those things I'll look back on when I'm older and think what a great experience it was. It was special, but temporary. Not something I could fall into a routine of doing every night.

Sleeping with Abigail alone, just me and her, felt more permanent. I could see myself spending a lot of time with her. That's the part I can't get past. How can I feel so strongly about a person who apparently feels nothing for me?

At 6:00 AM I give up on trying to sleep. I put on my robe and go downstairs to the kitchen to start coffee brewing. The house is dark and quiet. No one stirs. As I walk through the huge rooms it feels more like a graveyard than a residence.

While the coffee brews I sit on a barstool at the kitchen island. My thoughts are jumbled up inside my head bouncing off one another. If you could view my mind by peering through my ear canal, it would look like an image inside a kaleidoscope.

I hear flip-flops slapping on the tile floor coming closer. It's Nikki. She's in her robe, her hair is in tangles and her eyes are half shut. She pulls out the barstool next to mine and sits.

"Are you alright, little brother?"

"As good as can be expected, I guess."

"I worry about you."

"Thanks, but it isn't necessary. We'll be okay. Even if our song gets eliminated, we'll still have the income from the TV show and the recording of the song."

"That's not what I'm talking about. You're a kind-hearted soul. You see the good in people, and that's a fine quality. With some folks, I think you overlook their dark side sometimes."

"You're talking about Abigail, I take it."

"She's the latest, but she's not the first. You remember that boy who moved in down the street from us when you were nine? His name was Brady or Brodie, I think."

"Brandon. Yeah, I remember him. We were buds."

"He stole your basketball and you weren't going to do anything about it. I went to his house, took it away from him and brought it back to you. Do you remember that?"

"I do. You kicked his ass. He told his mom. Chandra made you apologize to him."

"That's beside the point. You thought he was your friend, but he didn't think of you as a friend. People don't steal from their friends."

"It wasn't a big deal. I never liked basketball that much. He did."

"How do you feel about winning the songwriting contest and getting one hundred thousand dollars? Are you going to tell me you don't like it, but Abigail does?"

"Apples and oranges, Nikki. Two completely different things."

"Not really. You may be older and more streetwise, now, but inside you're still that same kind-hearted little boy who thought Brandon deserved the basketball more than you."

I think about Nikki's words. She's tougher than me in many ways. She always has been. Willing to stick up for herself. To fight if need be. I'm the go along to get along sort. I hate confrontation.

I haven't thought about Brandon in years, or about Nikki intervening on my behalf. I didn't choose her as a sister and she didn't choose me as her brother. Nevertheless, here we are.

"I love you, Nikki."

"Ditto, little brother."

The sound of footfalls behind us draws our attention. Truman enters the kitchen wearing a robe over silk pajamas. His Hugh Hefner look.

"I thought I smelled coffee," he says.

"Help yourself. I just brewed it."

He takes three mugs from the cupboard, pours them full of steaming coffee and brings them over.

"What were you two talking about? And why'd you go all quiet when I came in here? Were you saying stuff about me?"

"Your name never came up," I say.

"That's true, Truman. We were talking about a kid who lived down the street from us when we were kids," Nikki says.

"Oh, yeah?"

Truman gives her a skeptical look over the rim of his mug as he raises it to his lips. Nikki explains further.

"Dylan thought he was a friend, but he wasn't."

"Oh, I get it now. You were talking about this kid down the street, but what you were really talking about is Abigail. Have I got that right?"

"Close enough," I say.

"Dylan, I love you like a brother. You know that. But there are a lot of people like Abigail and that kid down the street. People who will take advantage of you if you let them."

"That's exactly what I told him," Nikki says.

"I appreciate your concern, both of you. I do. I'm touched that you care about me. But I am who I am. I don't want to become some cold-hearted unfeeling narcissistic guy. It wouldn't be me."

More footfalls and Maddie appears dressed in a robe, the same as the rest of us.

"Have a seat Maddie," Truman offers. "I'll pour you some coffee."

He pulls a stool out and she plops down.

"What's everyone doing up so early?" she asks.

"I couldn't sleep," I say. "I can't speak for Nikki and Truman."

"I smelled coffee," Truman says. "That got me going."

"I heard Dylan get up and I thought I'd come spend some quality time with my little brother," Nikki says.

"What have you guys been talking about?"

"Oh, you know. This and that," Nikki tells her.

"Did Abigail come up in the conversation?"

"Mm-hmm."

"I hope you've learned your lesson this time, Dylan," Maddie says.

"I hope so too," I say.

More footfalls and Josh comes into the kitchen.

"What were you guys talking about?" he asks.

"Crap. Not another one," I mutter under my breath.

~62~

Everybody knows that smoking ain't allowed in school

The four of us ride in silence to the SOTY office in downtown LA. Truman drives. I sit in the front passenger seat. Josh and Maddie sit in the seat behind us. Our expressions are those of school kids who have been called out of class and ordered to the principal's office.

A young woman behind a desk greets us as we enter the reception area of the office. She's the only member of the SOTY staff in sight and not much older than me. She gives us a big smile. Why wouldn't she? She's not the one who's been called to the principal's office.

"You're the 'Love Transcends' songwriters," she states, rather than asks. "They're waiting for you. Follow me."

She leads us to a small conference room where Abigail and two women are seated with coffee cups in front of them. They're chitchatting among themselves like old friends until we walk in and the conversation comes to a screeching halt mid-sentence. Abigail doesn't look at me. One of the other women speaks.

"Good morning and thanks for coming. I'm Elaine Ferris with the Songwriter of the Year organization. This is Hillary Olsen, also with the organization. And I believe you know Abigail Collier."

A dirty look directed at me accompanies the mention of Abigail.

"Please, be seated."

The four of us sit at a table across from them. Elaine Ferris and Hillary Olsen are fortyish white women plucked straight out of Middle America and transported to LA. Not one thing about them is any less or any more than average. Elaine picks up a sheet of paper. Looks at it. Looks at us.

"Abigail Collier has filed a formal complaint regarding your song entry in this year's contest. That's the reason for this meeting. In keeping with the rules of the contest we will review the complaint and take the appropriate action following the review."

She barely glances at the sheet as she speaks. It's as if she's been rehearsing for this moment and the outcome is predetermined. I wonder if this meeting is just a formality.

"Do you understand?"

We tell her we do. She continues.

"This is not a courtroom. The procedure is not as formal. We'll take testimony from Abigail, then the four of you can speak. Hillary and I will render a decision once we've given your testimony due consideration."

"When do you think that will be?" I ask.

"Soon," she says curtly. "If there are no other questions, I'll begin with Abigail's testimony."

Hillary takes over from there.

"Abigail. In your complaint you state you were told by Dylan Jones that he and his partners did not write the contest-winning song, 'Love Transcends'. Is that correct?"

"Yes. He told me the song was written by his mother. They rearranged it and entered it in the contest."

"That's not entirely true," I say.

"Dylan. Please don't interrupt. You'll get your turn to speak, next," Hillary says. "What were the circumstances when he told you this? Was he under the influence of alcohol or drugs? Were you? Again, this is not a court of law. I'm trying to establish his and your state of mind at the time."

"We were both sober. It was early morning shortly after we woke. We slept together the night before. I thought I knew him better than I apparently did," Abigail says, with damp eyes and quivering lips. "Then he told me about falsely claiming the song was theirs. It completely freaked me out."

More dirty looks from Hillary and Elaine. Abigail is playing them and they're buying into it lock, stock and barrel.

"Alright Dylan," Hillary says. "Let's hear your side of this."

"I did tell Abigail the song idea came from my mother. My mother who died when I was so young I don't remember her. I had a dream or a vision or something. In it, my mother appears and sings the song. That's what I meant when I told Abigail our song began with an idea from my mother."

"You told me your mother wrote the song and that you and the others rewrote it for the contest," Abigail says.

Hillary doesn't admonish her for speaking out of turn, as she did me.

"Is that true, Dylan?"

"No, it's not."

My denial sounds convincing enough to me. I can't tell if Hillary and Elaine agree, though.

"Madeline, Truman and Josh. Do you support Dylan's testimony?"

"Yes."

"Absolutely."

"I do."

"Then that concludes this meeting. We'll inform you of our decision as soon as we've made it."

We all leave the SOTY office on the fifteenth floor at the same time. Abigail, too. The elevator is slow in coming. An awkward silence envelops us as we wait. Abigail stares at the digital display which tells her where the elevator is at the moment. I feel the need to say something to her. It's just who I am.

"Whatever happens, I want you to know there are no hard feelings."

Maddie hits me hard on my arm. I'll probably have a big purple bruise there by tomorrow.

"Would you stop being such a wussy," she says. "Don't you see what she's doing? She was runner-up to us in the contest. Get it? If we're disqualified, she's next in line."

It never occurred to me. Add stupid to naïve and easily manipulated. I look to Abigail for her reaction. There is none. She continues to stare at the display. The elevator arrives and the four of us get in. Abigail hesitates. Maddie hits the button to close the door. We leave her standing there.

"I don't like our chances," Josh says, as the elevator descends to the parking garage level. "Did you see the way Elaine and Hillary were looking at you when Abigail told them about you sleeping with her?"

I did. If looks could kill, theirs would have splattered my brains all over the walls of the conference room.

~63~

Heard ten thousand whispering and nobody listening

With the weekend upon us, it's not likely we'll hear from the SOTY women, Elaine and Hillary, before Monday. Whatever happens will happen. And since there's nothing we can do at this point to influence their decision, we try our best to put it out of our minds. Which is easier said than done.

"I need to get out of here," Maddie says. "I hate the feeling of being trapped in this house. Any of you want to come?"

"Sure, I'll come along," Josh tells her. "Give me twenty minutes to change clothes. Okay?"

"Anyone else?"

"Not me," I say. "I'm feeling a little glum over this thing with Abigail. I don't want to be a wet blanket."

"Dylan, she's not worth pining over," Maddie says.

"Oh, she's worth it. She may not deserve it, but she's definitely worth pining over."

"We'll stay here and keep Dylan company," Truman says. "You go out and have fun."

Maddie and Josh go upstairs to freshen up before leaving.

"I appreciate you care Truman, but you don't have to hang around for my sake. You know me. I enjoy my time alone. I might even try to play something on the piano. Go on with Maddie and Josh, if you want. Or better yet, take my sister out on the town."

Truman raises an eyebrow. I can tell he likes the idea. Nikki seems to be considering it. I give her a nudge.

"There are restaurants in Hollywood where movie stars sometimes eat. They're great places to see and be seen. You'd love it."

"Are you sure you'll be okay by yourself?" Nikki asks. "You won't do something stupid like call Abigail, will you?"

"I can't promise I won't do something stupid, but if I do it won't be that. You and Truman go on. I'll be fine."

"Okay, then. I'll go up and get ready. I can be ready in about an hour. Is that enough time for you, Truman?"

"Uh…, uh…, yeah," he stutters, as she hurries upstairs to prepare.

"Damn, Dylan. She's really going out with me. I don't know if I can pull this off. What's the name of the restaurant you were talking about?"

"Almost any restaurant in Hollywood probably has movie stars coming there. Pick one that looks nice and has a lot of people eating there. Nikki loves to be seen and people watch."

"What kind of food does she like? What do I talk about? I don't even know what to wear. I'm afraid I'll make a fool of myself."

"Stay calm, Truman. You can do this. Nikki will tell you where she wants to eat and she'll do most of the talking. It won't matter what you wear because everyone will be looking at her. She wouldn't have it any other way."

Near sunset I'm alone in the big house and sitting at the piano plinking on the keys. I'm trying to remember a melody that came to me recently, but having trouble concentrating.

There's a light rapping on the front door. Then I hear the latch rattle as someone attempts to open it. I go to the door, look through the peephole and see Natalie standing there.

"Hi, Dylan," she says, as I let her in.

We hug. We smile. We kiss.

"Abigail who?" I mutter.

"I came by to see how you're doing. The online chatter has been pretty brutal. I thought you might like a friend to talk to."

"I'm glad you're here. I've missed you."

We kiss again.

"I've missed you, too," she says. "Where is everyone?"

"They had to get away from here for a while. Come on in to the parlor. That's what I call the room where the grand piano is."

"What about Abigail? Are you still seeing her?"

"No. We broke up."

"Too bad," she says, without empathy.

"We sit side by side on the piano bench. Natalie strikes and hold a key down to listen to the sound resonate off the walls.

"How's Richard?" I ask.

"Alright, I suppose. He's with his wife, tonight."

"His wife?! I thought you two were engaged. As in engaged to marry one another. How can he be engaged to you and married to someone else?"

"You're so cute, Dylan. You always make me laugh. That's what I like about you the most."

I wait a beat for her to explain further. She doesn't.

"Natalie. This is none of my business, but you're smart and beautiful. I'm sure you could have pretty much any guy you want. Why Richard? It sounds like he's using you. You're his plaything. Something to put back in its box when he's through with it."

"You're right." For a second I think she's agreeing with me, then she says, "It isn't any of your business. But if you must know, we use each other. I get things from him. He gets things from me. It's a mutually beneficial arrangement."

"Do you love him?"

She gives me a look like it's the stupidest thing she's ever heard.

"What do you know about love, Dylan?" she says, bitterly. "Check that. What do you *think* you know about love? Have you ever been in love?"

"I don't know. I guess not. Have you?"

She lets out a sigh.

"I don't know, either. Probably not. I'm sorry. I'm feeling a little frustrated about how things are with Richard. I didn't mean to take it out on you."

"It's okay. I'm here and I'm not going anywhere. Talk to me. What has you so frustrated?"

"That's funny. I came here to listen to you tell me about your troubles. Not the other way around."

"Do you have to leave, soon?" I ask.

"No."

"We can trade off. You talk some, then I'll talk some."

We embrace. We kiss. This goes on for some time. Finally, our lips part and we gaze into each other's eyes.

"Who broke it off? You or Abigail?"

"She did."

"She's a fool, Dylan. You're a special guy."

"Apparently, dumping me was part of the plan from the start."

"Oh? Why do you say that?"

"She's the one who initiated our problems with SOTY. She filed a complaint stating we didn't write the song."

"I can't say I'm surprised she'd do something like that," Natalie says.

"Well, she sure had me fooled. I was ready to nominate her for sainthood until she pulled this."

"You're too naïve, sometimes, Dylan."

"So I've been told."

"I like it that you are. There are far worse things you could be."

She strikes a few more keys, then turns and looks thoughtfully at me.

"Have you ever done it on a grand piano?" she asks.

"Done what?" I joke.

"I'll take that as a no."

She begins to undress. The piano is made of hardwood. Material which isn't forgiving to knees and elbows.

"What are you waiting on, Dylan?"

"Wouldn't you rather go to my room, where there's a nice soft bed?"

"We can do that later. I've never done it on a grand piano. I might not have another opportunity."

One day I'd like to have a peek at her bucket list. I'll bet it's a doozy.

~64~

Don't ask me what I think of you,
I might not give the answer that you want me to

Elaine Ferris calls early Monday morning to deliver the bad news. I'm alone in the kitchen with a mug of coffee and a bowl of Honey Nut Cheerios in front of me. I thought the call would come before now. They obviously had made their decision long before we arrived at the SOTY office on Friday. In my opinion, the so-called review was nothing more than a charade designed to give the disqualification an air of legitimacy.

"Dylan Jones?" she asks.

"Yes."

"This is Elaine Ferris with SOTY. We've made our decision. Your entry in the contest has been disqualified."

I expected this, but it hits me hard, nonetheless.

"We wrote the song. We worked our asses off doing it," I tell her.

"Hillary and I debated over who was being truthful with us, you or Abigail. In the end it was your behavior with her which influenced our decision. Any man who mistreats a woman as you did Abigail is someone who is accustomed to being dishonest with others."

"What? You think I did something to Abigail?"

"She was obviously traumatized by you. Hillary and I couldn't in good conscience ignore this."

My disappointment is replaced by anger like I've never felt before.

"Let me tell you something. Abigail wasn't mistreated in any way. She used me. Not the other way around. She's no saint. She played me and she's playing you, too."

"You need to control your temper, young man."

"Oh, I do, do I? You're not my mother and I like my temper just like it is. And I'll tell you something else. This isn't over. We're going to appeal this. We'll go over your head."

"There is no appeals process. And there is no one over my head. Our decision is final. You're just going to have to learn to live with it."

"We'll see about that. I'll sue your ass."

"I doubt that. One more thing before I hang up. Your debit cards have been deactivated. Our accountants will be contacting you to arrange the repayment of your winnings."

"Good luck with that."

"And good day to you, Dylan."

I'm so mad I throw the phone against the refrigerator. It breaks into a dozen pieces that scatter across the floor.

"That's what I'm talking about," Truman says.

I turn to see Truman, Maddie, Josh and Nikki gawking at me like I've lost my mind.

"They disqualified us," I say.

"Oh, we figured that much out for ourselves," Truman says. "And you told her off. I didn't know you had it in you."

"Me either," Maddie says. "What'd she say when you told her we'd appeal the decision?"

"She said we couldn't. That she has the final word. She also said our debit cards are no good any longer and the accountants will contact us about repaying the hundred grand."

"Who knows, maybe we can sue them," Josh says.

"I just said that because she made me mad. I doubt we can do anything about being disqualified. What bothers me the most is their decision wasn't based on the song, alone. They thought I was lying about writing the song because of the way I treated Abigail. That's what she told me."

"Dylan!" Maddie rants at me. "What did you do to her? You didn't force yourself on her, did you? No means no."

"I didn't take advantage of Abigail in any way. Nothing bad happened. I'm naïve and easily manipulated, like everyone keeps telling me. I let her use me. That's what I did."

"What's done is done," Josh says. "Abigail is an outsider. She's not part of our group. We can't let an outsider divide us. We have to stay united. That's how we get through this."

"Well said, Josh. This is not about what I should or shouldn't have done. It's about what we do next. I think we need to get out in front of this as quickly as possible. Elaine Ferris will notify the media about her decision, soon. That's if she hasn't already."

"We need to start thinking about damage control," Josh says.

"Before we do anything else, we need to get Dylan another phone," Truman says. "He's the one Stella calls and she doesn't like it if she can't reach him."

"I wasn't thinking about that when I tossed the phone at the refrigerator."

"I know you weren't. You were venting your anger. Everyone has to do that sometime. That's okay. I'm looking out for you. So is Josh and Maddie. We're a team. We'll get through this together."

"I'll call Stella on my phone and let her know yours is out of commission for the time being," Maddie says.

~65~

All lies and jest,
Still a man hears what he wants to and disregards the rest

Stella said it could end as quickly as it started. I didn't believe her. I thought she was using our fear of failure to motivate us. I was wrong. She calls early one morning.

"I've got good, bad and worse news. Which do you want first?"

"Give me the good. I have a feeling it won't take long."

"The good news is 'Love Transcends' has sold fifty million downloads."

"And the bad?" I ask.

"Ha Yoon Ghim's people may file a lawsuit against you."

"Crap! You're kidding."

"I wish I was. They don't really have a choice. They have to distance themselves from the fallout in the event there's a problem with the song."

The fallout she's referring to is the domino effect toppling anyone who has benefitted financially from my mother's song in the event our copyright application is denied.

I'm hoping that won't happen. It would open up a can of worms and scare off those who wish to record or distribute the song or any we write in the future. Luckily, the copyright office doesn't use the same rule book in making their decision as Elaine Ferris and Hillary Olsen did. And Abigail has no say in the matter.

"What's the worse news, Stella?"

"You know the girl who took your place as the contest winner?"

"Abigail Collier. What about her?"

"The recording of her contest-winning song was released yesterday."

"It was only a week ago they took the title from us and gave it to her. How can she have a recording of the song so soon?"

"My guess is it was already recorded and the release was delayed until after the contest, so she'd get maximum exposure if and when she won. From what I hear, the song is featured on an album to be released in the next week or so. Abigail plays guitar and sings on all the songs."

Although I don't know much about making an album, I'm sure it involves a substantial amount of time, money and planning. In other words, it was in the works long before Abigail even entered the contest.

It bothers me to see Abigail's star on the rise while ours seems to be flaming out. What bothers me more is to realize she used me as a stepping stone to elevate herself to where she is, now.

The ripple effect from the disqualification threatens to turn into a tsunami. Filming for the second season of our TV show is put on hold. Our once-adoring fans give us dirty looks and whisper behind our backs when we go out in public. The restaurants where we always get a table, regardless of how busy they are. That's history.

In a little over a week, we go from being a hot commodity everyone wants a part of, to being a hot potato nobody will touch. Stella is among those who have been adversely affected by the downturn in our popularity, but so far she's been real stand-up about it.

"I got the SOTY people off your backs about the money. I told them you fulfilled your obligations to them by doing two weeks' worth of personal appearances without pay. So you earned the hundred grand. Don't worry. You're going to get through this in one piece. Every dark cloud has a silver lining."

"You really believe that?" I ask.

"Let's say I do and leave it at that."

I get a call from our money manager, Boyd Proctor. We've been wondering about our financial status.

"I thought I'd better give you a heads-up," he says. "I've been looking over your account balances. The money is going out quicker than it's coming in."

"I thought that might be the case," I reply. "What do you suggest?"

"That's simple. Make more money or spend less."

My bad. It was a stupid question.

"Give me an idea of how far apart we are. I mean, between what we're earning and what our expenses are."

"I'll put it this way. If your current income and expenses remain as they are, you'll be begging for change on street corners a month from now."

"That bad, huh. Can we borrow money until we get rolling again?"

"No. You're already overextended as it is."

"We can cut our expenses," I say. "It might buy us some time. We'll find someplace cheaper to live. What are we paying for rent here?"

"Twenty-five thousand a month."

"Seriously? I didn't realize it was that much. We can do without one of the Highlanders, too. Heck, we can give them both back. How much would that save us?"

"It won't save you anything. Not one dime. Here's why. You're bound to the lease on the house whether you're living there or not. The same with the Highlanders. They're leased and you're obligated to make the monthly payments for the term of the lease."

"Damned if we do and damned if we don't," I say.

"Pretty much. In lieu of a significant cash infusion, you're out of options. You'll have to file for bankruptcy protection."

I've heard the term, bankruptcy protection used before, but never in a complimentary way. It's always, "that deadbeat, he declared bankruptcy," or "that conniving little wench filed for bankruptcy".

"I don't know if I want to do that," I say.

"I don't know if you have a choice. Talk it over with the others and see how they feel about it. Let me know what you decide."

"Bankruptcy!" Truman exclaims, when I tell him and the others what Boyd advises. "I haven't even gotten used to being rich, yet."

"How would it work?" Josh asks. "Did Boyd say?"

"I don't think he knows. It's not really his area of expertise. We probably have to consult an attorney."

~66~

I went to my brother to ask for a loan 'cause I was busted

I've never understood the idiom, 'you can't squeeze blood out of a turnip'. In my defense, I'm not familiar with turnips. As far as I know, I've never seen one. I wouldn't know a turnip if one bit me on the ass. Is it fruit or vegetable? Do they bleed? I don't know, you tell me.

From an attorney referral service we get the name of one who specializes in bankruptcy. Dana Blackwell. We call her office number.

"Attorney's office," a woman answers.

"Dana Blackwell, please," I say.

"Your name?"

"Dylan Jones. I might want to go bankrupt. I'm hoping she can help."

"Please hold."

"I'm on hold," I tell the others, in case they're wondering.

"Mr. Jones. I'm Dana Blackwell. How can I help you?"

"My friends and I would like to find out what's involved in declaring ourselves bankrupt. My friends are Truman, Maddie and Josh. We're partners in a songwriting venture."

"Those names sound familiar. Why?"

"We won the Songwriter of the Year contest and we have a reality TV show. Maybe you've seen it."

"No. That's not it. Something I read somewhere. Your song was disqualified. You won the contest and they took the money back. Right?"

"Uh, yeah. That's us."

"Wow! What a bummer."

"Anywho," I continue. "The contest snafu caused some other problems, which led to financial troubles. Our money manager says our expenses exceed our income and we should file for bankruptcy protection."

"Alright. There are a few ways to go about this. There is debt relief or debt consolidation. And there is bankruptcy chapters seven or thirteen. Before I can advise you which is best I'll need to take a peek at your financial statement. You said you have a money manager who handles that. Could you have them fax a financial summary to me?"

"I can call him and ask."

"Splendid. I'll give you the fax number here. As soon as I look over the information I'll get back with you."

I do as she requests. A short while later she calls.

"I'm afraid there's not much I can do for you, Dylan."

"I don't understand," I say.

"You're not a candidate for bankruptcy because you have no assets. No real estate, boat, plane, auto, stocks and bonds or cash."

"I thought that's why people declare bankruptcy. Because they're broke and unable to pay their debts."

"That's what people often assume. Actually, bankruptcy is designed to protect your assets from creditors. And since you have no assets, you have nothing to gain from filing for bankruptcy protection. You see?"

"Not really. What about the other things you mentioned?"

"Debt relief and debt consolidation," she says. "Those are different means of accomplishing the same goal. Protecting your assets."

"I'm not sure why our money manager thought it was the thing to do. Thanks for taking the time to talk to me."

"You're welcome, Dylan. Before you hang up, I'd like to give you some free advice. This is off the record, you understand? I'm not speaking to you as an attorney."

"Okay."

"Not having any assets is an asset in itself. I'd use it to my advantage if I were you."

"How do you mean?"

"When your debts become so overwhelming you can't see even the dimmest light at the end of the tunnel, walk away and don't look back."

"That's it?"

"Yes, Dylan. That's it."

After the conversations with Boyd Proctor and Dana Blackwell, I call everyone to the parlor to discuss our situation.

"Walk away and don't look back? That's what she advises us to do? And she's an attorney?" Maddie questions.

"She wasn't speaking as an attorney. It was off the record," I say.

"Off the wall is more like it."

"I'm just repeating what she told me. From a purely pragmatic standpoint it makes perfect sense. We don't have any assets. Therefore, there's no incentive to sue us."

"It might make perfect sense," Truman says. "But that's the kind of thing deadbeats and losers do. When I look in the mirror, I don't want to see that guy looking back at me."

"You wouldn't have a mirror to look in," Josh says. "You'd be living under the interstate overpass in a cardboard box."

"I know you're joking, Josh, but I have to agree with Truman on this," Maddie says. "It's not the kind of person any of us wants to be. We can get jobs. Maybe those jobs won't pay much, but with four of us working, it will be enough to cover the bare necessities."

"Five of us," Nikki says. "I'll help out. I don't want to go back to Detroit any more than you do."

My thoughts drift back to cleaning the frying vats at Bubba's Catfish Restaurant.

"I'm not against working for a living," I say. "But it might be counterproductive. The best menial jobs pay around fifteen dollars an hour, twenty at most. Times forty hours equals eight hundred a week. Five people, four and a third weeks a month. It comes out to around seventeen thousand. And that's the absolute best case scenario."

"So what's wrong with that?"

"Boyd Proctor told me our rent is twenty-five thousand a month, and we're obligated to pay it for the full term of the lease. Otherwise we get sued by the landlord, along with everyone else who wants a part of us."

"Just to recap things," Truman says. "Boyd advises us to declare bankruptcy. But the lawyer tells us we can't. We can't afford the rent on this place, and it doesn't matter if we move because they're going to sue us anyway. If we find jobs that don't pay enough to cover the rent, they'll take what we make and sue us for the rest. As our money manager, what is it Boyd does for us? Maybe we should think about suing him."

"He's not the reason we're having these financial problems. It all started with Abigail's complaint," Maddie says. "I'd like to have a few minutes alone with her. I bet I could make her take it back."

"The damage is already done and we can't turn back the clock."

"I'd still like to get my hands on Abigail."

I'd like to get my hands on Abigail, too. But for an entirely different reason than what Maddie has in mind. She may have betrayed me—alright, she did betray me—but she's a heck of a lover.

~67~

You're nobody 'til somebody ~~loves~~ sues you

Nikki was a straight-A student in school. From the first day of class through the last day of high school, she made nothing but A's. I hated her for this because she always made me look bad.

When report cards were passed out, she'd hurry home to show Isiah and Chandra. They'd hug her and tell her how proud they were. She'd hold out her hand and Isiah would put a dollar in it.

Then I came dragging in saying I lost my report card on the way home. I'd hold out my hand and Isiah would do a give-me-five slap on it. Nikki, Chandra and Isiah all thought that was hilarious.

Anyway, my point being Nikki is super smart. It's an often overlooked attribute of hers, due to her often looked-over face and body. I've never really appreciated her intelligence until now.

"Can I say something?" Nikki asks. "You may feel like this is none of my business."

"This involves you too," Truman tells her. "Speak your mind."

"Having your song disqualified by the contest people isn't really the problem. You got to keep the money and the recording of the song is doing well. The problem is the public's opinion of you changed. You need to find a way to change it back. Take action. Actions speak louder than words and will do a better job of getting the public's attention."

"What kind of actions did you have in mind?"

"A court action. I think you should sue SOTY. Win or lose it will show people you're serious about defending yourselves."

"We'd have to find a lawyer," Maddie says. "And I doubt we could afford a good one."

"Actually, you don't have to have a lawyer to file a lawsuit in California," Nikki explains. "I've been looking into it. The California court system has a website where it tells you how to do it. There's a self-help page for people just like us."

"Interesting," I say. "Even if we don't win a lawsuit against them, it might be a lot of fun trying."

"Here it is," Nikki says, pointing to her laptop screen.

She sets it on a coffee table and we gather around it to watch.

"It says you have to decide if you're suing a person or a business."

"Elaine Ferris called it an organization. I guess that's the same as a business," I say.

"If they're a corporation, the California Secretary of State keeps a record of the names and addresses of the corporate officers," Nikki reads from a page of instructions. "That's where you start. Find out if the SOTY organization is incorporated and who their officers are."

She taps a few keys, then a few more. A page appears on the screen.

"The SOTY organization is a corporation," she tells us. "They go by the name, Songwriter Award Incorporated. If I go to the California Secretary of State's website and do a search for Songwriter Award Incorporated it gives me the name of the agent for service of process and their address. That's where the summons goes."

"Cool," I say. "Is it Elaine Ferris or Hillary Olsen?"

"No. It's Marcus Putnam. The address is here in LA."

"What was that about the summons?" Maddie asks.

"You have to file a complaint or a petition and a summons with the court. Then, you have Marcus Putnam served. That means you pay a process server to deliver a copy of the court papers to him."

"It sounds pretty complicated," Truman says.

"It's not really," Nikki says. "There are a few forms to fill out. I can download the forms. We'll need to fill them out and make copies. Once Marcus Putnam gets served, he has thirty days to respond. Then we request a court date. I'm not sure how long that will take."

We download the forms and begin filling them out. There's a line on one form where we put the amount of the lawsuit.

"What do you want to put there?" Nikki asks.

"One million dollars," Truman says. "We were on a roll. There's no telling how much we would have made in the next year or so if it hadn't been for Abigail."

All eyes turn to me at the mention of Abigail. It might be a while before I'm forgiven for trusting her.

"Unless anyone objects, one million dollars it is, then," Nikki says.

We can mail the forms or file them online, but there are lots of tales of lost or misplaced papers. To be certain the paperwork gets into the right hands, the five of us drive to the courthouse the next day. It's a two-hour wait before we're finally called to the window.

"One person at a time," the clerk says, as the five of us approach.

We let Nikki handle it. She hands things to the clerk, who scans all the documents, deems them acceptable and collects the fee. Then, the clerk stamps the appropriate forms with a case number.

"That's all we need to do here," Nikki tells us. "Next we hire a process server to deliver a copy to Marcus Putnam."

Wednesday we file the papers. Thursday Putnam is served. Friday I receive a phone call.

"Dylan?" the caller inquires.

"Yes," I reply.

"This is Elaine Ferris with SOTY. Do you remember me?"

"How could I forget? You ruined my life."

I know it's melodramatic, but I couldn't resist.

"The state of your life is your own doing, not mine. The reason for this call is, I've been informed by our corporate office you've filed a lawsuit against our organization. Is this true?"

"Yes, it is. Did you honestly believe we'd tuck tail and run because you told us we had no other choice?"

"You don't have other options. The contest rules are very clear on this. We have the right to disqualify any contestant if we see fit to do so. You have no legal recourse. A frivolous lawsuit will only cost you time and money, and you have nothing to gain from it."

"That's where you're wrong. It's not a frivolous lawsuit. We have everything to gain and nothing to lose by fighting to repair our reputation. And what you told me about there is no one over your head. Apparently, that was a lie. I'll see you in court, Elaine. Have a wonderful day."

I doubt Elaine is rattled by my words, but she's bothered about the lawsuit. Otherwise she wouldn't have called. Marcus Putnam either called her or spoke to someone who called her. Either way, we have their attention.

~68~

Ride a painted pony let the spinning wheel spin

Public opinion can be as volatile as a hurricane. There it is. Heading straight toward you, packing one hundred fifty mile-per-hour winds, one minute. Turning away and heading harmlessly out to sea, the next.

Natalie agrees to help with our social media campaign to inform the public of the lawsuit and try to garner their support. After a couple of days sending tweets across cyberspace I call to see how it's going.

"Hi Dylan. I only have a few minutes to talk."

"Sure. I understand. How is the social media world responding to us these days?"

"They're not really. When you guys were disqualified they loved it. Claiming you're innocent doesn't spark much interest. Abigail is a different story. The internet social media dweebs can't get enough of her."

I'm all too aware of Abigail's success and growing popularity. Every time I see her face or a blurb about her online it saddens me. I haven't told anyone I downloaded a copy of her recording, because I know they'd give me a hard time about it. I listen to it when I'm alone in my room.

"I was hoping for a better response from cyberspace, but thanks for helping us out, Nat."

"I'm glad to do it. I'll keep trying. Public opinion is unpredictable and tomorrow is a new day."

"Are you busy tonight? Would you like to come over?"

"I'd love to, but I can't. Richard has reservations at Chez Panisse. We're celebrating our three-month anniversary."

As refreshing as Natalie's candor is, I long for a girl to tell me lies, such as I'm the only one for her.

"Maybe we can get together some other time, then. I mean, unless things with Richard and you are going to become exclusive."

"I don't know what will happen with Richard, Dylan. I'm not ready to decide on one person. I don't know if I ever will be. I like our time together, you and me. Ever since I told Richard about you, it's like he's falling in love with me all over again."

"You told him about me?"

"Yes, I did. He threw a jealous fit. I've never seen him like that. It was a real turn-on. Now, any time I'm not with him, he worries I'm with you."

"Glad I could help," I deadpan.

"Me too. I wish I'd thought of it long ago. Look, I have to go. I'll call you when I have a free evening. Alright?"

"Alright. I'll talk to you, then."

As soon as I disconnect with Natalie my phone sounds its ringtone for an unknown caller. I answer cautiously.

"Hello."

"Who am I speaking with?" the caller asks.

Don't you know? I think to myself. You called me, after all.

"Who are you?" I shoot back.

"My name is Will McCormack, with the law firm of Wesson, Huntly, Zimmer and Fenton."

"Why didn't you just say that in the first place?"

"Sorry," he replies, curtly. "Are you Dylan Jones?"

"Yes."

"May I call you Dylan?"

"Yes."

"Thank you. Call me Will."

"I'm going to call you gone if you don't get to the point, Will."

He chuckles at that. I thought it was pretty funny, myself.

"I'm glad to see you have a sense of humor, Dylan. It will serve you well. My firm represents Songwriter Award Incorporated. I'm calling on their behalf regarding the lawsuit."

"Okay. What about it?"

"The court document doesn't give the name of your attorney. Do you intend to represent yourselves in this matter?"

"Yes."

"That's impressive. I admire your conviction. Not many people your age would challenge a corporation the size of this one in court. My hat's off to you."

"I'm flattered," I reply, sarcastically.

"As you've probably already discovered, the court system moves at a snail's pace. Even when the claim is valid, it can still take months, even years, to get a judgement. I'd like to meet with the four of you to discuss this. I'm hopeful we can resolve this without the hassle of litigation."

"I'll ask the others. When and where do you want to meet?"

"We can do it over lunch, tomorrow. My treat. Danielle's in West Hollywood. Do you know the place?"

"I'm sure we can find it."

"I'll reserve a table for twelve thirty. Check with the others and call me back to confirm. How's that?"

"Alright. I can do that."

"Great. I'm looking forward to meeting you all in person, tomorrow. I'll see you, then."

~69~

Send lawyers, guns and money, dad get me out of this

Danielle's is one those trendy places frequented at lunch by business types in suits, wannabe actors in shades and bored housewives on a break from shopping. We give our names to the hostess as we enter.

She leads us to a table for eight where three suits are already seated with cocktail glasses in front of them. Except for a few cubes of ice, the glasses are empty. All three men are chomping on ice and scanning the room for the waitress as we approach.

"I'm Dylan Jones," I announce to the three men. "This is Truman Dixon, Madeline Lee and Josh Martinez."

"And I'm Nikki Jones, Dylan's sister."

The suits stand up like their CO called them to attention.

"Will McCormack," suit number one says. "This is Charles Avery and Norman Denton. Please, have a seat."

We sit while he snaps his fingers at a waitress who seems frazzled and overwhelmed by the lunch crowd. She lets out a sigh and hurries over.

"Another round for us," Will tells her, and then gestures at us. "And whatever our friends would like."

"We'll have iced tea," I say, before Maddie and Josh can order something stronger.

"The food here is great," Will says. "Look over the menus and order whatever you want."

I don't have any firsthand experience with business lunches such as this one. I understand this much. When

Will said he'd treat, what he really meant was he'd stick Songwriter Award Incorporated with the bill.

The bone-weary waitress returns with our drinks and takes our food order. Prime rib and steaks for the suits. Pizza and hamburgers for us.

"Can we speak candidly?" Will says.

"I don't see why not," I reply.

"The recording of your song is doing well. You have a successful reality TV show. What do you hope to gain from suing our client?"

"You mean, besides a million bucks?"

"Christ!" one of the other suits exclaims. "You can't be serious."

"Calm down, Charles," Will says. "Every negotiation has to start somewhere. Isn't that right, Dylan?"

"I suppose so."

"I'm guessing this is about more than money. Winning the contest was a proud moment for the four of you. Dishonoring you by taking the title away must have been a tough pill to swallow. Am I right?"

"We didn't like it one bit, if that's what you're asking. We were punished for something we didn't do."

"Oh, boo-hoo," Charles says. "Somebody cue the violins."

"Shh, Charles. I'll handle this."

I can't tell whether the good lawyer, bad lawyer routine is part of the plan or if it's the cocktails talking. Our food order comes and we pause from the conversation while the waitress serves us.

"Do you need anything else?" she asks as the last plate is placed on the table.

"Another round," Charles tells her.

She leaves to fetch the drinks. We begin eating. I'm no slouch when it comes to chowing down on a nice chunk of red meat. But the three suits are gnawing on their fifth bites before I can place the napkin in my lap.

We eat in silence. The conversation doesn't resume until we've finished eating and the three suits are working on their fifth round of cocktails. I'm the first to speak.

"Can I ask you something?"

"Of course," Will answers. "Go ahead."

"What are Elaine Ferris and Hillary Olsen's positions with the corporation?"

He glances at the other suits. They shrug their shoulders.

"I'm not really sure. Why do you ask?"

"Are they corporate officers or vice presidents of a division? Elaine told me there was no one over her head."

"I think it's safe to say there are people within Songwriter Award Incorporated with more authority than her. What are you getting at?"

"Just this. If there had been a means for us to appeal their decision to disqualify us, we might have gone that route instead of filing a lawsuit."

"So you're saying if they were to reconsider their decision, you might be willing to withdraw your complaint?"

"We want to be reinstated as the rightful winners of the contest," Maddie tells them. "It's not enough to simply reconsider."

"And not only that," Truman says. "We want a public apology."

"I agree," Josh tells them. "We want our names and reputations completely cleared. We're willing to go to court, if that's what it takes."

"Well," Will begins. "Now that you've informed me of your demands I'll confer with our clients to see what we can work out."

"That's great," I say. "Thanks for the lunch. We're looking forward to hearing from you."

~70~

I'd rather be a hammer than a nail
Yes I would, if I could, I surely would

An optimist expects great things to happen, but is often disappointed. A pessimist expects nothing and on occasion, is pleasantly surprised. I choose to be a pessimist because I'm not cut out for the emotional roller coaster that awaits an optimist.

In hindsight, we probably shouldn't have set the figure for the lawsuit at one million dollars. We did so because it's an intimidating number, and we were hoping to scare the pants off of Elaine Ferris and Songwriter Award Incorporated. It raised our expectations to new heights. Disappointment is the inevitable outcome.

"What are you going to do with your share?" Truman asks me.

"I don't think I have to worry about that happening."

"Come on, Dylan. Just play along for a minute. If you had two hundred and fifty thousand dollars, what would you spend it on?"

It's a stupid game to play. A total waste of time, if you ask me. But Truman is my best friend. So I oblige him.

"Let me see," I say. "I'd buy a lifetime supply of macaroni and cheese. If there was any money left I'd spend it on ice cream and sodas."

"Be serious, man. You're not going to blow all that money on macaroni and cheese, sodas and ice cream."

"If you want me to be serious, I'm going to have to say I wouldn't spend the money. I'd put it in the bank, so it would be there when I need it."

"That makes no sense at all, Dylan. What is the point of having money if you're not going to spend it? You could die tomorrow. You might get hit by a car while you're crossing the street. The money in the bank would go to pay for your funeral. You wouldn't have enjoyed it for one second."

"Your turn, Truman. What would you buy?"

"I would buy my own music store. It doesn't have to be anything big. Just some place I could sell guitars, amplifiers and accessories."

"That wasn't what I expected you to say. I thought you'd say a big house or a fancy sports car."

"You don't know me as well as you thought you did."

"Yeah, I do."

"No, you don't."

"Yeah, I do."

"No, you don't."

Our banter is interrupted by the sound of my phone announcing an incoming call.

"To be continued," I say to Truman.

"No, it won't," he replies.

I really hate to let him have the last word, but the call might be important.

"Hello," I answer.

"This is Will McCormack."

"Hi Will. What can we do for you?"

"I've had a conversation or two with the folks at Songwriter Award Incorporated. I'd like to get together with you and the others to tell you what they're thinking."

"When and where?"

"Somewhere more private, this time. I can come by your house if that works for you? Say this afternoon around three?"

"Alright. I'll tell the others you're coming."

Maddie, Josh, Truman, Will, Nikki and I gather in the great room for the discussion. Will starts it off.

"Dylan. You asked about Elaine Ferris and Hillary Olsen. Their official titles are director and assistant director of operations for the Songwriter of the Year Organization, SOTY. That's a separate entity from Songwriter Award Incorporated, SAI. SAI is the parent corporation. I told you Elaine has no real authority within SAI. That's true. However, she does manage SOTY."

He doesn't have to say more in order for me to understand what that implies. She's going to be an obstacle when it comes to settling the lawsuit.

"Her father is the chief financial officer for SAI," Will continues. "As I understand it, he gives her free rein over SOTY."

"That doesn't give her the right to disqualify us without a good reason," Maddie says.

"Or to trash Dylan's reputation over something another contestant said but can't prove," Josh adds.

"We've said it all along," Truman says. "We'll do what we have to do to clear our names. If we have to go to court, we will."

"I don't blame you for wanting to reclaim what is rightfully yours. Whether or not the songwriting title is rightfully yours is not crystal clear. Every disagreement has two sides. Otherwise it wouldn't be a disagreement. Every case which goes in front of a judge or jury has two possible outcomes. Any experienced trial lawyer will tell you it's difficult to predict how a judge or jury will decide on any given day."

I'm assuming Will is here to discourage us from pursuing the lawsuit. That's his job. He's a lawyer for the opposing side.

"I know you have an obligation to your client to tell us we can't win this thing," I say. "But we feel like we have more to gain than lose in court. So go back to your client and tell them it didn't work."

"You're right. I have an obligation to my client and I'm going to fulfill that obligation. That doesn't mean I have to hurt you in the process. I think a compromise of some sort would be beneficial to all parties. I'd appreciate it if you'd give me a minute to explain."

No one objects, so he continues.

"I want to start by saying I'm paid by the hour. I bill the client for my time. More time, more money. The longer this drags on the more money I make. I'm telling you this so you'll understand it doesn't benefit me personally to settle this thing quickly. But it is unethical for me to prolong it any longer than necessary.

"That being said, if you go forward with the lawsuit, my client will instruct me to stall for as long as possible. As full as the court docket is with this sort of litigation, I'd think it could be as much as three years before it is finally heard in front of a judge."

"Will," Nikki says.

She hasn't spoken in his presence before now. Not here at the house or at Danielle's during lunch yesterday. He's not sure what to make of it.

"Yes, Nikki."

"I know what you're saying is true. You can keep it out of court for two or three years. Would SAI consider mediation or arbitration?"

"What are those?" Maddie asks.

"It's where both parties agree to have a third party decide their case."

Maddie is puzzled by this explanation.

"If I may," Will says. "Mediation or arbitration are options worth considering. Mediation is a procedure where the parties discuss their claim and counter-claim in front of a trained mediator. Arbitration is a private process similar to a trial. It's more formal than mediation. The opposing parties give opening statements and present evidence. If the parties agree in advance to adhere to the arbitrator's decision, then it is as binding as a court decision."

"Would SAI agree to mediation?" Nikki asks.

"I can't make that decision for them, but I think they might. I'm sure they'd like to avoid the publicity of a trial."

"I'll discuss it with Dylan, Maddie, Josh and Truman. If SAI is willing to have a mediator review the SOTY decision to disqualify them from the contest, how soon could that take place?"

"It could be scheduled for as soon as next week."

He takes a business card and writes a number on the back.

"Here's my personal phone number. Call me after the five of you have talked it over."

~71~

If I can just get off of this LA freeway
Without getting killed or caught

The word mediation doesn't have the same harsh connotation as lawsuit. Threatening to mediate someone doesn't carry the same weight as telling them you'll sue their ass for every dime they'll ever earn. So I'm not thrilled with the idea.

"The reason I think you should consider it is because three years is a long time to wait for it to get to court, if it ever does. During that time there will be three more contests with three more winners. The focus will be on the most recent contest winners. Nobody will remember or care who won three years ago."

"What about one million dollars?" Josh asks. "Isn't that worth waiting three years for?"

"The million dollars is what you're asking for. Even if you win the lawsuit, the jury decides how much you're entitled to," Nikki explains.

"No guarantees, a lot of unknowns and three years down the road," I say. "We have a lot to talk about before we decide."

"My head already aches from thinking about it," Maddie says.

"I feel the same," Truman says.

The strain of it all is taking its toll on us. It's evidenced by our furrowed brows and glum expressions.

"While I'm here in California, I'd like to see some of the sights outside of LA," Nikki says.

"I would too," I say. "Once we get past this lawsuit or at least know what the schedule is, you and I can go sightseeing."

"I'm thinking all five of us could go tomorrow. Put off making a decision about mediation for a day. Get away from LA where you can hear yourself think."

"I don't know if we should," I say.

"I think it's a great idea," Maddie says.

"Me too," Truman agrees.

"I'm in," says Josh. "What about you, Dylan?"

"It sounds like I'm getting left behind if I say no, so I guess I'm in, too."

~~~

Nikki maps out the trip. We leave early the next morning, heading south from LA. The first leg of the trip is on an unimpressive stretch of Interstate Five. We take it to Torrey Pines, and then go west to the Pacific Coast Highway and north from there. That's when it becomes interesting.

The ocean views are magnificent. We stop often so we can get out to feel the wind coming off the water and breathe in the salt air. I didn't realize how tense and stressed I was feeling, or how much I needed this.

"I read that gray whales migrate past here annually," Nikki tells us, at an overlook where we stop. "We're a little early for them. They go south to Baja, Mexico in mid-December, then back north to Alaska in April."

"I'd love to see whales go swimming by," Josh says. "Maybe we can do this again when they're around."

"That'd be fun," Maddie says. "I wouldn't mind living around here and walking down to stick my toes in the ocean every morning. That would be a dream come true, for me."

"I want a picture of the four of you together having a good time. Stand there with the Pacific Ocean behind you," Nikki says.

We line up side by side, smiling broadly with our arms around one another while Nikki snaps a photo of us with her phone. Farther north we stop for a late lunch at a roadside café which sits on a cliff overlooking the sea. After lunch we descend forty feet down a set of stairs behind the café to the beach below.

Maddie takes off her shoes to dip her feet in the water. Nikki joins her. They step in and come right back out, squealing and giggling from the sensation of the cold water against their skin.

"I didn't expect it to be that cold," Maddie says.

The air temperature is around seventy-five. The water temperature is ten degrees cooler. Truman and I grab her and pretend we're going to throw her in. She squeals some more. Then, we grab Nikki and do the same thing. Then, Maddie and Nikki try to drag me into the water, but I manage to wrestle free.

We walk the beach for a short while, then load back in the Highlander and head home. It's been a fun day for us, but the closer we get to LA the more melancholy our mood becomes. We hit traffic on Interstate Five and it takes us an hour and a half to traverse the final ten miles.

"Except for that last part I enjoyed the trip," Truman says, once we're home. "Thanks for suggesting it, Nikki."

"Yeah, thanks Nikki," Josh echoes.

"You're welcome, Truman. You too Josh. I hope taking your mind off of the lawsuit for a day helps you resolve a few things."

"It certainly made me think about whether I'm ready to commit to staying in LA for another three years," I say.

"And…," Maddie prompts.

"I'm not. LA is starting to lose its appeal. If we can mediate our issue with SOTY and be done with it in a couple of weeks, I vote we do it."

"Wow! This is kind of sudden."

"It's been on my mind for a while. The trip today made me realize I don't like LA that much. Everything is temporary."

"I didn't want to be the first to say it, but I feel the same way," Truman admits.

"I'm not sure I'm ready to leave LA," Josh says. "I'm okay with doing mediation, though. If everyone is in agreement."

"Does anyone object?" Nikki asks.

No one does.

"Let's call Will McCormack and tell him what you've decided."

~72~

Up and down, and in the end it's only round n round

After we tell Will McCormack of our decision, it takes only a day for SAI and SOTY to agree. A bad sign, I'm thinking. A voice in my head keeps saying, "Careful what you ask for, you just might get it".

"We can schedule it for early next week," Will McCormack calls to tell us. "I've spoken with a mediation service I've used in the past. They're competent, reliable and unbiased. It's subject to your approval, of course."

We accept the schedule and choice of mediator. On the first Monday in December we all meet in a conference room at the offices of Mediation Solutions. On one side of the table is Nikki, Truman, Maddie, Josh and me. On the other side is Elaine, Hillary, Will and Charles. At the head of the table is our mediator, Andrew Harris.

"Good morning," Andrew begins. "I'll explain how this procedure works. We have four people on one side of the table and five on the other. To simplify and streamline the process, each side will appoint a spokesperson. That spokesperson will give an opening statement outlining their complaint on this side and the response on that side.

"After the opening statements, you'll have a discussion. Oftentimes, possible solutions come to light during the discussion. The next step is I meet privately with each side. Then, we have a joint negotiation session. If you reach an agreement during the negotiations, we put it in writing. The settlement agreement is signed by both parties and the mediation process is complete. Any questions before we begin?"

"Can we have a minute to discuss which one of us will be the spokesperson?" I ask.

"Certainly. This is an informal procedure. If you'd like to talk in private, you can use that room."

The five of us file into the room he points to. We discussed this earlier and decided I should do most of the talking since the accusation of improper behavior was directed at me.

"I think Nikki should speak for us," I say. "Elaine and Hillary are giving me dirty looks. It makes me nervous. I'm afraid I'll forget what I came here to say. Nikki doesn't let stuff like that bother her."

"How do you feel about it, Nikki?" Maddie asks.

"I'll be glad to speak for you. Those people across the table don't bother me one bit. They're no better than us."

I give her my handwritten notes, though Nikki is pretty good at winging it. We return to the conference room.

"If you're ready we'll begin with the Plaintiffs' opening statement."

Nikki stands up.

"You're not required to stand," Andrew says.

"I'd prefer to," Nikki says. "My brother, Dylan Jones, and his partners entered an original song they wrote into the Songwriter of the Year contest. The song was picked to win the Pop music category. For the next month this team of songwriters represented the SOTY organization and their sponsors at various functions. During that time, not one complaint was lodged against the team.

"About a month after the contest, the contestant who was runner-up in the same category as our team, Abigail Collier, filed a complaint with SOTY. In her complaint she stated the winning song was not an original composition.

Elaine Ferris and Hillary Olsen reviewed the complaint on behalf of SOTY. They took testimony from Abigail Collier and conflicting testimony from Dylan Jones. It was basically a he-said-she-said situation.

"In the end, they chose to believe Abigail Collier, in spite of the fact there was no evidence whatsoever to support her allegation. Dylan, Josh, Maddie and Truman were eliminated from the competition. Abigail Collier replaced them as this year's winner. As a result of their elimination, they've suffered substantial financial losses. They seek to recoup those losses and are asking for one million dollars."

"Thank you, Nikki. Let's hear from the other side, now."

"Charles Avery will speak for us," Elaine says.

I flinch involuntarily when I hear this. At Danielle's Charles was antagonistic. The bad lawyer to Will's good lawyer.

"I've seen my share of frivolous lawsuits, but this one is the worst of all," Charles begins. "Not only are they paid one hundred thousand dollars in prize money—the biggest prize of any songwriting contest in the world—their agent demands payment for their promotional appearances on behalf of SOTY and their sponsors.

"From there, they parlay their contest win into a small fortune. The recording of their song has sold millions of copies and is still going strong. They are stars in their own reality TV show based on four impoverished teenagers who become rich and famous overnight.

"They made more from winning this contest than any previous contestant in the history of the SOTY awards. They are deeply indebted to SOTY, Elaine Ferris and Hillary Olsen. They should be eternally grateful. How do they show their gratitude? By filing a lawsuit and demanding one million dollars from them, that's how."

Charles ends his opening statement on that note. He did well for SAI and SOTY. He painted us as villains rather than victims. It left me feeling a little guilty over the lawsuit.

"Both sides have summarized their claim and counterclaim. Now we'll have a discussion to clarify each side's position. In this part of the process anyone is free to speak when it's your side's turn. Nikki, would you like to start it off?"

"Yes, I would. Charles is correct in saying the songwriting team parlayed their contest win into a small fortune. Winning the contest started the ball rolling, but their careers took off because of their own hard work. They became celebrities. That celebrity status gave them the earning potential which created their fortunes.

"SOTY is responsible for getting them started. And for that, they are grateful. SOTY is also responsible for stalling their careers. And for that, they're asking to be compensated for the damage done."

"What damage," Charles says, indignantly.

"Please don't speak out of turn, sir," Andrew cautions.

"We don't have to sit here and listen to her lies without responding."

"Let's take a short break to compose ourselves. We'll resume this session in fifteen minutes."

~73~

All in all it's just another brick in the wall

I don't know whether Charles losing his composure helps us or not. It's fun to watch, though. He's a big guy with a jowly face and ruddy complexion. When he's angry—which seems to happen often—he gets super red in the face. I think his sharp outbursts are nothing more than attempts to rattle his opponents.

Nikki is well aware of the effect she has on certain guys and she's not shy about using it to her advantage. I've been watching Andrew while Nikki is talking. She catches his attention as we return to the conference room after the break and smiles at him. He blushes.

"Would you like to continue, Nikki?"

"Yes, I would, Andrew," she replies. "As I was saying before the break, we're seeking compensation for loss of future income due to the untimely and irrational actions on the part of Elaine Ferris and Hillary Olsen, as director and assistant director of SOTY.

"Those future earnings would come from their reality TV show, personal appearances, song royalties and product endorsements. Obviously, future earnings can't be accurately calculated. But by using the known earnings of similar celebrities, we estimate our team's earning potential to be as much as one hundred times what we're asking."

"Elaine," Andrew says. "Do you want to respond?"

"I've said all along that we acted within the guidelines set by our organization. Dylan, Madeline, Truman and Josh were present when we took testimony and reviewed the complaint against them. We made our decision based on what we heard at that review and we stand by it."

"I'd like to respond to that," I say.

"Go ahead."

"Elaine. You told me over the phone your decision was influenced by my treatment of Abigail Collier. I told you I didn't mistreat her. You didn't ask her for proof of any kind and you didn't give me a chance to challenge her claim. Don't you think you acted hastily by disqualifying us?"

"No, I don't. We weighed the information and testimony from the review for forty-eight hours before making our decision. We thought it was the proper decision then, and we still do."

"Does anyone have anything to ask or add to the discussion?"

"I do," Maddie says. "We weren't given the opportunity to question Abigail's testimony at the review. I bet I could have poked holes in her claims of abuse or mistreatment. You say you didn't act hastily, but the review lasted only fifteen minutes. I think that's pretty hasty."

"I've already responded to that," Elaine retorts. "And as far as Abigail is concerned, I'll say this. She has represented SOTY quite remarkably in every way. As a songwriter, singer and guitarist, she is a perfect example of the kind of artist SOTY wants to promote.

"I don't believe the four of you represented us as well. As long as there was a shadow of doubt you wrote 'Love Transcends', there was a smudge on the reputation of our organization and any songwriter we support."

I hate to admit it, but there is some truth to that. We're not musicians. We set out to win a contest, not build careers as songwriters.

"If there is nothing more either side wants to add to the discussion, we'll move on to the next step. I'll meet privately with the songwriters, and then with Elaine, Hillary and their representatives. These sessions normally take twenty to thirty minutes each. Elaine if you and your group will wait in the next room, I'll begin with the songwriters."

We wait silently while Elaine, Hillary, Will and Charles shuffle out of the room and shut the door behind them. This isn't going well.

"At this point in a mediation, it's normal to feel like you haven't made much progress. It's the nature of the beast. Neither side wants to give too much, too quickly. With that in mind, I'd like you to look at this from a different perspective.

"Imagine leaving here with nothing resolved. Going home empty-handed and facing a lengthy wait to battle it out in court. Alright. Hold that image for a minute. It's ugly. Not at all the desirable outcome. You've wasted your time and have nothing to show for it.

"Now, set that image to the side for a moment. What would be even slightly better? What could they offer you that would give you some satisfaction and persuade you to abandon the lawsuit?"

"A million dollars," Josh answers.

"That's already on the table. It's stated in the court papers. What if we start at the bottom and work our way up? What if they offered one hundred dollars to each of you?"

"No way," Truman says, immediately.

"Not so quick, Truman," Andrew cautions. "What if that's their best offer. They say take it or leave it. Do you still say no? Do you walk out of here facing the uncertainty of pursuing the lawsuit? Or, do you take the sure thing? What's best for you in the long run?"

"One hundred dollars isn't squat. It doesn't matter how long I think about it. I'll still say no."

"Alright. What about one thousand dollars each?"

"Same answer," Maddie says. "It's not nearly enough."

"What about ten thousand dollars?"

Our hesitation lets him know he's getting closer.

"I want you to think about it. That's not chump change. It's real money and this issue is resolved. You can get on with your lives without this lawsuit hanging over your heads. While you're thinking about it, I'm going to speak privately with Elaine Ferris and Hillary Olsen."

~74~

Little by little we meet in the middle

Andrew's words have the desired effect. They force us to focus on tomorrow, not today. That's important. Because the here and now is big and requires immediate attention. Tomorrow is not a pressing matter. We can plan for it or we can worry about it later.

"What do you think Andrew is saying to them?" I ask the others, as we wait on them to finish their discussion.

"He's probably saying pretty much the same thing he said to us," Josh allows. "He's asking them what's the most they'd pay to make us go away."

"Do you think he's telling them we might settle for ten thousand dollars each?" Maddie asks. "I think he got that impression when we didn't say no to it, right off."

"I don't think he'll do that," Nikki comments.

"Why not?" Truman asks.

"I think he'll get them to think about a number in between forty thousand and one million. Like one hundred thousand. He'll tell them to think about having to pay out one million, or possibly more. He'll mention the time and expense involved with a lawsuit. Then he'll ask them if they can live with paying out one hundred thousand dollars and putting this whole thing behind them."

That's basically the same tactic he used with us. Start at the extreme end of the scale and work toward the middle.

The door to the conference room opens and Andrew peeks out.

"We're ready for you now," he says.

Elaine, Hillary, Will and Charles are wearing poker faces as we re-enter the room and take our seats across the table from them.

"Now, we'll begin joint negotiations. You may feel like you're too far apart to come to an agreement. I've spoken privately with both parties and I believe everyone agrees settling the dispute here is preferable to doing it in court. Elaine, are you prepared to make an offer?"

"I still maintain we are not responsible for any financial hardships you may have suffered, but in the interest of resolving our differences, we are willing to pay ten thousand dollars to end this dispute."

"To clarify," Andrew says. "The offer is for a total of ten thousand dollars, and not ten thousand to each of the four plaintiffs. Correct?"

"Yes, that's correct."

I didn't think Elaine would be so quick to make an offer. That much is encouraging, even if the offer falls short of our lowest expectations.

"I'm sorry," I say. "We can't accept that."

"Make a counteroffer, Dylan," Andrew suggests.

"We would agree to withdraw the complaint and abandon the lawsuit for one hundred thousand each, or four hundred thousand total. That's less than half of what we were asking for in the lawsuit and it's a fraction of the potential damage from the contest elimination. I think that's reasonable."

"Well, I don't," Elaine says. "We're not willing pay that amount."

"Your turn to counter, Elaine," Andrew coaxes.

"We will offer ten thousand to each of you. Forty thousand total. Not a penny more. Take it or leave it. Even if I wanted to pay you more, SOTY doesn't have the funding to do so."

It sounds like a bluff to me, but I can't be sure. Calling her bluff could be costly. I look at Maddie, Truman and Josh. I can tell they're thinking the same thing I am.

"SOTY may not have the funding," Nikki says to Elaine. "But Songwriter Award Incorporated is also liable and named in the lawsuit. They have more resources, and more to lose, as well."

"Can we discuss it privately for a moment?" I ask.

Nikki, Josh, Maddie, Truman and I go into the next room.

"What do you guys think?" I ask.

"I don't think it's enough," Truman states. "But she sounded pretty serious when she said, 'take it or leave it'."

"We still have the lawsuit as leverage," Maddie says. "She won't rescind her offer as long as the lawsuit is active."

"I agree with Maddie," Josh says.

"Nikki, what do you think?"

"Make a counteroffer. Your last offer was one hundred thousand each. Try half that. Fifty thousand each, or two hundred thousand total."

We return to the conference room and I do as Nikki suggests.

"No," Elaine says. "Absolutely not. We're still too far apart. I really hoped we could reach an agreement, but it doesn't look like that will happen. I think we're done."

"I urge you to reconsider," Andrew tells her. "We're making progress. We've gone from zero to forty thousand on this side, and one million to two hundred thousand on that side. Please, continue talking."

"We'd like to discuss this privately," Will says. "Give us a minute."

They go into the other room. It seems much longer than the five minutes the clock ticks off before they return.

"Okay. I'm going to make our final offer. It's a very generous offer and I urge you to accept it so we can all move on. One hundred thousand dollars, the same as you received for winning the contest."

I look at the others. They nod.

"Alright, we accept," I say. "On one condition."

"What's that?" Elaine asks.

"We'd like a public apology for disqualifying us. Word it however you like as long as it's clear we didn't steal our song from anyone."

She considers it for a long moment.

"Alright. I guess I can do that."

"I'll summarize the agreement and have everyone sign it," Andrew says. "It will just take a minute."

~75~

The answer my friend is blowing in the wind

It's an unseasonably cool sixty degrees in LA on this Wednesday, the first week of December. The five of us, Josh, Truman, Maddie, Nikki and I are lounging around the pool, shivering like it's twenty below. I heard two people talking earlier today.

"It was so cold in my house this morning, I didn't want to get out of bed," one says to the other.

"Don't worry it won't last long," the other replies.

"Nothing ever does," the first one retorts.

That pretty much sums up my feelings about this place. Everything is temporary and everyone is short-sighted as a result. What happens in the morning is forgotten by afternoon. The latest trend on Monday is as passé as a Princess phone by Tuesday.

I've seen more ups and downs in the three months I've been here than in my entire previous life. I came to LA to chase a dream. When I finally catch up to it, I discover it isn't a dream at all. It's my tail and I've simply been running around in circles.

Our silence is interrupted by the sound of the ringtone I selected and designated for Stella, 'I just called to say I love you', the Stevie Wonder song. Ironic, don't you think?

"Hi Stella," I answer.

"I've got bad news and I've got worse. Which do you want first?"

"Tough decision. Give me the bad and tell me it's the worse."

"You got it. Alfred Lehman has decided not to go forward with another season of your TV show. Now for the bad news. I was hoping all the publicity surrounding the lawsuit and mediation would revitalize your careers. It hasn't and with the way things ended, your future doesn't look good."

"It doesn't come as that big of a surprise. We were hoping for more of a boost with the public apology from SOTY. Her heart wasn't in it and I think people sensed it."

"I'm not defending her, but I understand her reasoning. She did what she had to do for herself and SOTY. The Songwriter of the Year contest and awards ceremony will go on in spite of everything that's happened."

There's an uncomfortable pause in the conversation. I'm thankful Stella has supported us as long as she has, but everyone has their limits.

"I know what you're going to say, Stella. It's okay. You've been great. We couldn't have asked for a better agent. You've gone way beyond and above in every way."

"Dylan," Maddie calls to me. "Let me speak to her."

I hand my phone to her.

"Stella. I just want to say thanks for everything. None of this would have been possible if it weren't for you. Josh wants to say something. I'm giving him the phone."

"It was great while it lasted, Stella. We'll miss you. Here's Truman."

"Stella. All I can say is, what a ride. You stay in touch. Okay?"

I take the phone from Truman and put it on speakerphone. The line is quiet for a moment.

"Stella," I prompt. "Are you still there?"

"Yeah, I'm here."

For a brief second, I think I hear her voice crack. But with Stella's normally scratchy voice, it's hard to tell.

"I'm not cutting you loose," she says. "I'm happy to manage whatever comes in, but I can't give you the same attention as before. You understand, don't you?"

"We do. What about the house and the vehicles? What's going to happen with those?"

"You'll have them until the end of the month. I'll square it with the leasing companies. There's enough money in your account to take care of those things and leave you with some change. Past that, you're on your own."

"I understand. We'll decide what we're going to do between now and the end of the month. Thanks again, Stella."

"You're welcome, kid. Take care of yourself."

I disconnect.

"One month," I say.

"Less," Maddie says. "Today's December fourth."

"Almost a month, twenty-seven days, four weeks, take your pick," Truman declares. "We have to decide what we're going to do before December thirty-first. But, we don't have to decide right this minute. And with that in mind, I think we should stop moping around and enjoy the time we have left here."

"Let's have a party," Josh says. "This weekend. We can invite some friends over. It could be sort of a going-away party."

"I like it," Maddie says. "I'm going to start calling some people I know, right now."

I'm not in a partying mood, but maybe by the weekend I'll feel differently. Either way, I'm not going to rain on their parade. Besides, it might be the perfect way to say goodbye to this house and the memories it holds. I wonder if Abigail might consider coming. The controversy over who won the contest is history. Maybe we could set aside our differences for an evening and get reacquainted.

"You better not invite her, Dylan," Maddie warns.

"Who?"

"You know who. Abigail. She's persona non grata in this house for as long as I'm here. And don't you forget it."

~76~

Only the lonely know the way I feel tonight

Contrary to what everyone keeps telling me, I'm not really naïve and easily manipulated by girls. I'm aware they're using me. But I allow it because I love being close to girls. I love everything about them. The way they feel and smell. The way they walk and talk.

A world without girls would be a world without love. A place I wouldn't want to live. I couldn't cope with the loneliness. Being used by a girl is a small price to pay for her company.

There's a place in Long Beach, called The Hub. It's a coffee house/brew pub. Abigail mentioned it the last time we were together. Tonight is open mike night. Musicians stop in to play an instrument or sing. They don't get paid. Not even tips. It's not about the money. It's about performing and interacting with a live audience.

Abigail said she likes to try out the songs she writes at this place. I can imagine her onstage, singing a song to be heard by ears other than hers for the first time and wondering how the crowd will respond. Will they love her or hate her? Will they applaud or boo?

I was envious when she told me about doing that. Envious for a couple of reasons. First because I wouldn't have the nerve to stand before an audience of strangers and lay myself open for them to scrutinize. And second because I'm not a songwriter. I'm a poser. A phony.

It's late when I leave the house. Well after dark. Open mike performances begin at nine. I don't tell anyone where I'm going. They wouldn't understand. Frankly, I don't understand it myself.

Abigail probably won't be there. Why would she? She's a rising star. From now on, her days and nights will be spent performing at concert halls, recording in studios or filming videos. Like me, The Hub is a part of her past. Something she's outgrown or no longer needs.

The Hub is almost full when I arrive. It's a casual setting. A wide open space with rows of long wooden picnic tables and bench seats. I find a seat between two girls. The girl on the left is engrossed in conversation with a guy. The girl on the right is talking idly with a couple across the table.

"Is anyone sitting here?" I ask her.

"I don't think so," she answers, without looking at me.

On the small stage, a girl is reading poetry. I can't hear what she's saying over the noise of the crowd. That's okay. I'm not that into poetry, anyway.

She finishes and another girl comes onstage carrying a boombox with her. She switches it on and turns up the volume. Just my luck. Hip-hop. She begins rapping lyrics which don't make sense or even rhyme. There's a smattering of applause afterward.

I go to the coffee bar to order a mocha latte between acts. While the barista makes my drink I watch a guy set up a Fender Twin Reverb amp and plug a Telecaster guitar into it. It makes me think of Truman.

The guitarist tunes his instrument as I return to my seat with the coffee. He plays a few blues riffs, then segues into 'The Thrill is Gone', by B.B. King, singing and playing without accompaniment. He sounds pretty good. I think Truman would agree.

The response from the crowd is lukewarm. I can see from his expression the guitarist is disappointed. It's a tough audience, tonight. Especially considering the performers are playing for free. I'm not sure what the people in the crowd were expecting or why they came here tonight. Then again, I'm not sure why I came here, myself.

The next person up is a young man with an acoustic guitar. He's really nervous. He doesn't look at the audience. Instead he focuses on the fretboard as he begins playing. He doesn't sing along. It's just him and his Martin guitar.

It's obvious he hasn't been playing very long. Soon, the audience is ignoring him and talking among themselves. The crowd grows louder and the guitarist slips further into the background. I feel sorry for him. I wish I could help him somehow. Give him encouragement by clapping my hands in time to his music.

"Help him, Dylan," a voice says.

It's like my conscience is speaking to me, but in my mother's voice. The same one I heard as a baby. The same one I hear when she visits in my dreams. I scan the people around me to be certain it wasn't one of them. The voice comes again.

"He needs you, Dylan. Don't let him down. He doesn't want to be up there by himself. You can do this. There's nothing to fear. Trust your instincts. You are a songwriter. Show them. Prove it to yourself."

I rise from my seat and walk to the stage. The young man watches me approach with a look of relief in his eyes. I gesture for him to continue playing, position myself behind the mike and begin singing.

"Well I've had fun in California, it's been a hoot but I should inform ya,

I'll only be here for a while.

So much to see, so much to do, so much a guy can get into,

I'm going to leave here with a smile."

The young guitarist starts to get into it, swaying to the rhythm, tapping his feet and strumming with more intensity. One by one, heads turn to watch. The crowd starts clapping their hands to the beat.

The words have been bouncing around in my head for a couple of weeks, coming to me one line at a time. I sing another verse.

"I flew from Detroit to LA, I never thought that I would stay,
It wasn't long until I changed my mind.
Hollywood and movie stars, pretty girls and fancy cars,
And marijuana if you're so inclined.
"I'm a long way from home, and I'm traveling alone,
Doesn't anybody really care?
Such a long way to get home, and I'm tired to the bone
Wishing I was already there."

I look at the young guitarist and give a nod to let him know that was the last line. Hit strikes a final chord and kills it. The audience applauds. A few even give a standing ovation.

"What's your name?" the guitarist shouts over the applause.

"Dylan Jones," I shout back.

"I'm Thomas Pate."

He steps up to the microphone and introduces me to the audience.

"Dylan Jones, everyone."

I do the same for him.

"Thomas Pate, on acoustic guitar."

We vacate the stage for the next act as the applause fades.

~77~

I have done all that I could to see the evil and the good

Walking onto the stage and performing without any rehearsal or preplanning was scary. Something I never in a million years thought I'd do. Now that I have, I don't know what I was afraid of. I'll probably never see anyone in this place again. So what if I'd made a fool of myself. The audience would have a good laugh. By tomorrow I'd be forgotten.

"Hi, I'm Susan," the girl sitting next to me says.

Susan has a pretty face, which I didn't notice before because she hasn't as much as turned her head my way until now.

"I'm Dylan."

"Yeah, I know. Dylan Jones. Who does that song? The one you sang."

"Besides me, I don't know."

She's puzzled by that.

"I heard it somewhere and remembered the words," I explain.

"You must have a photographic memory or something."

"Yeah, I must have."

The next act is a two-man steel drum band. It's difficult to talk over them, so we pause in the conversation to listen. Thomas catches my eye and gestures for me to come over. He's standing by the coffee bar with another guy. I excuse myself.

"Dylan. I want you to meet someone," Thomas says, when I'm near enough for him to be heard over the music. "This is Paul Nelson. He's the manager here."

"Great to meet you, Dylan," Paul says. "You're the guy who won that songwriter contest, aren't you?"

"That's me."

"Thanks for coming by tonight to sing for us. Anytime you want to come in, you're always welcome."

"Thanks, Paul. Good to meet you. I'll see you next time I'm here."

"Dylan, can we talk?" Thomas asks. "Let's go outside where it's quieter."

I follow him to the parking lot on the side of the building. Several people are out there talking and smoking. He pulls out a joint.

"This okay with you?"

"Yeah, it's fine."

He lights it, takes a hit and passes it to me.

"I thought we really sounded good together. That was totally unrehearsed. The people went crazy. What do you think? Would you like to try and put something together?"

I pass the joint back to him.

"I have a lot going on, right now. Other commitments, you know. I doubt I'd be able to devote as much time as necessary. Sorry."

He passes it to me, again.

"No problem. I figured it couldn't hurt to ask."

"Are you guys going keep that all to yourselves, or can a girl have some?" someone asks.

I recognize the voice.

"Say, Abigail. Remember me, Thomas Pate?"

"Sorry, no."

"Yeah, I guess it's been a while. Meet my buddy, Dylan Jones."

I turn to face her. Her expression reveals nothing. I hand the joint to her, but she doesn't put it to her lips.

"We've met. Thomas, would you mind if Dylan and I speak privately?"

"Uh, no. Of course not." He starts to reach for the joint, but thinks better of it. "You guys enjoy that. I'll see you later."

"So, what are you doing here, Dylan? Slumming it?"

"These are the slums? You should see the neighborhood I grew up in."

"Did you come here expecting to find me? And don't tell me you happened to be in the area."

"The truth is I remember you telling me about open mike night. I thought I might enjoy it. I didn't think I'd find you here. Not with your busy schedule and all."

She takes a hit, then passes it to me.

"I've earned everything I have. I paid my dues, playing in places like this. Can you say the same? I deserved to win the contest. You're a fake. I knew it the first time we met. I hope you didn't come here thinking you'd get an apology from me for exposing you, because it's not going to happen."

This is a side of Abigail I haven't seen until now. I don't care for it. I hand the joint back to her, hoping she'll inhale a lungful and hold it long enough to mellow out some. She has more to say before she smokes.

"I saw you onstage. Was that another one of your mom's songs?"

That's a low blow. It's lucky for her Maddie isn't here.

"I was just singing along to what Thomas was playing. The words just came to me. I might have heard them somewhere. I don't know."

"Read them somewhere is more like it."

I've taken about as much as I'm going to from her. I should probably leave before things turn ugly.

"It's been fun chatting with you, Abigail. I'm going to take off. Have a great life."

I turn to leave.

"Say hello to those other losers. Truman, Josh and Maddie."

Snap! I turn to face her.

"I bought a copy of your song, 'Make it Me'. There's nothing original about it. You stole lyrics from a dozen different songs and guitar riffs from just as many. The chord progressions are commonplace, too. They've probably been used in hundreds of songs. Even the title has been used before. You pretend to be someone you're not. You're the faker. I'm glad I got the chance to meet the real you. Now I'm certain the Abigail I fell for never even existed."

"Oh yeah," she starts.

I struck a nerve. She's steamed, but can't think of a clever retort.

"Abigail! You're up next," someone calls to her.

She gives me the evil eye one last time, then turns and goes inside. I can hear the crowd applaud and scream her name as she takes the stage. Through the window I see her strap on her guitar and smile at her audience. Underneath the smiling façade is an unhappy soul. Knowing that gives me no pleasure. I get in the Highlander and leave.

~78~

It's my party and I'll cry if I want to

As parties go, ours is probably a two on a scale of one to ten. We decided to invite only our closest friends. The list was too short, so we broadened it to include anyone who would come.

A couple of guys Maddie knows say they might come by. A couple of guys Josh knows say they will come by. A group of zombies from California Sounds promise to stop in. I invite Natalie. She says maybe. We invite Stella. She's the first to arrive.

"I know I'm early, but it's already past my bedtime and I can't stay. I wanted to give you a little going away gift, in person."

She hands each of us a small box with a bow atop it.

"Go ahead, open them," she urges. "I want to see your reaction."

We do. Inside each is Stella's address, phone number and email engraved on a business card-size piece of bronze-plated metal.

"It's permanent," she says. "When I say I'll always be there for you, I mean it."

"I don't know what to say, Stella," I tell her.

I'm truly touched by the gesture. I start to tear up.

"Stop that," Stella says.

I go to give her a hug.

"You don't need to do that," she tells me. "Really, it's not necessary."

343

I wrap my arms around her anyway. The smell of tobacco smoke on her clothing and whiskey on her breath is overpowering. One at a time Josh, Truman and Maddie joins us. We stand there in a group embrace for only a matter of seconds.

"Are we done, yet?" Stella asks. "Because I really need to leave."

We release her. She says goodbye. But it isn't goodbye. It's more like I'll see you later. A really classy woman, Stella is.

The other party guests start arriving a few at a time an hour later. It's a quiet affair. Probably the tamest party this big house has ever seen. Maddie takes her friends into the great room to talk. Josh does the same with his friends. Truman, Nikki and I hang out in the parlor close to the front door until three zombies show up.

Truman takes them upstairs where his Marshall amplifier is set up. I hear him playing the Stratocaster at low volume. I doubt it will stay that way for long. There are two people left without party dates or friends. Me and Nikki.

"I guess we're stuck with each other tonight," I say.

"Not that I mind being stuck with you, little brother, but I invited someone. They should be here soon."

The doorbell sounds.

"I suspect that's him now."

Nikki opens the door. Andrew Harris, the guy with Mediation Solutions, steps in.

"You remember Andrew, don't you Dylan?"

"I do. Welcome to our humble abode, Andrew."

He takes it all in.

"Nice digs," he says.

"It will do in a pinch," I reply.

"Come on in here with the other guests, Andrew," Nikki says.

She takes his arm and leads him toward the great room. I start to follow. The doorbell rings. I answer it. Natalie greets me with a hug and a kiss. Then she introduces the guy with her.

"Dylan. This is my fiancé, Richard."

He offers his hand to me.

"Nice to finally meet you, Dylan," he says.

I'm thinking things can't get any more awkward than this. Then Natalie excuses herself to powder her nose.

"You guys get acquainted, I'll be right back."

We sit in the parlor. Richard in an arm chair. Me across from him in another. I'm not any good with small talk in the best of situations and this is a far cry from that.

"Natalie is some girl, don't you think?" I say.

"She is that," says he.

We go quiet, hoping Natalie will hurry back. Five minutes go by. He feels the need to talk.

"Sometimes I wish I'd never met her. Then I have a moment of clarity when I realize I'd be completely lost without her."

"I've been there," I tell him. "I mean, not with Natalie, but I've felt that way with another girl or two."

"It sucks," he says.

"Tell me about it. It rips your heart out."

"You know, Natalie came up with this crazy idea the other day. She wants to get to know my wife."

"Whoa. That's pretty scary."

"That's what I thought, too. She has a plan for how it could happen. We start double dating. You're with Natalie. I'm with my wife. My wife thinks you and I are friends. She gets to know Natalie as your fiancé. This way if she ever catches us together we have an alibi. Friend of a friend who just happened to bump into one another."

"Pretty clever," I say.

"No kidding. She has the whole package. Beauty and brains."

I'm starting to like Richard and we seem to be bonding. Who'd have thought that could happen?

"You did a great job on her boobs, by the way. I'd swear they were real."

"Thanks. Most people don't realize how difficult it is to get them just right. Too many women think bigger is better. They want me to stuff them so full they look lumpy."

"Do you do a lot of boob jobs?"

"About twenty a week."

"You must get tired of looking at them."

"Sometimes, but you have to remember. Most of these women aren't nearly as easy to look at as Natalie."

Natalie returns from the ladies room.

"Are you talking about my boobs?"

"Not yours really. Just breast augmentation in general," Richard answers.

"Don't get him started on boobs, Dylan. He could talk for hours about his work."

"Sorry," he says. "It's true. My work is my passion."

Our discussion of boobs is interrupted by the doorbell.

"I'll be right back," I say.

I open the door to find three men with stern faces. One is in a suit. The other two are wearing police uniforms. The suit flashes a badge.

"The Mercedes convertible parked in your drive is registered to Richard Creighton. Is he here?"

"I'm not sure."

I look toward the parlor where Richard was standing a minute earlier. He's gone. Natalie is wide-eyed with her hand covering her mouth. She's looking in the direction of the veranda.

"That's him," suit says.

I look to where he's pointing and catch a flash of someone running. Richard I presume. The uniforms take off after him. It isn't much of a chase. They tackle him to the deck on the veranda and cuff his hands. They walk him out as the suit Mirandizes him.

"Richard Creighton, you're under arrest for the unauthorized practice of medicine. You have the right to remain silent....."

"I'm really sorry, Natalie," I say, though what I'm thinking is I hope they put him away for a long time, and I finally can have Natalie to myself.

"I can't believe that just happened," she says.

"You didn't have any idea this was coming?"

"None whatsoever. I have to go. He'll need an attorney and I'll need to start getting the bail money together."

"Shouldn't his wife handle that?"

"He can't depend on her. She'll let him sit in jail for a week before she does anything."

She walks quickly out the door, and possibly out of my life as well. Another one bites the dust? With Natalie, you never know.

~79~

I was so much older then, I'm younger than that now

Ten days before Christmas we walk out of the house on Sunset Boulevard for the last time. We leave a lot of great memories behind. That's okay. We'll make more. Whether those memories are made in California, Detroit or somewhere else remains to be seen.

The leased Highlanders are gone. The dealership picked them up the day before. Josh and Maddie are renting a car to drive south.

"We're going to find a place to rent north of San Diego," Maddie tells me. "We want to be a short drive from the ocean, so we can watch the whales and walk the beach picking up shells. Once our money runs out, we'll get jobs to pay the bills."

"Stella gave me the name of an agent that specializes in modeling gigs. I'm hoping to do some of that," Josh says.

"That sounds like a plan," I say. "I wish you luck. Call me whenever you're back in the LA area."

Between the contest prize money and the mediation payoff, Truman was able to save enough to invest in the music store, California Sounds.

"That goth-looking kid who we thought was a salesperson. He owns the place. His father fronted him the money. He's a bigwig with some oil company. I bought twenty percent of it. There's a small apartment above the store. That's mine as part of the deal."

"I'm really happy for you, Truman. It sounds like a perfect fit. I'm not that far away. I found a studio apartment in Santa Monica. I won't have a car initially, but I can always hop on the bus to meet you somewhere."

"Same here, man. We'll see a lot of each other. We've been through too much together to say goodbye. I still got your back, Dylan. Don't ever forget that."

"Ditto, Truman. I won't forget it."

I ride in a taxi with Nikki to see her off at the airport. The last few days she went back and forth over whether to stay in LA or not.

"I had fun and it was good of you to let me stay with you. California just doesn't feel right for me. I'm more of an East Coast girl."

"I know Chandra and Isiah will be happy to see you. And you can always come visit whenever you want."

"You can come back home anytime you like, too. You know that, right little brother?"

"I do. And I will come to visit. I miss Isiah and Chandra. But there aren't many opportunities for me in Detroit and I feel like I still have unfinished business here. Take care of yourself, Nikki."

An overwhelming sadness envelops me as I watch my sister go through the checkpoint and down the concourse toward the departure gate. Once she's out of sight, I go outside to find the bus to Santa Monica.

I have a pen and a pocket-size spiral notebook with me. I bought it the other day, so I can jot down any song lyrics which come to mind. I have a feeling I'll be searching my mind for words which rhyme with loneliness on the bus ride home.

~80~

This is the end, my only friend the end

For as far back as I can remember, I've felt like there was something missing in my life. The void created by the untimely death of my parents, perhaps. An emptiness inside me. One I don't understand, but can't ignore. As Nikki boards the plane to leave LA, I realize what it is.

Isiah and Chandra accepted me as their son from the day my parents died. And after a while, Nikki accepted me as her brother. I was the only holdout. I never accepted them as my family. To do so meant admitting to myself mom and dad were gone forever.

I've finally come to terms with it. I'm not sure exactly when it happened, but the emptiness is no longer there. Whenever I hear the word family, Isiah, Chandra and Nikki come immediately to mind.

On Christmas Eve six inches of snow covers the Detroit landscape. The walk and porch to the Jones' house has been cleared and salted, in case carolers or one of Nikki's friends drops by. I didn't tell them I was coming. It was a last-minute decision.

I have the taxi stop at the curb of the house next door to theirs. I pay the cabbie and get out with my sack of gifts. The lights are on throughout the house. I see shadows of people moving as I approach. I hear music as I step onto the porch. A Motown Christmas. I could knock, but I don't. Instead I take out my phone and call Isiah.

"Dylan!" he answers. "I was hoping we'd hear from you."

"Hi, Isiah. Merry Christmas. How is everyone?"

"Just great. We're having hot chocolate and listening to music."

"I can hear the Temptations singing 'Silent Night' in the background."

"I know how you always liked that album. I sure wish you were here. This is our first Christmas without you."

"Funny you should say that, because I'm...,"

"Dylan, hold on a second. Chandra wants to say something."

I hear the phone being transferred from his hand to hers.

"Dylan! We're having a white Christmas here. There's almost a foot of snow on the ground. I'll bet you're running around in short sleeves sipping iced tea, right now."

"Well, as a matter of fact, I'm...,"

"Nikki wants to talk to you, Dylan. Here she is."

I hear the phone go from hand to hand, again.

"Hello little brother. Did you get the card I sent?"

"Yes, I got it. Thanks. It was sweet of you."

"We didn't get a card from you. Did you forget to mail it?"

"I didn't get you a card, but I did get you a gift."

"You did? I didn't get that, either. When did you send it?"

"I didn't send it, I brought it with me."

I expect to hear her squeal with excitement. Instead the door opens and Isiah, Chandra and Nikki are standing there laughing at me.

"We were wondering how long you were going to stand out here," Nikki tells me.

"We saw you get out of the taxi," Chandra says.

"I wanted to surprise you," I tell them.

"Oh, you did. Now, get in here out of the cold. You must be freezing. You're dressed like you're still in LA."

Once again, I'm the butt of the joke. Some things never change, and the ones that do, I wish they hadn't.

Where Credit is Due

The chapter sub-titles used throughout this book are borrowed from the lyrics of popular songs. In the course of reading it, I'm sure you've recognized many of them. Here's the entire list of the lyrics used and the band or artist responsible for each one.

(1)   Like a complete unknown, like a rolling stone
         Like a Rolling Stone, Bob Dylan

(2)   While my guitar gently weeps
         Song by that title, The Beatles

(3)   Ebony and ivory live together in perfect harmony
         Ebony and Ivory, Paul McCartney and Stevie Wonder

(4)   Now if six turned out to be nine, I don't mind
         If 6 was 9, Jimi Hendrix

(5)   Hot town, summer in the city
         Summer in the City, Lovin Spoonful

(6)   She's a brick….house
         Brick House, Commodores

(7)   Running on empty, running blind, running behind
         Running on Empty, Jackson Browne

(8)   Takin' what they're givin' cause I'm workin' for a livin'
         Workin' for a Livin', Huey Lewis and the News

(9)   All you got to do is pick up your telephone
         6345789, Wilson Pickett

(10)   She takes just like a woman
         Just Like a Woman, Bob Dylan

(11)   You were always on my mind
         Always On My Mind, Willie Nelson

(12)   I've got sunshine on a cloudy day
         My Girl, The Temptations

(13)   Tell me something I don't know
        Song by that title, Selena Gomez
(14)   Hit me with your best shot
        Song by that title, Pat Benatar
(15)   Where am I to go now that I've gone too far
        Twilight Zone, Golden Earring
(16)   You are the sun, I am the moon, You are the words,
        I am the tune
        Play Me, Neil Diamond
(17)   Call out the instigators, because there's something in
        the air
        Something in the Air, Thunderclap Newman
(18)   If you'll be my dixie chicken, I'll be your Tennessee
        lamb
        Dixie Chicken, Lowell George
(19)   It's like trying to spin the world the other way
        What Can I Say, Carrie Underwood
(20)   It's love's illusions I recall
        Both Sides Now, Joni Mitchell
(21)   Just push play, they're gonna bleep it anyway
        Just Push Play, Aerosmith
(22)   And you can tell everybody, this is your song
        Your Song, Elton John
(23)   Don't ask me no questions, I won't tell you no lies
        Don't Ask Me No Questions, Lynyrd Skynyrd
(24)   I've been waiting a long time for this moment to
        come
        Waiting, Green Day
(25)   One step closer to knowing
        One Step Closer, U2
(26)   The story of my life is very plain to read
        The Story of My Life, Neil Diamond
(27)   And I wonder should I laugh or cry
        Should I Laugh or Cry, ABBA

(28)   Going to California with an aching in my heart
       Going to California, Led Zeppelin
(29)   Learning to fly, but I ain't got wings
       Learning To Fly, Tom Petty
(30)   People are strange when you're a stranger
       People Are Strange, The Doors
(31)   Follow, follow, follow the yellow brick road
       We're Off to See the Wizard, Judy Garland
(32)   Boom shaka-laka-laka, boom shaka-laka-laka
       I Want to Take You Higher, Sly and the Family
       Stone
(33)   Gonna live while I'm alive, I'll sleep when I'm dead
       I'll Sleep When I'm Dead, Bon Jovi
(34)   I'll find my limo driver, mister take us to the show
       What's Your Name, Lynyrd Skynyrd
(35)   When you smile for the camera, I know I love you
       better
       Peg, Steely Dan
(36)   Turn it up, bring the noise
       Bring the Noise, Public Enemy
(37)   You're a shining star, no matter who you are
       Shining Star, Earth, Wind and Fire
(38)   Yes, you look wonderful tonight
       Wonderful Tonight, Eric Clapton
(39)   The winner takes it all, the loser has to fall
       The Winner Takes it All, ABBA
(40)   Because I'm falling down with people standing
       around
       Falling Down, Duran Duran
(41)   This could be the start of something big
       Song by that title, Steve Allen
(42)   Got to give the people, give the people what they
       want
       Give the People What They Want, O'Jays

(43)   Turn out the lights, the party's over
        The Party's Over, Willie Nelson
(44)   Taking care of business and working overtime
        Taking Care of Business, Bachman Turner
        Overdrive
(45)   Money for nothin' and your chicks for free
        Money for Nothing, Dire Straits
(46)   Want you to sign your contract, want you to sign
        today
        Working for MCA, Lynyrd Skynyrd
(47)   I'll light the fire, you put the flowers in the vase that
        you bought today
        Our House, Crosby, Stills and Nash
(48)   I need it, you know I'm a fiend, getting freaky in my
        limousine
        Peaches and Cream, 112
(49)   You go back Jack do it again
        Do It Again, Steely Dan
(50)   My friends all drive Porsches, I must make amends
        Mercedes Benz, Janis Joplin
(51)   Time goes by so slowly and time can do so much
        Unchained Melody, The Righteous Brothers
(52)   You can't fake it when you're naked
        Naked, Bon Jovi
(53)   You just keep on using me until you use me up
        Use Me, Bill Withers
(54)   All I gotta do is act naturally
        Act Naturally, Buck Owens
(55)   You gotta stomp, whistle and scream, you gotta
        wake
        right up in your dreams
        Puttin' on the Dog, Tom Waits
(56)   Everybody just have a good time
        Party Rock Anthem, LMFAO

(57)   Where are the clowns, there ought to be clowns
Send in the Clowns, Judy Collins

(58)   When the moon is in the seventh house, and Jupiter aligns with Mars
Aquarius, The Fifth Dimension

(59)   Son can you play me a memory, I'm not really sure how it goes
Piano Man, Billy Joel

(60)   All the time they want to take your place, the back stabbers
Back Stabbers, O'Jays

(61)   'Cause I can't make you love me if you don't
I Can't Make You Love Me, Bonnie Raitt

(62)   Everybody knows that smokin' ain't allowed in school
Smokin' in the Boy's Room, Brownsville Station

(63)   Heard ten thousand whispering and nobody listening
A Hard Rain's Gonna Fall, Bob Dylan

(64)   Don't ask me what I think of you, I might not give the answer that you want me to
Oh Well, Fleetwood Mac

(65)   All lies in jest, still a man hears what he wants to and disregards the rest
The Boxer, Simon and Garfunkel

(66)   I went to my brother to ask for a loan 'cause I was busted
Busted, Ray Charles

(67)   You're nobody until somebody ~~loves~~ sues you
Song by that title, Dean Martin

(68)   Ride a painted pony let the spinning wheel spin
Spinning Wheel, Blood, Sweat and Tears

(69) Send lawyers, guns and money, dad get me out of this
      Lawyers, Guns and Money, Warren Zevon

(70) I'd rather be a hammer than a nail, yes I would, if I could, I surely would
      El Condor Pasa, Simon and Garfunkel

(71) If I can just get off of this LA freeway without getting
      killed or caught
      LA Freeway, Guy Clark

(72) Up and down, and in the end it's only round and round
      Us and Them, Pink Floyd

(73) All in all it's just another brick in the wall
      The Wall, Pink Floyd

(74) Little by little, we meet in the middle
      Guilty, Barbara Streisand and Barry Gibbs

(75) The answer my friend is blowing in the wind
      Blowing in the Wind, Bob Dylan

(76) Only the lonely know the way I feel tonight
      Only the Lonely, Roy Orbison

(77) I have done all that I could to see the evil and the good
      Doctor My Eyes, Jackson Browne

(78) It's my party and I'll cry if I want to
      It's My Party, Leslie Gore

(79) I was so much older then, I'm younger than that now
      My Back Pages, Bob Dylan

(80) This is the end, my only friend the end
      The End, The Doors

Mason is hard at work on his next novel. To find out what's coming next or to leave comments or ask Mason a question:
Please visit:
masonmalone.com